Rick Gangraw

Secrets in the Ice

Published by White Feather Press, LLC in 2012

ISBN 978-1-61808-043-1

Printed in the United States of America

Cover design created by Ron Bell of AdVision Design Group (www.advisiondesigngroup.com)

White Feather Press

Reaffirming Faith in God, Family, and Country!

Acknowledgments

A special thanks to Wayne and Martha Flusek, my favorite Yoopers, best friends, and neighbors in the UP.

Thanks also to Christian and Linda Selden for early feedback and encouragement.

Thanks to my friends and colleagues in the Melbourne Writer's Group who provided many pointers, tips, suggestions, and more.

And last but not least, thanks to my wife, Denise, who constantly provides support and love.

Chapter One

THE EARLY EVENING MIST MOVED gradually across the frozen lake's surface and between the trees, enveloping cabins and boats in a ghostly motion, claiming ownership over every part of the town.

Tim fell in and out of sleep this evening, and wasn't sure which part was real and which was a dream. This was going to be another restless night in Upper Michigan, as his thoughts drifted back to looking across the lake. It didn't take long before he was in another world again.

He trudged through the deep snow as he made his way to the lake, his boots crunching noisily as he walked through the thick woods, holding on to branches as he stepped over fallen logs. Following a snow-covered path through the woods, it was challenging to see where to step. Tim was a strong, six-foot outdoorsman, who spent a lot of time outside even in the winter. A carpenter by trade, he could fix any problem his neighbors had around Kisinaw Lake and in Manitow, and was well-liked by everyone he worked with.

The clean smell of white pines and cedars was barely noticeable throughout the woods this time of year, but he didn't slow down to savor it the way he usually did. Fresh snow dusted the tree branches and covered the ground. It was a beautiful scene, but he was not in a state of mind to stop and take in the view. The cedar trees had snow on every branch, like a store bought Christmas tree made up perfectly in a window display, but he clumsily knocked the branches on his way past these silent giants. The trees just stood there, as they had for many years, not interfering, unable to reach out to him. Loud and noticeable, each breath escaped his mouth and nostrils like smoke from a chimney. With no sounds of traffic from the nearby highway, Tim heard only the noises he made as he continued his solitary march through the woods.

Eventually, the path led up to the frozen lake, where he stood and looked out over the ice for a minute. Along the lake's edge, a thinly drawn line separated where the land ended and the lake began. Spectacular. Many of the trees leaned out over the lake as though they offered something to the water or pointed out hidden secrets. Tim eased his way down the two-foot drop from the woods to the icy surface, but slipped when his shoes met the ice. He slid on his back for several feet onto the frozen lake, but immediately got up and walked out farther.

He felt as though he was wrapped in a blanket of silence. Hearing no signs of life, not even from the residents living around the lake or from the train that regularly traveled alongside the highway about this time. He only recognized the sounds of his own labored breathing and his hard foot-steps as they crushed the ice crystals on the frozen surface. By this time, the cold air burned as he breathed it in, but he was used to feeling like this from all the times he spent outside this time of year working on a neighbor's roof or fixing a shed.

He looked down at the ice as he walked carefully, like a toddler planning each step, then after a couple of minutes, he stopped. Tim thought he heard something from the woods along the edge of the lake. He looked up, followed the shore-line with his eyes, and saw the cabin set back into the trees. The dark stained log cabin had snow on the roof and looked much like an island in a sea of white with cedar and birch trees on each side.

Tim was no more than twenty yards from shore when he stopped to catch his breath and listen for another sound. His mouth was dry, but he ignored his thirst. While standing in the stillness of the cold air, something moved slightly in the ice under his hiking boots and he tried to stabilize himself. The ice was getting thinner now with the warmer weather on its way, and it wouldn't be able to support a man's weight for much longer. He wondered if he was on a thin section of the ice now.

A hand punched up through the surface of the ice and grabbed one of his ankles. The pale, bluish-grey hand didn't look healthy; in fact it looked like old, rotted flesh. Tim felt as though he might lose his balance and fall through the ice, when another grisly hand reached up through the thin ice and grabbed his other leg. Terror engulfed him as he looked down at the ice cracking below him. Horrible faces with blank white eyes peered up at him through the ice with anticipation. The ice gave way beneath him with a loud crack, and as he fell, he reached out grasping at anything in a panicked effort to keep his head from going under the black water. Rotting hands beneath the surface kept pulling him down by his legs, as he struggled to get himself back up onto the ice. Another hand reached up from the freezing water behind him, grabbed the top of his head, and pulled him backward as Tim's hands slid helplessly across the icy surface. Unable to hold himself up any longer, he was pulled down into the darkness of the cold water.

Tim woke up from the dream gasping for breath and sat up quickly, covered with sweat, as he looked around the room terrified. He was in the cabin from his dream, and as his eyes adjusted to the darkness, he eventually saw things in the room that brought him back to reality: the pictures of

3

his parents on the wall, the knickknacks he bought in town on the shelves, the familiar lamps on the dressers, all helped him to relax a little bit and realize he just woke up from a nightmare. He fell back on the pillow, breathing hard just like in his dream, and stared up into the dim light of the cabin for several minutes.

He had been staying in the cabin for almost a year, and this wasn't the first nightmare he experienced while living there. Some of the townspeople warned him it was haunted, but he told everyone he didn't believe in ghosts. After this nightmare, he wasn't so certain anymore. It had all seemed so real, and his heart pounded even after being awake for several minutes. Everything in the dream was accurate and vividly clear: the way the path looked after a snowfall, the way the cabin looked from the frozen lake, and even the faint winter smells of the trees as he walked by them in the dream.

It was still dark, and Tim wanted desperately to fall back to sleep. However, a pulse of fear gripped him mercilessly at the thought of having another terrible dream. As far as he could remember, he hadn't experienced any nightmares except for when he was a little child, but since he'd been at the cabin, this was the third or fourth one. Could there truly be something with this cabin that gave him these realistic night terrors? Fortunately, his exhausted body won out over his fear, and he dozed off again for a few hours of restless sleep.

Chapter Two

LISA SPOKE EXCITEDLY TO HER HUS-
band as he drove their SUV to a cabin getaway
in Upper Michigan. Paul looked forward to time
with her on this vacation, and tried to keep up with all of
her planning. It was too easy for him to get distracted and
not follow her conversation, so he workrd hard to stay focused on his wife. He didn't want her to get mad at him and
think he had tuned her out. He marveled at the beauty of
the snow on the trees and on the ground beside the road as
they drove by it in their four-wheel drive. In Detroit, as in
any large city, the snow often looked dirty and unattractive,
but out here it seemed like an artist had painted the scene.

"Ever since we dated in college, I knew I wanted to spend
my life with you, Paul. When I graduated with a Nursing
Degree and was hired at the hospital in town, then you graduated with your Engineering Degree and took a job with that
software company near the hospital, it was as though we were
meant to be together."

"Lisa, I wanted to marry you long before we graduated,
but I knew that would have been challenging. I only wish
we could have gone on a honeymoon last year right after the
wedding. That's the only thing I regret. We've had to save up
vacation time and money, but I want to make it up to you
now. After a year of working hard, I'm determined to relax

in this cabin on a lake with you, and I hope we can do some skating, frozen waterfall exploring, and maybe even ice fishing. I feel that I need this break to get rejuvenated for my next assignment at work too."

"I know you've been interested in coming here for a while, since your parents first told you about it a couple of years ago, and since we've had to work harder for it, we're going to appreciate it that much more. I'm glad we're finally getting the chance to take a vacation. You've had to put in a lot of extra hours over the last few months, and I've missed you. I think we both need this time away together."

Paul smiled, and leaned over to kiss his wife. They drove in silence for a few minutes.

"I always strive to look professional at work, but today it feels good to be dressed casual with flannel and jeans, without shaving. I feel like a new man experiencing the freedom that comes with a rare long weekend or a vacation. I might not even shower all week."

"You drive me wild with your mountain man look, your blue eyes and dark brown hair. I have a craving to run my fingers through your hair right now," and she did just that while he kept his eyes on the road, scooting over toward him as close as she could get. "You're a classy, handsome man, but I'll have to insist that you take at least a few showers this week."

Paul enjoyed the unexpected attention, and glanced over at his wife. She was everything he had ever dreamed of and more, and he was consumed with pleasant thoughts about her as she purred like a kitten while snuggling up next to him and slowly messed up his hair. He loved it that Lisa was a tall, attractive young woman with long, straight blonde hair, and was amazed that she looked good in anything she wore. He knew she didn't care much for makeup, and agreed that she certainly didn't need it. Her natural beauty impressed Paul so much that he enjoyed staring at her when she wasn't aware and even looking at photos he took of his very own private model. In addition, she was so much fun to be around that he knew she would be his wife for the rest of his life. He was a lucky man indeed.

"Hmm, there's another deer, hit by a car," said Lisa abruptly. "I'll never get used to seeing them like that."

She turned and stared at it through the back window until it was out of sight. Paul noticed a sadness in her eyes as she pondered the deer on the cold ground, slowly being covered by the snow.

"Have you ever thought about how alive their eyes look, even after they're dead? I could just envision that deer's eyes looking up at us, pleading, as we drove by."

Paul knew she didn't expect a response, and just looked over at her as she stared behind the SUV. He enjoyed a brief glance at her and was awestruck at how pretty her face was. Looking forward to watching her for the rest of his life, Paul realized that he would never tire from catching a glimpse of his better half.

"I can't wait to get inside and snuggle up with you by the fire tonight, Lisa. I've been waiting for this for a long time."

Lisa looked over at him, and gave him one of her incomparable smiles.

"I know. It's like a dream come true for me. The past year has been so busy for us, and now we're finally going to do some fun things together without thinking about work schedules."

"Hey, I brought you a treat for being good on the drive today. It's your favorite dark chocolate."

Lisa's eyes widened and her lips revealed her perfect teeth as she reached to collect her reward. Paul was glad to see her so happy over a simple chocolate bar.

"Oh, now I know that you really do love me, Paul."

She leaned over and kissed him on the cheek, and he

turned his head to give her a quick smooch on the lips. He couldn't help but watch the expression on her face as she enjoyed each bite with her eyes closed and made "Mmmmmmm" noises. She had a weakness for chocolate, so he smiled inside at his plan to leave her special treats throughout the cabin for her to find over the next week. She savored the delicacy, even offering one bite to Paul, and finished off the rest in no time at all. It was a challenge for him to keep his eyes on the road, but he saw signs of a town coming up.

A few minutes later, he found their turn off from the highway, and followed what looked like a tunnel, with white frosted tree branches from each side of the road touching overhead to cover them about ten feet over the roof of their SUV. Driving through here was like going into an ice cave, with glistening white all around them, and they smiled at each other as they slowly drove through their 'tunnel of love'.

"I think this was our turn," Paul said, "but I still don't see anything that looks like a lake."

"Keep going. Even if this was a wrong turn, it was worth it for us to drive through these trees."

It wasn't quite dark yet, as they followed this storybook road, which he assumed went around the lake. To his surprise, the first clearing on the left revealed a cozy log cabin framed in by several tall cedars, so he slowed down to get a better view. Paul watched Lisa's expressions as her eyes raced from the chimney to the flower boxes under the windows to the dark stained log walls.

"This is it!" Lisa exclaimed, while her husband sighed in relief.

As Paul pulled into the driveway and parked, he looked around in awe, neither of them saying a word. He was enchanted by the cabin in front of them, the thick forest on each side, and the snow covering everything in sight. It was perfect, and exactly what he had hoped for. Paul got out of the SUV and went around to open the door for Lisa. When she stepped out, she gave him a bear hug then helped him carry their luggage from the SUV to the cabin.

The air was cold and crisp, and the fresh smells from nearby fireplaces made him stop and breathe it in for a few seconds before continuing with his suitcase. There was a snow-covered branch from a cedar tree between the SUV and the cabin, and Lisa closely followed Paul toward the cabin's door. As Paul walked under it, he nonchalantly reached up with his hand and pulled on the branch, immediately dumping snow on Lisa's head. She stood there for a few seconds with a smile while Paul continued up to the door as if nothing had happened. Just as she ran up to him with a handful of snow for his face, Paul quickly set the suitcase down and ran around the cabin with Lisa close behind. When he turned the corner to the lakeside of the cabin and saw the frozen lake up close, he was mesmerized and stopped to stare at it, while Lisa came running up and stood beside him.

She dropped the snow on the ground as they both watched the mist moving slowly over the lake. He turned and put his arm around her, forgetting about Lisa's revenge for the moment. Paul looked into her blue eyes and gently brushed the snow out of her hair with his other hand. It felt colder since the sun sets early up here in winter, and he looked as far across the lake as the mist would let him. It seemed eerily silent now, with no sounds from nearby neighbors, and no traffic noises from the highway.

"I wonder if there are many birds here in the winter. It seems too quiet. Maybe they're not singing this late in the afternoon."

Lisa looked over toward the woods, and commented, "How do you like how dark it is in the woods over there? Now that's a little spooky."

Paul followed her gaze, and added, "Yeah, the trees are

very close together, so there's little room for the sun to shine any light into the woods."

As he said this, a feeling came over Paul that made him look around to see who was with them, but there was nobody there. His eyes darted across the yard, in the woods, and even up on the roof of the cabin, but he still saw nothing unusual. Something didn't seem right, but he said nothing to Lisa. He wondered again about the hush that surrounded them both, almost feeling as though it suffocated him, and he listened closely for any sounds at all.

******

A small, overgrown path led through the trees, and Lisa thought she saw a pair of eyes watching them from the dark woods beside the path. Her heartbeat quickened as she held her breath and tried to focus on the mysterious set of eyes. She heard a branch crack, and the eyes were gone.

She felt a chill, and Paul said, "Let's finish up and go inside."

Lisa figured that Paul was unaware of the eyes in the woods, and felt it was definitely colder now. She wasn't sure if she had really seen anything and wondered if it was just her imagination, so she didn't mention it. She immediately put it behind her and got her mind back into vacation mode. They both walked the rest of the way around the cabin and Paul found the key that unlocked the door. Maybe it was because she had been cooped up in the SUV for a few hours, but Lisa became giggly and playful as she kissed Paul on the cheek when he tried to carry her suitcase up the front step. He smiled and stopped for a minute, sat the suitcase down while she gave him another big hug and locked her lips with his. She could tell he didn't mind these kinds of interruptions and delays since he made no effort to stop her. However, Paul obviously wasn't prepared for her to put all of her weight on him and kick her legs up backward, so with a surprised look in his eyes, he wrapped his arms around his wife and regained his balance while he held her in the air.

When she put her feet back down on the ground, he stepped back, held up one finger and without saying a word, picked her up and tried to romantically carry her across the threshold of the cabin, much to her surprise. As he stepped through the door frame, he 'accidentally' but gently pushed Lisa's left shoulder and left ankle into the wall on each side of the door frame, not turning to fit her through the doorway, and she laughed. Paul stepped back and thought for a moment, making comical expressions with his mouth and eyebrows as he pretended to think about his situation. He turned to walk backwards through the doorway, but this time gently bumping Lisa's right shoulder and right ankle on the outside wall of each side of the door frame, again pretending not to realize that he needed to turn sideways to fit her through the doorway. By this time, Lisa had a difficult time controlling her laughter at his silliness.

Finally, with a look of enlightenment, Paul said "Aha!" and quickly tossed Lisa up over his shoulder. With her head hanging over his back and her feet kicking in front of him, he walked through the doorway while she playfully pounded on his back. Once inside, Paul set Lisa down in the living room and she snuck another kiss.

He turned on a light and looked around the interior of the cabin. Lisa could tell from Paul's face that he was very happy with what he saw. She was too. The stone fireplace was impressive, and the log siding on the inside walls gave it a rustic feel. She liked wood floors, and these were the most perfect she had ever seen. Paul gave her another kiss, and then led her back outside.

It didn't take long to finish bringing the rest of their things into the cabin, but it was already darker and colder.

Lisa was glad to get inside for the night, start a nice, warm fire soon after sunset, and sip on hot tea while lying down on the big, soft rug in front of the fireplace. This would certainly be the honeymoon they never had.

Chapter Three

THE NEXT DAY, ON THE SOUTHERN part of the lake, Axel Johansson checked the frozen lake in front of his house. Before going to bed, he had sprayed fresh water on the surface of the ice, smoothing it with a large squeegee, and let it freeze overnight. He enjoyed providing a big ice-skating surface for the neighboring kids, and they all stood standing along the shore waiting for him to finish examining the ice. Axel's three boys were in the waiting crowd, and his oldest son, Arvid, excitedly watched his dad with pride as he looked at their 'natural' skating rink. It didn't take long to make sure the new water had frozen evenly on the cold surface, so within a few minutes, his job was finished, and he gave the kids a thumbs-up with a big smile. Immediately, a cheering group of kids started ice-skating on the frozen surface, obviously having a good time chasing each other, racing, and playing tag. Clouds blanketed the skies, but it was perfect for some outdoor play in the snow and on the ice this time of the year. Arvid led the way and skated out farther than the rest of the kids.

He shouted, "Catch me now guys, if you can!" and sped off in a burst of speed.

These kids were teenagers and 'wannabe' teenagers, and all of them were expert ice skaters. They had a lot of practice, since the lake stayed frozen for so much of the winter and early spring each year. The rest of the kids chased Arvid, and he glanced back over his shoulder to see where they were. He heard their collective shouts and enjoyed their adulation, since many of the kids tried to imitate him. Puffing cold breath like a locomotive, his leg muscles pushed him faster. His throat burned after breathing in this cold air, but he wouldn't miss this kind of fun for anything. He was out farther away from where his dad had smoothed out the ice for the kids, and the surface of the ice was a little rougher there. He smiled and looked ahead again, when he tripped over something sticking up through the ice, slamming down hard onto the surface of the lake. The wind was knocked out of him briefly as he tried to catch it again.

"What was that?" he asked himself in a rough, whispered voice as he laid there for a couple of seconds.

While he checked to make sure his teeth were still there, and then rubbed his chin, the other kids came up to him to see what happened, and circled around him. His elbows and chin hurt from the impact since he had been skating fast, but he got back up and skated through the crowd with determination to get the stick that tripped him. Sometimes the trees that fell down into the water near the shore had branches that poked up above the lake's surface, so when the water froze, a few of the branches stuck up through the ice. Arvid thought it was odd because he had been farther away from shore, where none of the trees would have fallen. Plus, it was too deep here for a typical tree branch to reach up to the surface.

When he found the place where he tripped, he got down on his knees and cleared the snow around it. Brushing the area clean, he gasped and jumped backward falling on his backside with a thud and an astonished look on his face.

The other kids watched him, assuming he would get his

revenge on that pesky stick, and talked about playing hockey when they saw Arvid fall backward. They all quickly gathered around closer to see the stick that their friend had tripped over. As they inched forward, then peered over his shoulder and beside him, they saw that it wasn't a stick at all, but was someone's frozen fingers sticking partially up through the ice. The kids screamed in perfect harmony and skated away in different directions at different speeds, each to his own house to tell his parents.

******

A neighbor called the police and one of the younger officers, named Jake Haley, soon came to the spot where the kids had been skating. Jake had only been settled here about six months, and was still in the process of learning who everyone was in the small town. Out of school for only a few years, he looked older than he really was. His hair was buzzed short, military style, and he was very serious when on the job. He spoke clearly and was an organized person in every way. Some of the older locals gave him a hard time since he was a newcomer, but most of the townspeople welcomed him. He hoped that his no-nonsense attitude while on the job made people feel safe and his fun-loving attitude after work made him approachable to the residents.

Jake admired Axel's two-story log cabin, especially the picture windows overlooking the lake, and he wondered if he would ever be able to afford something like this. Jake talked to the kids and several of their parents about what they had found, and recruited the help of two of the fathers, along with a local ice fishing expert from town named Dave Bramwell, to help dig through the ice. Dave was very much the opposite of Jake in many ways, in that he was unshaven with long hair, drove a rusty old truck, and spoke with a thick Upper Peninsula accent that was sometimes challenging to understand. Dave was called a 'Yooper', since he was born in the UP of Michigan, above the Mackinac Bridge which separates Lower Michigan from Upper Michigan. Jake was born in Bay City, which is south of the bridge and Dave constantly called Jake a 'troll', since he came from below the bridge. Dave was entertaining to be around, but Jake often felt he was too silly. He hoped Dave wouldn't goof around today.

Jake asked the other parents to take the kids back home so the adults could continue in private with their grisly task. Most of the kids complained at first, but did as they were told, while only a few of the adults stayed on the lake shore in front of their homes to help if needed.

"Dave, I appreciate you coming out this morning on short notice to help with this."

Dave just nodded his head and kept on working.

After he had spent some time skillfully cutting through the ice with what looked like a modified chainsaw or a gas-powered auger, Dave motioned for the neighbors that it was time for their help. Jake was impressed with how quickly Dave finished the hole and knew right away he had called the right person. It took the strength of four men and ropes to lift up this very cold, dead body, and they were exhausted when they finally got the man up onto the frozen surface.

"It's Eddie Larson, one of the older guys from around the lake," said Jake, a little out of breath.

"He's almost frozen solid," commented Axel. "How long do you think he's been there?"

"Hard to say. I just saw him a couple of days ago at the pub, so has to be less than two days. As a matter of fact, he was wearing that same grungy old jacket, but I guess he always wore that jacket."

Jake noticed that Dave was fixated with the expression on Eddie's face, since it was frozen in a horrible terror. His eyes and mouth told a story that sent chills up Jake's spine, but nobody said anything about it while the men were all together.

As soon as the two of them were off by themselves away from the others, Dave asked, "Jake, have you ever seen anything like this before?"

Jake just shook his head. Although he didn't let Dave know his feelings at this point, Jake was also bothered by the look on Eddie's face when they got him out of the water. It affected him more than he realized as they finished up their work on the ice, and he noticed several times that his own hands shook. The chills and the shaking were certainly not the results of the cold weather this time though, despite his attempts to convince himself otherwise. Eddie was one of the older locals who constantly gave Jake a hard time, and everyone knew that these two men were not the best of friends.

Without looking at Dave, Jake finally commented, "Well, it was probably an accident."

"What about his eyes and the fear in his face?" Dave quietly responded so the two fathers who helped them couldn't hear.

"Falling through the ice will put that kind of fear on a person's face, and in this case, that expression was frozen for all to see."

"Be careful what you say, especially in front of the neighbors, until the autopsy, ay? Once that's done, it should help us better understand what really happened to this guy."

Jake didn't acknowledge what Dave said, but kept walking on the ice toward shore, looking down deep in thought while the other men followed. Dave picked up his tools as the police officer paced around the shore about thirty feet away, casually scuffing up the footprints in the snow while he talked to some of the dads who had watched them get the man's body out of the lake.

Jake commented to these men, "He must have fallen

17

through the ice, moved under the surface away from the hole for a few minutes, couldn't find the hole again, and tried to punch his hand up through the ice to pull himself out before succumbing to the frigid water."

Axel nodded his head in agreement, as did most of the other men, and added, "Can't say that I'll miss the old jerk."

******

Dave heard the discussion carrying across the ice and thought it almost sounded like a pre-rehearsed statement from Officer Haley. It was as though the verdict had been decided before any investigation was carried out, but Dave didn't say anything more. He was frustrated at the way Jake ignored his input, going ahead with his theory before getting any of the facts, but this wasn't the first time. It was no secret that Jake didn't care much for Dave, but the feelings were mutual between the two. Dave thought Jake was too inexperienced, and tried too hard to fit in with the locals. Maybe that's what people need to do when they move to a new town, but he believed that Jake overdid it. He also figured that Jake wasn't respected by the police force, and was given this assignment in the Manitow area as a kind of punishment. At least that's what he hoped had gone down.

He scanned the shoreline, wondering what really happened to Eddie. A motive was not an issue, since Eddie was a mean person and there were probably plenty of people who would be glad to see him dead. Why at this spot though? Did the trees here offer good cover while a person worked on the ice? Another thing that bothered Dave was that the ice was over four inches thick here. There was no way a man could punch his hand up through that much ice and get his fingers to stick up through the surface. Someone must have deliberately left this guy's hand up, keeping his head underwater, while the ice froze around his fingers. Dave knew there was no use in arguing with Jake though, especially in front of the neighbors.

While he walked back to shore, Dave looked around to see if he could spot where Eddie might have gone through the ice, but didn't see anything that looked obvious. If the moon was hidden by clouds that night, then just about anywhere on the lake would be a good place to dump a body, since the ice freezes quickly again to cover up a hole. Where the man's fingers reached through the ice was probably where he was put into the water.

Dave put the tools and rope back in his truck and, after a bit of heavy lifting by the four of them, loaded Eddie the iceman into the ambulance to finish their job. This wasn't how he expected to spend the morning, but at least he had the rest of the day to get some real work done that would earn a paycheck.

The police officer continued talking to the neighbors who lived there on the shore and had helped lift the old man out of the lake, while the ambulance drove away. Dave checked the area once more to make sure he hadn't missed any of his tools, and then walked back to his truck. He couldn't get the dead man's expression out of his mind, and doubted that he ever would. He was convinced by the fact that Eddie's eyes were opened wide with intense fear and his mouth was also open, frozen in a scream, that something terrible had happened to him against his will, more than just falling through the ice. It was no accident.

Chapter Four

PAUL WAS UP EARLY AND LIT A FIRE in the fireplace since the cold permeated the cabin this morning. He worked up the will-power to go out into the arctic weather, looking forward to exploring outside. The smell of bacon and eggs wafted throughout the cabin while Lisa cooked breakfast. He walked into the small kitchen and gave her a hug from behind. He spun her around and danced briefly with her while she held a spatula in one hand and his hand in the other, then spun her back around to let her continue with breakfast.

"Let's eat on the porch overlooking the lake," he suggested.

"Hmmm. OK."

He gathered up a few plates, forks, and napkins and went out to setup the table on the porch for their meal as she finished up the eggs. While he was out there, Paul hid a few of Lisa's favorite chocolates in places where she would easily find them, and smiled as he imagined what her expression would be when she found one of these hidden treasures.

Once back in the kitchen, he poured coffee for both of them and said, "It is a little colder out there, but I think it'll build character."

She smiled and said, "I'll be ready for it," as he took their cups out to the porch.

It looked like at one time this room was just a screened in porch which could only be enjoyed during the summers on the lake, but the screens had since been replaced with almost a dozen windows, and insulation had been partially put in to help keep the porch warmer in cold weather. It didn't help much when the temperature was below zero outside, but it did make the room a relaxing area that could at least be used in the winters now. Paul liked the couch that overlooked the lake, but thought he would enjoy sitting next to it, at the small table with his wife as they ate breakfast out there. He helped her carry their food out to the table, and they sat down to eat while looking at the frozen lake.

"This is an awesome view," Paul commented with interest as he looked through all of the windows as far as he could see. "Notice that long stretch of undisturbed shoreline, then a cabin, then another long stretch of white birch and cedar trees, and another cabin. The ice goes right up to the trees, but I'll bet during the summer there's a sandy beach that almost touches the woods."

Lisa joined him at the window and followed his gaze as Paul continued.

"And look across the middle of the lake. There are several small cabins and a large building way off in the distance, with a lot of trees on each side. That must be the 'popular lakeside restaurant with cabin rentals' you mentioned on the way here."

She sat down at the table and looked up at her husband.

"Paul, when you first suggested coming to this area, I did some investigating to see what kind of interesting things are nearby. I'm looking forward to visiting that lighthouse on Lake Superior, just a few miles away from the cabin, so let's check it out today."

"Are you sure it'll be open in the winter? A lot of the

things around here are closed from October to May?"

"I checked, and the website said it would be open for visitors today," Lisa confirmed. "It's been here over a hundred years and has been made into a museum."

"It sounds good to me. It would be even better if they let us climb up to the top and look around from up there."

"Don't get your hopes up, but that would be a nice view, wouldn't it?" as Paul nodded with a mouthful of breakfast.

They finished eating and cleaned up the kitchen, then braved the cold, running out to their SUV. They were dressed for it, with jackets, gloves, hats and each had a cup of coffee for the short drive.

******

Lisa said, "The lighthouse is just up the highway, then turn right to follow a long road to Lake Superior. It's a good thing we have a road map, since neither my cell phone nor the GPS are getting a signal."

"We'll just have to rough it and find the lighthouse the old fashioned way, like they did a hundred years ago. With the roads covered in snow the way they are now, it may take us just as long to get there as it would back then."

After driving for ten minutes and not seeing a single car or house along the desolate road, Paul wondered if he had missed a turn. His eyes occasionally glanced up at the rear-view mirror, and it occurred to him that they were so far off the beaten path nobody would find them for weeks if anything happened to the SUV, especially with no cell phone service way out here. It's a good thing they packed extra blankets, snacks, and other supplies in the back. If someone wanted to dispose of a dead body, this would be just as good a place as any. Maybe better. The road curved to the left, and he saw Lisa looking at the roadside with piles of snow pushed up on each side. Paul realized someone must have plowed this area, so that was some relief, since he figured that all civilization had been left behind miles ago. People around here probably had a snow-plow attached to the front of their truck so this may not have been done by the city or county. However, even finding a house and a truck with a plow would be a little more reassuring. He hoped Lisa hadn't noticed how far out they were now.

"Look at the footprints in the snow. I think they're moose tracks. Wouldn't it be great to see a moose here?"

Paul nodded and said, "Well, let's keep our eyes open. This looks like an ideal place to see one. I think they like to munch on those branches along the road there."

He was ready to admit defeat and confess that he was lost, when all of a sudden there was an opening in the trees and, centered in the middle, the lighthouse loomed ahead like a giant staring down on them. Paul felt his stress melt away as he watched Lisa out of the corner of his eye. It seemed as though she never felt lost, and actually just enjoyed the scenery along the way, so he would leave it at that. He parked next to a truck, and they walked around outside to look up at the incredible structure. Painted white with red trim at the top to match the light keeper's house connected to it, neither looked anywhere near a century old. There was very little breeze from the lake here, which surprised Paul, but he was glad because it was cold enough without the wind's icy fingers reaching through their winter outfits.

******

"Wow, they've done a great job fixing this place up."

A man came around the corner of the light keeper's house and walked up to Paul.

"Hi folks. My name's Larry Olson. Just wait until you see the inside," and he reached out to shake Paul's hand.

Paul quickly turned, shaking Larry's hand.

"Good morning. Is it open for visitors now?"

"Yes, please come on in and look around. If you'd like, I'll take you up into the lighthouse. It is a beautiful view from up there."

Lisa replied, "Oh, we'd like that very much," and they followed Larry into the main house.

Larry was an older gentleman with flecks of grey in his hair, and he dressed warmly in layers with the traditional plaid jacket that all the locals wore around here. His face was weathered, but Lisa could tell it was a friendly face. He had wrinkles at the edges of his eyes, but her first thought was that they were from years of smiling. She believed his hands felt as though they had worked hard all his life, and figured he was probably a trustworthy man. Paul often told her that she was a good judge of character.

"Some loyal people from the area worked for several years to restore the lighthouse, the house where the lighthouse keeper lived, and a small museum next door. It's all in good shape now, but it was in disrepair for decades. This is where the lighthouse keepers and their families lived over the years. We've brought out all of the original furniture, dishes, household supplies, and such, and picked up a few antique items that we thought would enhance the feel of the place."

"You all have done a wonderful job. It looks like we've stepped back in time a hundred years."

Larry smiled at her and said, "Feel free to walk around here and upstairs, and when you're ready to climb the lighthouse, let me know."

Lisa took her time examining each room, and commented, "Did you see that old-fashioned kitchen with its icebox and iron stove? I could just see myself making a wonderful dinner for us in there."

"I especially like the authentic Victorian furniture and the turn-of-the-century harpsichord in the living room."

"I think my favorites were the old bedrooms upstairs with genuine antique beds, dressers, and vintage clothes."

While they still looked around, Larry came up to them and said, "So I hope you're enjoying yourselves. Let me know if you have any questions."

"Thanks for letting us look around. It's very interesting."

"How many steps is it up to the top of the lighthouse?" Lisa asked.

"It's ninety-six steps to the top. Are you ready to make the climb?"

"Let's go," said Lisa with a mischievous grin, and they followed him through the door to the lighthouse.

As they climbed, Larry said, "I always enjoy taking people up to the top to see the view, but you can't imagine how much fun it is taking kids up the stairs. They have such a sense of wonder about how high up it is, and the expression on their faces when they look out the window at the top is priceless."

Lisa envisioned a herd of preteens ascending in front of her and listened to the excitement in their voices as they anticipated the prize that awaited them at the end of their climb. She considered what it would be like to bring her own kids here one day, and she shared in their sense of wonder. She looked forward to being a mom someday and hoped that day would be in the next nine months. She smiled at the thought.

After walking the spiral staircase for several minutes, they came up through an opening in the floor, and saw the enormous light which was used to warn ships that the rocky shoreline was near. Lisa was also surprised when she came up and stood next to the large windows overlooking the water. The silence said everything for a couple of minutes as Lisa took it all in. It provided a 360-degree view, so they saw the snow-covered trees, the house, and Lake Superior. Larry broke the silence.

"On a clear day in the summer, you can see all the way to an island out there, but it's a little overcast now."

"This view makes it all worthwhile," said Lisa, and Paul nodded.

They all stepped around the small walkway that surrounded the large light bulb and made sure they saw everything they could in every direction.

"I like those giant boulders on the shore down there. Some of them look as big as a car and probably weigh a lot more than my SUV."

From this angle, Lisa then noticed what appeared to be a hidden trail through the trees from the lighthouse all the way to Lake Superior, and was immediately captivated. It gave the impression that someone might be able to sneak through that section of the woods from the lighthouse to the lake without being seen, providing a secret path that wouldn't be noticeable. From up here however, it would be possible to see someone go in the woods and come out at the lakeshore. Just then, she thought she saw a man standing at the edge of the woods. That got her full attention, as she tried to find the person again. It looked like he wore a dark brown jacket and a hat, but he was nowhere to be found now. She questioned whether or not she really saw someone way down there. Maybe it was just the bushes and trees.

"Is there anyone else here today besides us?" Lisa asked without taking her eyes away from the entrance to the secret path.

"No, just you two so far. By the way, if you feel the call of nature, we have a 'His and Her' outhouse near the big rocks on the way to the shore."

"Yeah, I'm looking forward to that experience, Larry," Paul replied sarcastically as Lisa ignored their conversation.

She remained silent as she searched the woods at both

ends of the path, and then confirmed there were only two cars at the base of the lighthouse – Paul's SUV and Larry's truck that Paul parked next to.

Paul leaned over toward Larry and said, "Thanks for taking us up here today."

"It's my pleasure. As you walk down the steps, stay to the right and watch your head as we go down through the door in the floor."

Lisa reluctantly followed them down the hole, and wondered who might have been way out here without a car. It seemed odd, but maybe there was nothing to be concerned about. She figured that someone may live close by and they just didn't notice the driveway that gave this person access to the road they came in on, or maybe there's another road that led out of this area.

It took them a few minutes to get all the way down, and when they reached the exit, Paul asked, "How old is this lighthouse?"

"It was finished in 1895, so it is now 117 years old."

Paul handed Larry some cash, and said, "Here's a donation to keep up the repairs."

"Thanks. We appreciate it."

"Are there any other items of interest nearby?"

Larry glanced at Lisa and paused for a few seconds.

"Well, downtown Manitow is nice, with several good restaurants. There's a small lake a little closer that has a lot of old Ojibwa Indian legends about it, if you're interested in that. Some mysterious things have happened there over the years."

"Which lake is that?" Paul asked.

"Oh, it's called Kisinaw Lake, about eight miles up the road, just off the highway."

Lisa looked at Paul, astonished, and said, "That's where we're staying. What kinds of mysterious things?"

"So you already know about it. Yeah, the legends say that a lot of people have died in the lake over the generations, but I only know of a few in my lifetime. Supposedly, people were found sitting cross-legged at the bottom of the lake, others have been found stuck under trees that had fallen over and sunk to the bottom years before. The Ojibwa have a lot of these kinds of stories, but don't have any explanation for the deaths. From what I hear, they were all strong swimmers, and it appeared that someone or something pulled them under against their will."

Lisa looked up at Paul, and he just smiled at her.

"Sounds like some old ghost stories to me," he answered while putting his arm around Lisa.

"Yep, take them with a grain of salt, but remember these legends are very real to many of the Ojibwa. Also, check out downtown Manitow as well. I think you'll like it."

Paul said, "Thanks a lot Larry," then he and Lisa walked down the path to the gravel parking lot.

As her boots crunched the gravel with each footstep, Lisa wondered if there was anything more to the old legends and she looked around in the woods toward that hidden path to see if she saw a pair of eyes watching them.

Chapter Five

MANY OF THE TOWNSPEOPLE MET each weekend at a lakeside restaurant and bar called 'Old Deerfield', quite a few of them almost every night, and there was a homey feel to the old pub. It had been there on the southeast part of the lake since at least the 1930's, and was owned by the same family during most of that time. The building was very rustic, but had been well taken care of over the years. The most recognizable landmark on the lake, it was a popular spot to meet friends, have a drink, or eat. From the outside, it looked similar to the kind of structure Daniel Boone would have visited in Kentucky, with hand-cut logs stacked up and gaps filled in with mud or clay. It was like going back in time to walk around the outside of the pub, especially when no cars were parked out front. Obviously, that was part of the appeal of Old Deerfield, and most people probably wouldn't want it any other way.

Once inside, there were dozens of old photos on all of the walls, with pictures of the locals, their fishing prizes from the lake, their cabins around the lake, and more. Some of the catches included large pike, walleye, and bass, and the record fish and fishermen were proudly displayed in the timeworn photos. A couple of the prize-winning fish themselves even hung on the walls, along with the heads of deer, moose, bear, and a stuffed lynx on a shelf high up in the corner.

The large stone fireplace in another corner, used for decoration much of the year but crackling with warmth all throughout the winter, was a main attraction of Old Deerfield and many people asked to sit near it while they ate. Ancient rifles hung above the impressive mantle, which was lined with antiques that were probably placed there when the pub first opened. People had been coming here for decades, and the stories that were told within these walls over the years could have filled volumes.

Jake sat here winding down, and was quieter than usual, listening to the conversations. This evening the locals discussed their neighbor's body being found in the lake, so he was interested to hear the thoughts from these folks.

"His death was determined to be an accident. Eddie just somehow fell through the ice and couldn't get out in time."

"Yeah, but Eddie lived on this lake all his life and wouldn't have gone out on thin ice."

"The place where his body was found wasn't an area where the ice would have been thin anyway."

"But he might have fallen through somewhere else, moved under the ice looking for a thin part to break through, and ended up freezing to death at the spot where he was found."

"Isn't it coincidental that just as some visitors came to stay on the lake, we have a murder?"

"Murder? I heard it was an accident?"

"Yeah. I wonder what this 'newlywed' couple is really like."

"Could they have already targeted someone and killed him the first night they arrived in town?"

"What would they be after, since Eddie didn't have any money?"

"Maybe they've been in town longer than anyone realizes and only checked-in the day before to try to remove any suspicion from themselves."

A few of these locals were overly cautious of any visitors for some reason or another, and never cared for tourists at all. Ironically though, tourism brought in money to the businesses in town and around the lake and was good for the overall community. Jake thought they may have been jealous that these tourists had money to spend on vacations, while most of the locals barely made enough to buy food and drop a little bit of change into the casino off the highway. Many of them weren't even friendly with people they had known for decades, so a tourist or even a person like Jake, only recently moving in to town, just couldn't win with a crowd like this.

******

About this time, Paul and Lisa walked through the front door. It was their first time in the restaurant, and everyone became quiet. Out of the cold wind but exposed to icy glares.

Paul waved to the crowd at the bar on the left, said "Hey guys," and a couple of the younger locals looked over at him and nodded.

They strolled toward an empty table in the corner and at once he detected all eyes watching them cross the room. As he walked, Paul felt odd and things started moving as if time slowed down. He knew that everyone was watching him, but from the corner of his eyes he only noticed blurred faces. He almost believed he saw them as faces with angry expressions now, although he wasn't sure for certain whether that was the case. Even though the room was silent, he heard angry voices too with each slowed-down step he took. The second hand on the large clock became louder and louder, and had slowed to tick once every few seconds. It was a strange feeling that he had never encountered, and it gave him reason for concern. He wondered if he might be getting ready to blackout and wanted to hurry over to the table to sit down in case he did fall to the floor.

Once he made it to the table across the room and quickly took his seat, however, everything went back to normal. Footsteps echoed quickly as they stepped on the hardwood floor, and there was a friendly murmur of voices in the room. Not many people looked at him and the crowd seemed to move at normal speed again, some with smiles and some laughing. This was quite an experience for Paul, who wondered if it really happened or if it was just his imagination.

Lisa talked and grinned, appearing as radiant as ever as she sat down across from him. She obviously didn't go through the same episode he just went through, so he decided to forget about it and not mention it to her. A friendly waitress almost immediately brought them a menu, as people around them talked more about other topics. Paul looked around the pub, saw the large fireplace at the end of the dining room, and noticed stained wooden beams across the ceiling.

"I really like the ambiance of this place," said Paul, and Lisa nodded as she surveyed the room.

The policeman, Jake Haley, was there and asked Little Frank, "How many portions did you get out of that deer you picked up off the road?"

"Over 35 portions," replied Frank, with a proud look on his face.

Everyone nodded. Paul glanced at Lisa, and knew they were talking about roadkill. He gave her a 'yuck,' look, and laughed about it. He remembered the deer they saw while driving in to town yesterday, and wondered if they were discussing that same deer. People called the man Little Frank again, which was a bit peculiar, since the man was at least six feet tall and weighed easily over 300 pounds.

Paul said, "I wonder why they call that big guy Little Frank. He's bigger than you and I combined," then Lisa shrugged her shoulders.

******

A little while later, Tim walked in and sat at the bar. He talked with the bartender, looking around at the usual crowd. He responded to the person at his right when he asked Tim a question. A pretty waitress came up and chatted with him, but he didn't eat anything. He just had a few drinks, like a lot of the locals, and enjoyed conversations with a few of the people there. Jake watched the new couple when the waitress brought them their dinner, and stopped by their table to introduce himself. They both seemed pleased to meet one of the locals, and Jake was glad he made them feel at home. They spent quite a while talking to Jake and listening to him tell them about the town, the pub, and some of the townspeople.

Jake tried to see what the couple knew about Eddie being found dead in the lake, and also showed the townspeople that he was 'unofficially' investigating this couple over dinner. He didn't mention anything about a body being found in the lake, since it never came up in conversation. If this couple was not involved with the death, he didn't want to cause any unnecessary concern for the honeymooners. He also came over there to join them as a non-verbal warning for the locals to not mention Eddie's death in front of these 'out-of-towners'. Anyway, the three of them had a lot of laughs while they ate dinner, and eventually people began to return home for the evening.

Jake told the couple, "Maybe I'll see you two around town this week," and they walked toward the door. The waitress cleaned up their table and they headed out to the parking lot. The cabin they stayed at was halfway around the lake, and Jake added, "Since the moon's out and it's not overcast tonight, it should be a pleasant five-minute drive back to your cabin, with a great view of the frozen lake all along the way."

Paul and Lisa waved as Jake watched them drive off. He then came back inside to give a report on these out-of-town-ers to a dozen waiting locals who listened closely, as if he was a camp leader telling a ghost story around a fire.

Chapter Six

PAUL AND **L**ISA DROVE AROUND the lake from their cabin the next morning, and went to the park on the southwest corner of Kisinaw Lake.

Lisa exclaimed excitedly, "Let's get out and try to walk on the ice here!"

Across the lake and to the left, she saw the cabin they rented, as it stood out from the shoreline of trees on each side of it. She noticed that the park on the shore had some swings, a slide, a carousel that spun around, an old-fashioned water pump that stood about six feet tall, and grills for cookouts on the lakeshore. Most of these items were over halfway buried in snow. This would be a nice place in the summer, but it looked as though it didn't get as much activity during the winter, for obvious reasons. She figured that in the summer, people pumped their own water here for the cookouts or even for use in the cabins, since Jake had mentioned that a couple of the cabins didn't have a well.

While Paul eyed the tall trees across the road, Lisa nailed him in the back of the head with a snowball, and he turned to see her innocently looking away as if she hadn't thrown a thing. He bent down to scoop up a weapon for himself, and saw her trying to conceal her laughter as she cunningly distanced herself from her husband.

Lisa made her way down to the edge of the lake at a frozen boat ramp, and stepped carefully out onto the ice in front of the park. Slipping and laughing hysterically at her efforts to walk on the slippery surface, she was obviously having a good time, while Paul got into position to retaliate with his own snow arsenal from the shore.

"When I finally make it back to the shore, I'd like for you to spin me on the carousel," but as Lisa said this, she immediately fell forward over a small batch of snow.

She landed over some clear ice and was surprised when she saw a face looking up at her that wasn't her reflection. Little Frank was under the ice, eyes wide open and mouth frozen in a scream, right under her face. Terrified, she gasped and jumped back quickly, then scrambled over to her husband, who had started sliding on the ice toward her.

"Lisa, are you OK?"

She couldn't catch her breath to say anything and noticed Paul staring at her with a concerned expression while she pointed at the ice. He looked down as well, and saw the same familiar face that she too had recognized from Old Deerfield the previous night.

Paul checked to find that his cell phone had a signal on this part of the lake, and called the police immediately. He put his arms around Lisa to lead her back to the shore, and they waited.

Once he arrived at the lake, Officer Jake Haley confirmed, "This is Little Frank, one of the older guys from around the lake. I just talked to him last night."

After speaking to some of the townspeople who had showed up at the park, Lisa found out, to her surprise, that this was the second body pulled from the lake in the past couple of days.

Paul asked Officer Haley, "Why didn't you mention this last night?"

"I honestly thought Eddie's death was just a one-time thing that wouldn't happen again; an accident where he slipped and fell through the ice. I just didn't want to bother your vacation with that kind of bad news, since I figured that could ruin your belated honeymoon."

"Well, that makes sense. Thanks for that."

Lisa, however, thought that he should have at least mentioned it in case there really was a murderer on the loose, but she didn't say anything.

******

Jake said, "I believe Little Frank's death will be ruled an accident, just like Eddie's."

That just got the crowd talking even more all around the scene, and everyone had their own theory. Jake sensed that not many people believed there could be two accidental drownings in a small frozen lake within days, especially if the two people had lived here all their lives and knew the lake so well. He recognized that he would be under pressure to either prove they were accidental or find clues that helped catch a murderer as quickly as possible, and that meant he would be working long hours over the next few days. The pressure was on him now, almost as though he was the one down under the lake at this moment.

******

Paul and Lisa went into town with Officer Haley to help him complete some paperwork, and while they were there, Paul wanted to stop by the fishing store next door to look around. They answered all of Jake's questions, and filled out the necessary forms for finding a dead body, then walked down to the bait and tackle shop.

"I've always wanted to go ice fishing," Paul mentioned.

He hoped to get Lisa's mind off of Little Frank, but even

changing the subject to fishing didn't help.

"What if you're fishing and you snag another dead body?" she asked.

He turned away from her and made a face, frustrated that she was focused on the dead man, then heard a man talking at the register about ice fishing on Kisinaw Lake the next day. That piqued Paul's interest right away, so he walked up to the man.

"I've never been ice fishing, but I'm staying in a cabin on Kisinaw Lake this week. I heard you mention something about fishing there tomorrow, and wondered if I could join you."

The other man at the register looked at Paul and said, "Well you came to the right place. This guy wrote the book on ice fishing in this area, and sets up on the ice better than anyone I know."

Dave Bramwell smiled, and shook Paul's hand.

"I'd enjoy some company, don'cha know. Which cabin are you staying in?"

"Great! I think it's the third driveway on the lakeside after coming off of the highway, the log cabin. Oh, and this is my wife, Lisa. We're visiting from just outside Lansing."

"Hi Dave."

"It's nice to meet you, Lisa. Yah, I know which one that is. It's in a perfect location with the woods on each side, ay. How about if I pick you up about 8:00 tomorrow morning? You don't need to bring anything, since I already have everything ready to go."

"Thanks Dave. I look forward to it."

He and Lisa walked out of the store to see if Officer Haley needed anything else before he took them back to their cabin.

******

That evening, Paul and Lisa ate at the pub again, and Paul noticed that several of the locals were hesitant to speak to them about finding the old man. By the way people talked to him, Paul had the feeling that a lot of these men suspected he and Lisa had something to do with the two deaths, especially since the bodies were discovered soon after he and Lisa arrived in town. What a vacation this was turning out to be.

While sitting at the table, Paul noticed everything slowed down and people's faces became blurred again. He looked around, but as he turned his head, it seemed as if the room moved in slow motion again. Paul tried to determine why this was happening, and wondered if Lisa realized he was experiencing this. Anger and hatred pounced on him from every corner of the room, and as he looked across the pub, people had the meanest expressions he had ever seen, all staring at him. Every step someone made on the hard wood floors echoed much louder than normal and seemed to take seconds for each echo to finish. It sounded as though an angry man near the bar was about to throw a glass at him, and Paul wondered if he would be able to protect Lisa.

He slowly turned to look at Lisa, still reading the menu, and just as suddenly as it had started, Paul was back to normal. It was like it had never happened. He glanced over at the bar, and nobody even gave the impression that they were going to throw anything at him. The men at the bar smiled and talked calmly with each other now. Paul considered discussing this with Lisa, hoping that he wasn't coming down with something at the beginning of their vacation, but again chose not to mention anything unless it happened a third time. He hoped there wouldn't be a third time.

******

Tim was at the bar again, and listened intently to the talk around the room. This wasn't the first he had heard about Eddie's death, but now that a second person had been found dead, he seemed a little concerned. He knew he wasn't considered a local, since he had only been staying at his cabin for less than a year. Some of the older people called him an 'out-of-towner' or a 'newcomer'. There was certainly a kind of strange pride in living on the lake longer than anyone else, and a person who was 'newer' than the others was almost treated like a second-class citizen by a few of these guys.

The conversation buzzed this evening at the pub, which made for some interesting ideas being brought up.

"Don'cha know you just can't trust those Indians? They're always involved with things like this, and I don't like them one bit."

"Ah, you and your Indians. They're not as bad as you make 'em out to be."

"Yeah, the one at the souvenir shop's alright."

An elderly gentleman added, "There's a ghost that's haunted this lake for decades, and it might finally be seeking revenge against the men who've lived on the lake for a long time."

That got everyone's attention, especially Tim's.

"How could Little Frank's and Eddie's deaths be related to a ghostly revenge?" asked another person at the bar.

"Less than thirty years ago, a young local couple, Stephen and Laura Nelson, were found frozen in the lake, and it was ruled an accidental drowning, just like these two recent ones. However, the word around the town at the time was that those two were murdered, and their bodies put into the freezing lake to make it look like an accident."

There was murmuring around the pub, but it was strangely quiet as they all waited to hear more. Tim noticed that some who appeared to remember these events or had heard the story years ago just nodded or took a drink. He observed people's expressions to see who seemed surprised and who already knew about it.

"Several people made claims about the couple being dangerous fanatics, and someone said they had made threats against a few of the men on the lake that night when they died. It seemed odd that two people would have drowned at the same time, especially people who had grown up on the lake, but nobody questioned it further."

People looked at each other, but no words were spoken for a few seconds.

"Nothing was ever proven, and life went on for the rest of the town."

The guy next to Tim said loudly, "Hey, didn't those two people drown right in front of the same cabin Tim's staying at? That's the one just up the road there past the empty lot."

Someone else shook his head and replied, "It's just your luck to be living in a haunted cabin."

A few people smiled, including Tim, and somebody laughed.

"Out of all of the cabins on the lake, why did I get the haunted one? Someone mentioned it last year when I was looking for a place to stay, but I didn't believe any of it."

The bartender stared at him as he dried off another glass with a towel.

Tim sat close to Paul and Lisa's table and overheard Lisa comment quietly to Paul, "As outrageous as this sounds, it almost seems as though most of the people here believe it could be a ghost that murdered these two men."

He also heard Paul reply, "It's more likely that nobody's even taking the ghost story seriously. It is just a good story to tell at an old pub."

Tim wasn't sure what to believe now, and gulped another drink. He wanted to forget that he had consistent nightmares, and was in no hurry to make his way home to get some sleep.

Chapter Seven

DURING THE NIGHT, PAUL WAS awakened by voices, and realized it was still pitch black all around the room. He looked toward Lisa in the dark, probably sleeping peacefully, and was determined not to wake her, although he felt that he needed to make sure everything was OK.

It must be three in the morning. Who would be outside at this hour?

Immediately, he heard the voices again, but they sounded as though they came from the hall or living room, not from outside. He quietly slid out of bed in one stealthy movement, and stepped softly toward the door to listen for the intruders. Leaving the comfort of the cozy bed, the cold hit him instantly but he ignored it for now. It occurred to him that he didn't have anything to protect himself with, and wondered what he should do if someone waltzed into the bedroom unexpectedly. Paul's eyes became adjusted to the lack of light as he stood against the wall for just a minute. The whispering started again, but suddenly the hair on the back of his neck stood up and his heart rate began to increase. The voice appeared to be directly in front of him, but he saw in the dark room that nobody was there. Hesitantly, his arm reached up to be certain, but it waved right through nothing. It was very cold in the room when he climbed out of bed, but he noticed his fear had warmed him up to where he actually felt sweat on his forehead.

Determined to stay calm and protect his wife, Paul peered around the corner in case his senses were playing tricks on him. He was surprised when the living room revealed nothing unusual, and he stepped out of the bedroom all the way to investigate further. The whispering began again behind him, very breathy, but nothing legible, almost unearthly. None of this made sense, because Paul knew he was alone out here, but there was something making noises in this room, causing him to feel as though evil entities planned some dastardly event. It unnerved him since whoever made the noises didn't appear to consider Paul a threat and discussed their plans right in his presence.

As his eyes darted around the room to catch any sudden movement, he realized the whispering had stopped, so he glanced around the corner again into the bedroom. He barely recognized the lump under the quilts and was glad that he hadn't interrupted her sleep. Several minutes went by and he still wasn't able to find the source of the voices, or detect any new sound or movement in the cabin. Paul wondered if he had been dreaming, and shook his head at how foolish he must look, wandering around the silent, freezing cabin in the blackness of 3:00 AM.

He slipped back into the warmth of the bed, and was instantly glad to be back with the levelheaded again. He wondered how he could have thought there was someone else in the cabin, and chose to forget the incident ever happened. With his eyes adjusted to the lack of light, he adored the look on Lisa's face, and yearned for that same serene feeling as it came to him sooner than he expected. Within a few minutes, he was asleep again and was unable to tell whether or not the voices had returned within the walls of the cabin.

* * * * * *

After a restful night's sleep, Lisa made plans for the day as she ate breakfast. It was a cold but clear morning around the lake, and she kissed her husband as he waited for Dave Bramwell to arrive and take him to go ice fishing. They had met Dave in town at the fishing store the day before, and he and Paul hit it off right away. Dave had a pronounced traditional 'Yooper' accent, more than most of the town.

"I enjoy hearing him talk. I've read that the accent is actually the Finnish language coming out in words used by some of the families that emigrated from Finland a hundred years ago."

"He probably doesn't even know he's Finnish," Paul replied casually as he finished getting his hiking boots on.

Lisa disregarded his comment and continued, "Finnish doesn't have the 'th' sound, so Dave and others who have Finnish ancestry don't pronounce the 'th' in their words."

"Well, according to the bait and tackle store owner we talked to yesterday, Dave is an ice fishing expert, and can setup for fishing on the ice better than anyone. That's all I'm interested in right now."

Lisa heard Dave's truck drive up, and Paul went out to greet him. She followed in just her robe and slippers, then waved when she saw him wave from inside the truck.

"Hey Dave," said Paul as he quickly climbed in and joined him.

Lisa came over by Paul on the passenger side and said, "Good morning Dave. It's freezing out here!"

"Hi Paul. Good morning, Lisa. Are you sure you won't join us? It should be a lot of fun, don'cha know."

"No, thanks anyway. I'm interested in a ghost story we heard from the pub last night about the people who died in the lake almost thirty years ago. I was thinking about doing a little research about it today in town."

Dave looked at her inquisitively and said, "I'm dating a girl who works at the library in town, near the old church with the bell tower. You should go and talk to her, and she can help you look some things up on the library equipment, ay?"

Now this piqued Lisa's interest, and she agreed, "Yes, I believe I'll do that. What's her name?"

"Marta, and she's working today. I'll let her know you might stop by to see her."

"Thanks Dave," Lisa said as she kissed her husband once more, and stepped away from the truck.

"Just for the record, Dave, I don't believe in ghosts and I don't think Lisa does either. She's just interested in seeing how the story ties in to these recent deaths."

Dave nodded, then pulled out of the driveway and headed around the lake to their fishing destination.

Lisa ran back inside the cabin to finish getting dressed, and decided to take a few photographs of the scenery around the cabin when she felt more prepared to walk out in the cold air again. She had never seen trees lean out from the shoreline over a lake as far as these trees did, and she figured these quiet sentinels would provide some thought-provoking pictures. They reached out over the edge of the frozen surface as if they tried to help someone or something. Lisa stood in the yard by the shore and summed up which trees had the most character. She then positioned herself to get the right photos, sometimes kneeling on one knee, brushing aside her long hair since she had forgotten to put on a hat. She took several from each direction, some of the white birch trees and a few of the cedar trees, all with generous amounts of snow on their branches. She was happy with the subjects she picked out for these photos, and looked forward to seeing the finished results.

Next she went down the path to photograph several of the trees in the wooded section, and found a frozen creek. Lisa was stunned by the beauty, and she slowly examined each aspect of the woods as she planned out her next angles. She wondered about the eyes she had seen on their first day here, and tried to figure out if they were really eyes or just her imagination. She knew there were several wild animals that could be here in the woods, and was cautious as she made her way down the path.

It was darker in many areas here, since the trees were so thick that not much sunlight made it past the impressive branches overhead. Lisa found she had to adjust her camera settings to account for the lack of light, and with the skills of a professional photographer, she wisely made the correct changes. Again, the fallen trees were her targets, especially some of the larger ones, and she wondered what would have knocked down these massive titans with trunks over two feet in diameter. On at least two occasions, Lisa had the strangest feeling that she was being watched, but she didn't see anyone or anything suspicious around her. It gave her the creeps, but she kept walking, not giving anyone the satisfaction of knowing that she was a little intimidated. She looked for the eyes that had startled her on that first day, but saw nothing unusual near the frozen creek. Those eyes would be great in a photograph.

The creek had snow on the banks of each side, connected by a large sheet of ice, and after studying the area for a few minutes, she found exactly what she wanted. Click, click, click, and the scenes were captured forever on film. There were some kind of animal footprints on the other side of the creek, but she couldn't tell what made them. They looked like they might be deer tracks from where she stood. Lisa then followed the creek up to the road, and walked on the edge of the road along the woods back to the cabin. A homemade fence was there, which she photographed from the creek end of the property toward the cabin, as well as from the cabin back to the creek, and then she found the best angles from which to capture the cabin from the road. She liked seeing the frozen lake in the background, especially with the trees and cabins from the opposite shore in the background of the pictures. She also took a few good views of the 'front' of the cabin from the lakeshore, and smiled as she looked around again to see the lake, the trees, and the cabin before packing up her camera. She figured this had been a productive and enjoyable morning already.

Once satisfied she put on film all of the images she had initially wanted to preserve, she went back into the cabin to get ready for a trip to Manitow by herself. As she put things away, a glimmer caught her attention when she walked past the living room door. She stepped back through the doorway and looked on top of a painting on the wall, only to find a small dark chocolate candy bar hidden on top of the frame. She laughed out loud at her husband's creativity, and set the chocolate free from its hiding place. Without delay, she sampled the indulgence, and enjoyed every bite as if she had never tasted anything like it before. The taste was so enjoyable she had to look to see if her other half had planted any more surprises for her, and was delighted to find another one tucked away on the mantle. When a woman has chocolate it doesn't last long, and this one soon disappeared as well.

After she had enough of the delicacies, she locked up the cabin and drove into town. She planned to meet with the young local girl, who Dave called 'Marta', supposedly working at the library this morning. Dave said he would call his girlfriend to let her know that Lisa would be stopping by to talk to her, and she looked forward to meeting this local librarian.

The downtown area was about a 15-minute drive from

the lake, and was where most of the locals went to do their shopping. The library was an old brick building that hadn't changed much in the past century, and Lisa admired the entry way as she walked up to the front of the building. She wondered if it had always been a library, or if it was something else all those years ago. Lisa couldn't see in the high windows, but recognized that they were probably just to let in some of the sunlight for people inside. She also noticed that the snowdrifts were over six feet high, so these windows were even useful in the winter. Lower windows would be covered up by snow and wouldn't allow in any light. She gazed up at the trees along the sidewalk, noticing they were majestic white pines, and thought that they made excellent greeters, welcoming patrons into the library. She heard Chick-a-dees singing joyfully, as her eyes traced up one side of the wooden door frame, across the top, and down the other side.

Lisa didn't realize it, but she hummed along with the birds as she stepped into the old building. The February wind blew the door closed behind Lisa, and the slamming door embarrassed her. She looked around sheepishly as the echo seemed to go on forever across the open library. All eyes had immediately zoomed in on Lisa standing inside the front door, but within a few seconds, the sound had dissipated and everyone's head turned back to their books or newspapers. There was a large table in front of the desk, with rows of shelves, each offering hundreds of books to her. The colors on the walls were relaxing and cheerful as she stepped toward the desk. She expected there to be a musty smell from all the old books, but was pleasantly surprised at the relaxing aroma that surrounded her as she walked past each aisle. It smelled like someone had brewed coffee, and the room had a freshness that was very welcoming, just like walking into someone's home after a spring cleaning or when homemade cookies were in the oven.

A smartly dressed, attractive young woman with shoulder length hair stood behind the desk, and Lisa assumed she was probably Dave's girlfriend.

"Is Marta here?"

The girl behind the desk said, "Yes, I'm Martha."

Lisa realized the young librarian was named 'Martha', not 'Marta', but Dave just didn't pronounce the 'th' sound in her name. She laughed out loud when Martha said it, causing Martha to give her a confused expression.

"Dave said your name was 'Marta.'"

Martha smiled at that and agreed, "Yah, he has quite an accent, ay?" while they both busted out laughing at her imitation.

"I enjoy hearing him talk because of the accent."

"Yes, so do I, but don't let Dave know because it'll build up his ego too much."

After brief introductions and small talk, Lisa found that they were almost the same age, and had a lot of the same interests. She was impressed with Martha's taste in clothes, since they were professional yet very flattering. If she had seen Martha in a shopping mall in Lansing, she could have easily been mistaken for a lawyer or a manager, but was here instead in this small town library. Lisa wanted to ask where she shopped, but figured it would be best to focus first on why she came to the library. They could talk clothes later.

They discussed the old rumors, the local tales, some of the new rumors, etc, and the librarian suggested, "Why don't you look up the newspapers from back then on the micro-fiche machine? I'll set you up, and then I need to go and file a stack of books that came in today."

Lisa did that, and eventually found the articles of the couple's death twenty-four years ago. She just stared at the faces on the page for a minute or so because she realized that someone's story was about to be discovered many years after their death, and she felt like a combination between an archaeologist and a detective. As a child, she had wanted to be an archaeologist so she could investigate and study about ancient dinosaurs and cities from the Bible, and even though she went into nursing, Lisa still had an interest in investigating things from the past.

She now had a photograph of the couple, their names, and the exact date of the couple's death, but was surprised by the lack of additional information presented. The story was continued on another page, but Lisa couldn't find that other page. She got up and looked for Martha, who had gone back up front after helping her get setup with the microfiche, but only saw an older librarian at the desk this time. She had dark brown hair, was dressed well, like Martha, and looked through a stack of books while humming a pleasant tune from many years ago.

"Would you be able to help me with something?" Lisa asked the older lady.

She wore a nametag that read 'Abigail' and glowed cheerfully as she came over with Lisa to the machine.

"I'm looking for an old article that was supposed to be continued on another page," Lisa began, but when the older lady sat down, she looked at the article in horror with an audible gasp.

Her eyes were wide open, and she stared at the picture of the Nelsons without saying anything.

This took Lisa aback and with real concern she asked, "Are you OK?"

Abigail just stood up and stepped back with her hand over her mouth, and looked as though she had tears in her eyes.

"Is something wrong?"

Martha had come back by this time, and saw the look on Abigail's face. She rushed over to her.

The older woman said, "I think I'd like to go home and rest for a while."

"Excuse us for just a minute," Martha quickly said to Lisa, and she walked toward the entrance of the library to help Abigail with her coat.

"I'm feeling very tired now and just want to lay down for a bit," Lisa overheard Abigail tell Martha. She realized Abigail didn't want to talk about anything at this point.

"I don't know if you should drive now if you're not feeling well."

"It's only a two-minute trip to the house. I'll be fine."

Martha nodded, and walked her outside to her car. She came back inside the library as Abigail slowly drove away and sat down by the microfiche machine while Lisa told her what had happened. They looked again for the missing part of the paper, but were unable to locate it.

"I really don't understand how a piece of the newspaper could be missing from the library's records."

They talked a little bit about the older librarian and what might have upset her so much.

"I hope Abigail will be OK."

"I'll ask her later today what it was about this article that bothered her, or if there was something else, and I'll let you know what I found out. Maybe she'll know what happened to the second page, since she's been here at the library for so long. Now I'm intrigued by this article I've never heard of."

Lisa walked toward the door with Martha close behind, and she turned to look at her.

"I'd like to stop by and have lunch with you sometime this week, if that's OK with you."

"I'd like that very much. Let me know which day you're coming in again. There's plenty of great little café's just up the road within walking distance."

"Will do. Thanks again for your help today. I'll see you in

a day or two," and then Lisa left the library deep in thought about what had just happened.

Chapter Eight

RATHER THAN DRIVE BACK TO THE cabin right away, Lisa looked around outside of the library, and decided to take a stroll down toward the town's main street, thinking as she walked. The library was just around the corner, and the weather was perfect for a leisurely stroll. She felt stylish yet casual in her overcoat, gloves, and winter hat, and thought she fit right in with the townspeople. Lisa was dressed warm enough to be outside in the colder temperature, even when the icy wind picked up and raced along the sidewalks down both sides of the street, and she didn't mind it at all. She walked past the old church, which Dave had mentioned, then turned and saw the little shops that lined the historic street. When she scanned down the street, the scene made her go back to get her camera from the SUV, since she saw a few great 'post-card opportunities' and wanted to take some photographs of the town to bring back home with her.

Lisa adjusted her camera settings again to account for the brighter day, as compared to the darkness she had in the woods earlier. She started her walk again, taking a few pictures of the church and its bell tower before turning onto Main street for the second time. It was a nice relaxing walk, as she considered the exterior of some of the old shops. She and Paul were amateur photographers, and she had the camera out snapping pictures of the old buildings. She really enjoyed seeing this architecture, and in the wintery setting with snow positioned in strategic places, it made for interesting shots.

Most of these buildings had probably not changed much in 100 years, and it gave her a yearning to learn more about this old logging town. She read that in the late 1800's, many of the men in town were lumberjacks and would spend the days cutting down trees, carrying the logs to the river on large horse-drawn sleds, and floating them to the lumber company in town. Pasties were the working-man's meal, mostly for the miners, and apparently these were still a favorite at all the restaurants around here, as she just noticed on a menu posted outside of a little restaurant. It was a flattened kind of pie crust that was filled with meat, potatoes, carrots, and other vegetables, then folded over and cooked with everything inside the bread. The Finnish miners could keep this with them throughout the day and eat it when it was time for lunch. Lisa had tried one already at Old Deerfield and liked it covered in gravy.

As she thought about pasties, Lisa was hit with a delicious aroma from the restaurant next to her, and it instantly made her hungry. She wondered what it was, and found that she was able to figure out several of the tasty ingredients that made up that wonderful scent. Lisa looked again at the menu posted outside of the place, and was tempted by several of the items listed. She already made the decision that she liked this restaurant and would have to bring Paul here to try it in the next few days.

Just then, a few people came out of the restaurant full of laughter, and they all greeted her with a pleasant "Hi," to which she instantly responded.

Lisa looked in the restaurant and was waved at by a woman inside, probably the owner or manager. Lisa waved back and gave her a smile. Despite the cold temperature outside, she was warmed by the hospitality and it gave her a good feeling inside. She continued walking on the Main Street sidewalk.

Many of the restaurants and other stores along the sidewalks had black and white photographs of their logging ancestors, with men standing on top of sleds stacked thirty feet high with a dozen or more large white pine trees, or of the waterways filled with logs being floated down the Manitow River to the local lumber mill here in town. Lisa stopped occasionally to look at these pictures in the different shops. Some of the logs looked to be over six feet in diameter in these old pictures. What an impressive forest they would have made. She was saddened that these great trees were gone now, and wished she would have been able to see them and walk among these tremendous works of art.

Lisa wondered if Paul would have made a good lumberjack in those days, and smiled at the idea as she kept walking past the store windows. She had bought him flannel shirts and hiking boots for the trip, and told him that he would be her 'rugged mountain man.' Compared with these old pictures, it looked as though he would fit right in with these loggers. She imagined what it might have been like for these men as they worked in the forests, brought the trees into town for lumber, and faced the harsh winter conditions back then without today's modern conveniences. She couldn't wait to tell Paul about these photos of the lumberjacks, and continued her tour. Every once in a while, she would hold the camera up and snap another picture of a building across the street or down the sidewalk.

The bank on the corner looked like it had always been a bank, and indeed it had been there for over a century, since she noticed the date on the second floor front of the building. She figured this was probably when the bank was built because the address of the bank was displayed on the first floor over the front doors. It had a majestic architecture that almost seemed out of place in this small town, but she was glad it was there to look out over Main Street all of these years.

Another gem was the movie theater, which had an old fashioned façade since it had been a theater all the way from the 1920's to the present day. She tried to imagine what it would have been like to attend the theater back in those days, where someone there played dramatically on a piano to help increase the tension in a silent movie, or played faster during a chase scene in such a movie to build up excitement. She pictured the floor-length fancy dresses that the women would have worn to a show and how grand that must have been. She then looked at her casual clothes in the reflection of a store window. It was a little more formal back in those days than it would be going to a movie today.

From one intersection, she saw three church steeples standing over the housetops just outside of the business district, and Lisa thought she and Paul should go to one of the oldest churches in the town this coming weekend to see what it was like inside. Her preference so far was to attend the Lutheran Church on the corner, the first church she had seen, with the beautiful bell tower, but she would leave it up to Paul. He would want to do whatever made Lisa happy, so she would give him the opportunity to make her happy in 'his' decision.

One of the largest houses on the end of the street was actually a funeral home, and it was strangely beautiful. It crossed her mind that many of the people who lived and died in this area over the past century probably ended up going through this house before being laid at their church or home and moved on to the cemetery. For the rest of the downtown stores, the residents had done an excellent job of putting new businesses in the old buildings, then restoring the exteriors and interiors so that they retained their original look and feel. It was nice to glance in and see the old brick on the interior walls, and the original wood floors in many of the stores and restaurants.

There were a couple of antique stores, a laundromat, several charming restaurants, a fishing shop, a couple of bars that also served food, some small clothing stores, an old book shop that caught her interest, and an enticing little ice cream shop. Eventually, she made her way back to the SUV, thankful that she had good weather in which to walk outside and take some photographs. As she drove back to the cabin, Lisa decided that she would like to bring Paul to the bookshop and the antique store to add a few antique books and knick-knacks to their collection, and then stop by the ice cream shop while they were in town. She looked forward to coming back here with him.

Chapter Nine

PAUL AND **D**AVE WENT WAY around the north side of the lake, far away from the lake's pub and the cabin Paul and Lisa rented. Dave explained what a great spot this was for fishing, and had already began cutting the hole while Paul remained fascinated by the difference in the shoreline on this side of the lake. Over here, there were a lot of large rocks that decorated the shore.

Dave said, "This is the rockiest part of the lake." While Paul scanned the shoreline, he continued, "The rocks provide a good nesting ground for many of the fish, and safe places for the young ones while they're growing up. We want them to grow up so we can catch them when they're bigger, ay?"

Impressed by Dave's knowledge and expertise, as it did take skill to be able to cut the hole in the ice in order to do some fishing from it, Paul watched Dave with great interest as he worked. To Paul's surprise, someone rushed up to the lake's edge and shouted at them, so Dave stopped to look up. An elderly gentleman came out of a hidden cabin back in the woods on the shore, and he didn't look happy. He had a rough grey beard, and actually dressed like a settler from another century, reminding Paul of Daniel Boone in a way. Paul didn't even realize there was a cabin nearby, until he saw the man coming from that direction.

"Uh oh. That's an old hermit called Robert Vallee, and he's not a pleasant fellow."

Paul soon noticed that Vallee had a large rifle with him, so he gave him the attention that the man was expecting.

"You two need to get away from my land and do your fishing somewhere else."

"But we're out on the lake and aren't even on your property."

Paul wasn't too happy that Dave argued with this wild man who waved a gun.

"Dave, I think we could move on farther down the shoreline and still have some good fishing, so let's go."

"If I can see you from my front porch, then you're too close to my house," and the hermit pointed his rifle at Dave.

Paul pulled insistently at Dave's arm by this time, and Dave reluctantly agreed that they would move along. They picked up their tools and fishing gear, and walked farther west, away from Robert Vallee's old place, while Vallee just glared at them with his gun on his shoulder until they were out of his view.

"What's that old man hiding up here?" Dave grumbled as he pulled his tools and supplies behind him.

Paul helped carry some of them too. Dave did find an alternate spot for the new hole to be cut, and worked on it right away. He was obviously not too happy about being chased away from his first spot. Paul tried to figure out from Dave why the old man was so agitated, but realized that the conversation only made Dave angrier. He changed the subject to get Dave's mind off of the old man.

It was noisy for a few minutes while Dave worked his magic with the special drill, but once the hole was cut into the ice and they were positioned around the hole, Paul started enjoying himself again and was intrigued by the interesting conversation while they set up. It was as though Dave was part of the town's history, since his family had been here for several generations, and he knew a great deal of the local folklore.

They setup a little shack over the hole, and sat inside out of the wind while they fished. Dave had a few beers, but Paul brought along pop for himself since he enjoyed the local root beer. There was no need for an ice chest, since the air was much colder in the shack than inside a freezer, but the cold didn't bother the two outdoorsmen. They were dressed warm, fishing on the ice, and had a nice day planned on the lake.

"So what's a couple of trolls doing over the bridge this time of year?"

Paul looked at him curiously, and asked, "So Lisa and I are 'trolls'?"

"Yeah, trolls live under the bridge, don'cha know. You're both from Lansing, which is below the Mackinac Bridge, so you're 'trolls.'"

"No, I haven't heard that. So what are you, a goat?"

Dave laughed, "No, I'm a 'Yooper', born up here in the UP. you know, the Upper peninsula of Michigan. I couldn't live anywhere else. We call it 'The Superior State' for obvious reasons."

Paul thought about that for a minute, and remembered hearing that term 'Yooper' years ago. He reached inside a bag and offered Dave smoked fish and homemade beef jerky he had picked up in town.

Well, well, well Paul. Are you sure you're not a Yooper? These are some of my favorite foods, besides a seven course meal made up of a pasty and a six pack."

They both laughed and Paul shook his head.

While they waited for a bite, Dave said, "In the summer, the skies are so clear here at night that you wouldn't believe it when you look up at the stars. That's one of the things I like

61

about this area compared to being near the big city lights."

"What's so different?"

"In the winter here, the clouds are often in the way so you really can't see the stars, ay, but on a summer night, you'll see more stars than you've ever seen in your life. In the big city, the lights make it so you can't see as many stars, but out here where there are miles and miles of forests and very few city lights, the stars come out by the trillions."

"Maybe Lisa and I will make a trip out here one summer to see what you mean. I think she would like that. She loves it here."

"Well, you know if you're in London or New York City or even Detroit, it'll cost you a fortune to make a phone call to Heaven, but its free from the UP.

Paul tried to read Dave's eyes, but had to ask, "A call to heaven? OK, why is it free from the UP?"

"From the UP, it's a local call, don'cha know?"

Paul had to laugh, while his new friend focused down into the ice hole expressionless.

Dave's fishing line got a good tug, and they were both silent as they waited.

After a few minutes and no further bites, Dave said, "There's a great little souvenir shop off the highway as you go into town. You and your missus should stop by and see what they have."

"I did see a big casino off the highway, but I don't remember a souvenir shop."

"Well, you were probably looking over on the right side of the road at the casino, and didn't see the souvenir shop on the left side of the road. It's just across from the casino, don'cha know."

Paul nodded, realizing that's probably what happened.

"The owner is a great guy to talk to, very interesting. It's not busy in the winter, but he still opens up during the day and a few of us stop in and keep him company when we're not busy. I think you'll like him once you meet him, ay?"

"Yeah, that sounds good. Lisa would probably enjoy looking around to see what they have, since she wants to pick up a few things to take back with us when we go home."

They sat in silence for a few minutes, and Dave laughed to himself.

"In a few weeks, the ice will start to get pretty thin, but of the die-hards still go out on Lake Superior to get in some last minute ice fishing. The funny thing is that several of these bozos end up sitting on ice that breaks away, and they drift out into the big lake."

"You mean they actually get stranded on a little iceberg? How often does this happen?"

"Yeah, every year. I've been in a small plane flying near the shore, and saw three or four little icebergs, each with a shack on them, just floating farther out into the big lake. It's quite a sight, ay? These guys have to be rescued, and many of the same guys have done it more than once. You have to wonder about someone who doesn't learn from his mistakes."

Paul had never heard of this before, and shook his head with a smile. He realized they're only a few hours from Lansing, but it's a different world out here.

"Dave, how did you get to be an expert at cutting holes in the ice? Is there some kind of technique that you had to master?"

Dave laughed and said, "I'm only considered an expert because I'm the only one who has a gas-powered ice auger. If everyone had one of those, they'd all be 'experts' too. You do need to hold it right so it doesn't fall through the hole and sink to the bottom, don'cha know. There may be a little skill in using it to enlarge a small hole, but with a little practice anyone could do it."

"Well, the guy in the fishing store sure seemed to think

you had special skills."

"Yeah, just don't give away my secret, OK?"

Paul talked a little bit about the bodies that were discovered in the lake recently, and Dave looked over at Paul, then back at the hole in the ice.

"I'm a little puzzled about something with one of the men we pulled out of the ice water." Paul looked up at him, and Dave continued, still looking down at the dark hole into which his fishing line disappeared. "After we had brought Eddie's body up, I watched that new police officer as he appeared to cover up tracks in the snow on the shore of the lake while he talked to the neighbors. I just wonder why he would have done that."

"Maybe Jake was just helping the neighbor with something on the shore, and wasn't too concerned about where they stood."

Paul didn't think this was too unusual, but Dave kept going.

"Jake also came up with the idea that Eddie must have fallen through by accident, before even seeing the results of the autopsy or investigating some of the clues from the site." Paul looked over at Dave, as he continued, "I thought it would have been better to not tell anyone such a theory unless he had evidence to support it, but Jake didn't listen to me. He went ahead and told the neighbors right away that it was an accident."

"When Jake first told Lisa and I about the other guy that was found by the kids, he said he figured it must have been an accident. However, finding two bodies within a few days seems a little more suspicious, which Jake did acknowledge. Maybe he just didn't want to worry the neighbors that a murderer could be on the loose."

"Well, I think the neighbors should be warned that a killer may be out there so they would be able to keep their guard up and be prepared, rather than not even knowing they should be concerned. Keeping the town relaxed and off their guard is exactly what a killer would want, don'cha think?"

They both looked at each other in silence for a few seconds, when Paul's line pulled hard and got their attention away from the bodies found in the lake.

Paul had never been ice fishing before, so he immensely enjoyed catching his first Northern Pike, a giant toothy predator that put up a great fight. They both also caught a couple of perch and Paul noticed that Dave seemed extremely happy to catch a good-sized Walleye, which is an elusive favorite on the lake in any season, especially in the winter. The weather was cold, of course, but the sky was clearer than normal so the two great hunters had a perfect day on the ice, not counting their trespassing experience with Daniel Boone. Paul couldn't wait to tell Lisa about the ice fishing, although he knew she would have very little interest in sitting out in the cold for hours waiting for fish to bite. However, she would humor him and listen to his adventurous story nonetheless. He wondered what she would think about the man coming after them with a gun, and considered leaving out that part.

Chapter Ten

MANY OF THE OLD TIMERS AND NEWER families around the lake met with Officer Haley at the Community Center, just down the road from Old Deerfield, to talk about details of the two recent deaths in the lake. This was just a plain rectangular building with log siding and a dark green metal roof that matched the shutters, and it was an ideal meeting place in any weather. Jake sat at the end of the two rows of long tables, facing the crowd of people, as they lined the tables and looked at him while he spoke to them with his back to the big fireplace at the end of the room. He briefly enjoyed the warmth on his back and the relaxing sounds coming from it as the fire crackled, feeling as though he was about to get 'thrown into the fire' by the local residents. Jake expected someone to accuse the tourists that had just arrived in town on vacation, as well as a few other favorites that these people tended to pick on regularly, and he knew they would hound him for immediate action.

One of the older gentlemen asked, "Why all of a sudden have there been two deaths on our normally peaceful lake right after that young couple arrived in town?"

"So far they both seem harmless and I don't think they are the type of people who would murder elderly folks in a small town while on vacation. However, I'm still investigating all possibilities."

He knew that these people would get fixed on the idea that these vacationers came right when bodies were found, and could tie up the whole meeting with discussions on who they were, what are they doing, etc, etc. Jake steered the conversation back to the place where Eddie was found, and got people talking about him for a few minutes.

"I'm hoping to see what kinds of details you all might be able to provide about both deaths, and that's the main reason why I asked all of the lake property owners to come out here today. Maybe there's something you might remember that hadn't been mentioned yet. I also want to reassure everyone that I am indeed investigating these two cases, and you'll all be safe while the investigation is underway."

Jake paused and looked around to read the expressions on people's faces, then added, "It seems odd that Eddie would have been over on that section of the lake, where several families with children and teenagers lived, when Eddie lived in a more secluded area of the lake. I'm having a problem trying to figure out why Eddie would have even been there in the first place."

Everyone seemed to agree, or at least didn't violently disagree, so Jake continued, "If Eddie was going to fall through the ice, it should have been closer to his own home and he would have been found there, right? He would have had no business being over where the kids found him. Someone suggested that perhaps Eddie was doing something he shouldn't have been doing," but several of the older men scoffed at him immediately for suggesting that.

One gentleman added, "I don't think anyone believes Eddie would have been doing something wrong. I do think someone deliberately killed Eddie and put him in this area for whatever reason. That's what you need to find out, Haley, and quick."

Jake nodded in agreement. He still couldn't dismiss the possibility that Eddie may have been up to something he shouldn't have been doing, but he knew this wasn't the time or place to bring it up again. Eddie had been in the town all of his life, and despite being a cranky senior citizen (or at least he was weathered so much that he looked older than he really was), friendships ran deep in these parts of the country. Other people discussed Eddie's track record as an honest citizen over the years, and Jake just listened as the conversation carried itself for a few minutes without him.

Jake's interaction with Eddie in the past few months was minimal, but the few times they talked together, Eddie criticized him for being too young, inexperienced, too new to the area, and overly friendly. Jake didn't care for the man, but he tried not to let his personal feelings interfere with his investigation.

Suddenly, Jake felt a little strange, as though he was light-headed or groggy, and as he looked around the room, people's faces were blurred, words were not clearly spoken. He was actually afraid he might pass out. Jake wanted to find out what was going on, but he just looked around the room trying to make sense of what he now felt. It occurred to him that someone may have drugged him, and he noticed that several of the blurred faces looked mean while the unidentifiable voices sounded angrier. He had never experienced anything like this before, and wondered if anyone there could tell he was having a particular kind of episode.

For a few seconds, it seemed like he was in the middle of an angry mob that needed to be broken up, but just as quickly as it had started, everything was back to normal. The conversations went on between the townspeople and were not overly angry, and most of the faces were just as friendly as before, with a little bit of fear due to the recent deaths in the lake. Jake looked around into some of those faces, and it appeared that nobody even realized he had just been in a bizarre state during their discussions. Jake was fine now, as if it had never happened, so he elected to just continue with the questioning and ask the local doctor to check him out this week for anything unusual, just in case.

August Johnson, one of the men that lived near the area where Little Frank was found, did mention, "It's too coincidental for Eddie to be involved with something bad and get killed, then have Little Frank also be involved with something bad and get killed a couple of days later. We've all known these men for decades, and none of us can see either of them doing activities that would get them into any kind of trouble, let alone something that would get both of them murdered."

"It's also coincidental to have two accidental drownings in a frozen lake within a couple of days," Jake added, then paused while there was a murmur of agreement along both rows of tables.

August then asked, "What suspects do you have so far?"

"We really can't disclose that kind of information to the public at this point in time. I think you can understand that. I do want to assure you though that we are taking this seriously, and are looking out for your safety and the safety of your families."

"You know who the most likely suspect is, don't you Haley? It's that Indian, Dufresne, over by the casino. He's been trouble his whole life, and you should be checking on him before someone else gets killed."

Jake thought to himself, "Oh no, not again," but responded quickly as more people acknowledged this comment and a buzz picked up around the room.

"I know who he is, August, and I'm already planning to follow up my investigation by looking into his recent activities."

He knew that several of the people around the lake

didn't like Michael Dufresne, probably just because he was an Ojibwa Indian, although Jake never found anything suspicious about him. In fact, Dufresne appeared to be a nice guy, but Jake constantly had to fight off these kinds of prejudiced claims around here from one person or another.

"I also wanted to find out if someone noticed anything similar in the two recent deaths, since I'm hoping you all might come up with additional clues that could help lead to what really happened. Does anyone here have more input from what you've seen and not yet reported to the police?"

Louise Erlandson said, "When I saw Little Frank's face under the ice, he looked terrified."

"Yes, Eddie had the same frightened expression," said August's wife, Alma.

"This fact implies that both deaths were accidental, and both men could have fallen through a thin section of ice, panicked trying to get back out of the water, but were unable to find the hole where they fell through. Anyone would be filled with terror as they tried to feel the surface of the ice to escape from the freezing water."

Again, people agreed with the logic there, but an angry older gentleman named Virgil Moreau stood up and talked directly to Jake.

"Two of my neighbors have died this past week on the same lake they had lived on for more than fifty years. These men knew the ice, and neither of them would have been in areas where it wasn't safe. There's something suspicious about these events, and if you're not going to take this seriously, I'm going to get someone else to start investigating these deaths."

This caused discussions to start up again around the tables, as Jake shook his head and raised both his hands to try to regain order, and he saw that many people there were in agreement with Virgil.

"Look, I am indeed taking these deaths very seriously, and

even though they've not been ruled as murders, homicide is certainly still a possibility."

Disappointed, he saw that this wasn't going to be an effective way to gather information, since so many of the people were too opinionated to discuss other possibilities, and he said, "I want to thank everyone for coming out for this discussion. I'll keep you all apprised of our progress, and will be available if any of you have any other information that could be useful. Please call me anytime if you think of something that might be important."

All of the townspeople got up, still chattering among themselves, and headed back to his or her warm homes. He watched as the residents filed out of the front door and drove away, then glanced up a the ceiling. He noticed the wood rafters running from wall to wall above him and thought about the open space above them up to the ceiling. Although he felt peaceful now, a little while ago he wondered if that space was filled with evil spirits trying to stir up the crowd. He had heard some of the legends about this area since he arrived last summer, but never took them seriously. Now after what he experienced, he wondered if there could be any truth in them.

A little frustrated about the biting comments from a few of those people, Jake decided to go back to the police station and plan out his next step in the investigation. The dizzy spell weighed heavy on his thoughts now, and he considered how real the angry feelings were as they attempted to smother him during the meeting. Jake tried to convince himself that the anger wasn't genuine, just in his mind, and he was able to get back to reality within a couple of minutes. However, he couldn't shake the feeling that the hatred probably did exist, hidden deep within several of those prejudiced men, and what he experienced today was just a glimpse of what must be lingering around the lake.

Chapter Eleven

MOST EVENINGS AROUND THE cabin were quiet with a hint of wind or wolf howling, but this one was a stormy, thunderous night, and the lightning flashes created a brief, eerie light in the cabin every minute or so. Tim's worried face was visible in one of the lightning flashes, covered in sweat, rain, or both. It was dark again as soon as the lightening finished its display, and the thunder seemed to roll from the back of the cabin, the middle, past the front porch, and out across the lake as though it was some kind of giant animal growling outside of and over the top of the cabin. It rolled on for over a minute when another lightening flash briefly lit up the rooms again. This time, a horrible, rotted, rain-soaked face could be seen looking in the master bedroom window near where Tim was standing, and it didn't look alive.

The face's discolored skin appeared as though it had been underwater for a long time, and was partially falling off, while the white eyes apparently searched the cabin for its prey. When Tim saw this face in the window, his heart began beating rapidly like the sound of a punching bag hit quickly over and over by a boxer, and he felt as though it would burst forth from his chest. The room went dark again, which terrified Tim even more than when he could see the face, and the thunder rolled across the cabin again. He clicked the lamp by the bed, but figured the power must be out, since it gave no response. He tried to quickly make his way down the hall to a different room, bumping into things in the dark as he forced himself to remember his way through the blackness. His eyes were wide open, looking to see anything in the room to give him a hint as to where he was while he reached to feel a bedpost, dresser, or doorknob. He frantically tried the light switch by the door, but it's only answer was more darkness and despair.

The next lightening flash clearly showed Tim's fear, and it gave him a momentary view of the room so he saw where he was going. With this quick little bit of light, he stumbled his way out of the bedroom, into the hallway toward the other bedroom before it went black again. The thunder growled over him and around him, rattling the entire cabin as he moved in the dark. He let his hand slide along the wall, took a few more timid steps, and wondered to himself how it could be so dark. Usually there was at least a little bit of light, whether moonlight or a nearby house light, but tonight there was none.

It didn't take long before another light show briefly appeared, revealing a second horrible, rotting face looking into the guest bedroom window behind him. He glimpsed it for a second in the mirror, just before everything went dark, and his heart pounded so hard it caused his chest to ache. He wanted his heart to quiet down due to his fear that whoever stalked him might be able to hear it and find out exactly where he was, even in the darkness. Tim wasn't sure which was worse, the complete darkness where he didn't know what was around him, or the quick lightning flash that revealed his greatest fear so close to him. He went from one bedroom, where he briefly saw a horrific face in the window, to the other bedroom, where he now saw a second disturbing face in that window.

He gasped, and ran tripping back into the hallway, toward the living room, and then into the kitchen, only to see yet another ghastly face lit up right in front of him with the next lightening flash. For a moment, Tim saw soaked hair and torn clothes, with discolored grayish skin, and then the light was gone again. It was standing in a puddle of water in the kitchen with the back door wide open. Whoever these people were, one of them was now inside the cabin. He had to retrace his steps through the cabin to the front door to get outside into the rainstorm, get away from these people, and get help. He didn't want to be drenched outside in the freezing rain, or be a target for the lightning that was stretching its fingers close to the trees, but he didn't care anymore. Something told him that he just had to find his way outside now. Tim felt certain someone was trying to get him but he didn't know why. Before he made it to the front door and ran outside, lightening lit up the room again and he screamed at what he saw...

Tim woke up with a real scream, and sat up quickly in bed, only to find that there really was thunder rumbling outside. It took several seconds before he realized that it had been another dream, but he wasn't as reassured as he had hoped to be. He looked around in the dark, barely seeing the room's contents, and then he lay down hard with a sigh. His heart finally slowed down as he realized there was now a little bit of light from outside barely shining into his room, and felt relieved that it wasn't totally black like it was in the dream. However, he was almost afraid to look over at the windows because he thought he might see some horrible face. These nightmares were more frightening each time, and he didn't want to face another dream like this one. He knew it had to be a dream because this kind of lightning didn't really occur in the winter around here, but that still didn't give him any comfort.

He remembered the discussions from the pub about ghosts from a couple supposedly murdered over twenty years ago coming back to haunt the townspeople and even getting revenge on their killers. Tim had never believed in ghosts, but he didn't know what to think about the dreams he had experienced since he started staying in this cabin. He wondered if he should move into another cabin somewhere else around the lake to see if the dreams stopped, but what would that prove? If they stopped, then the problem was with the cabin, but if they didn't stop, was the problem with him?

Can a place truly be haunted? He had been raised to understand that there was no such thing as ghosts, and that when a person's body died, that person either went to Heaven or to Hell. There was none of this lingering around on Earth in some kind of confused state, not realizing that the soul should be passed on. However, if this cabin wasn't haunted, then why was he having these terrifying dreams? Something dreadful must have happened here, but he wasn't sure if he wanted to know anything more.

Chapter Twelve

LISA WOKE UP EARLY THIS MORNING and saw that a new snowfall in the night had blanketed the world outside the cabin. She was fascinated as she looked out over the front yard and the lake. The porch had double-paned windows, but wasn't heated, so it was noticeably cooler than in the other rooms. Out here, she sat wrapped up in a blanket on the couch that faced the lake and held a hot cup of coffee. It was interesting that people called this part of land between the cabin and the lake 'the front yard', while the land between the cabin and the road was 'the back yard'. This was just the opposite of what she had always heard from people who live in neighborhoods without lakes. It was another little quirk that she liked about being in a cabin on a lake, and she smiled as she sipped her coffee.

She saw her breath as she exhaled, and observed smoke coming from chimneys of some of the other cabins across the lake. The cold out here gripped every part of her body now, so she thought Paul needed to get up soon and warm up the cabin. She liked the smell of a crackling fire, and thought today would be the perfect day to be lazy and snuggle up in front of the fireplace for a while. She figured they should just go out for lunch or dinner nearby and not even go into town today, while she took another drink of coffee to try to warm herself up a little bit. She wondered if the hot coffee in the cup would actually freeze if she stayed out here for much longer.

Just then, from the corner of her eye, Lisa saw something move outside, and she peered up near the woods. Slowly, a large moose came walking out between two white birch trees, providing quite a contrast with his dark brown hair, the white trees, and white snow. She was speechless as she carefully sat her cup down before she spilled it all over herself, and realized that she couldn't take her eyes off of the magnificent creature. He stepped gracefully in the snow and moved out of the woods into their 'front yard', while she slowly peeled off the blanket and got up to find her camera.

The moose was visibly cautious, probably from many encounters with predators and hunters, and displayed a wisdom that surprised Lisa as it worked its way out of the woods. Lisa pondered what she would have done if she had encountered this fellow when she walked down that same path through the woods the other day, since she had been told they can be confrontational if they felt threatened. Lisa didn't want to startle the moose, since she knew he might be able to see her through the windows if she made a sudden movement, so she crawled to the door and went into the living room where her camera was. She heard Paul complain about the temperature, making noises as he struggled to get out of bed and walked around in the bedroom.

"Paul, there's a moose outside the cabin, so please be very quiet while I photograph him."

That got Paul's attention, and he peeked out his bedroom window to see for himself. Then he quickly and quietly came out to join Lisa in the living room. She could tell it felt extremely cold to Paul in the cabin too, especially since he had just been under the warm blankets in bed, and when he looked over at the cold fireplace, he scowled. He realized, he forgot to set the gas heater above forty degrees the night before, so the temperature had dropped to little more than freezing inside the cabin once the fire went out. That wouldn't happen again.

Lisa hoped he would realize that he needed to start a fire as he held his arms across his chest and said, "Brrrr."

She laughed out loud and had to snap a quick picture of him like this, with his hair messed up, in his long underwear and socks, and he protested to no avail. This shot was candid, but his expression at having his picture taken made the second photograph even funnier. She then quietly led the way onto the porch to see where the moose was, and Paul followed, watching his wife with interest.

"You look incredibly beautiful in long underwear and thick socks," and she gave him a quick glance over her shoulder with a smile and then raised her eyebrows at him.

As they stepped in silent unison onto the porch, she saw that the moose had walked out in front of the cabin only a little ways, eating branches near the edge of the woods. They both watched as little clouds puffed out of the moose's nostrils when it exhaled, then dissipated into the air within a few seconds. Lisa excitedly, yet professionally, snapped several pictures of the giant animal, with the snowy branches in the background. She wasn't sure how many pictures she would be able to get before it was scared off, so she took as many as possible. She hoped that the pictures would still turn out well, since she had to take them through the glass in the windows, but she had no choice other than to go outside and risk scaring the moose away.

At one point, it seemed as though the moose saw them through the windows when she changed positions to get him from another angle, but if he did notice them, he didn't seem to mind their presence so close by. Lisa figured that he felt safer since they were inside and apparently not an immediate threat. Paul had just mentioned yesterday to Lisa that he liked moose and wanted to have a moose theme in one of their rooms if they ever had a cabin, and after seeing this one outside, Lisa knew that Paul would insist on it.

He whispered to Lisa, "This is the most impressive animal I have ever seen up close," and she agreed with a nod and snapped another picture.

"I never dreamed we would be able to photograph one in the snow like this. I've always heard how difficult it is to get these kinds of pictures in winter."

"Just be thankful that you're inside a cabin and haven't been out there in the sub-zero weather with him all this time."

She was indeed thankful to be given this opportunity.

Paul commented, "I thought their antlers were much bigger than this, but maybe I just see the summer pictures when they're at the fullest. I don't think I've ever even seen a picture of a moose this time of year."

After taking more than a dozen pictures, Lisa held the camera under her chin and Paul, who was standing behind her watching the moose over her shoulder, put his arms around her. They stood there watching him eat and saw him slowly make his way back into the woods closer to the lake's edge.

"Pinch me," and Paul did so.

"It's not a dream" then she turned and hugged him with a kiss on the lips. They looked out the windows one last time as the moose disappeared, and Paul added, "I'm going to start a fire in the fireplace now. I can't wait any longer." He walked into the living room to see if he could warm up the cabin, while his wife stared longingly out the window where her moose once stood.

Chapter Thirteen

IT DIDN'T TAKE **P**AUL LONG TO GET the fire going, since the cold was quite an incentive for him. While he worked diligently by the fireplace, Lisa made Swedish pancakes with Lingonberries, an old family favorite of hers, and they ate on the big rug in front of the fireplace while they recalled their adventure with the giant mammal. With a fire crackling away and generating some much-needed heat in the cabin, Paul and Lisa ate a leisurely breakfast with more hot coffee.

"I can't believe it walked up that close to the cabin and let me take so many pictures of it," Lisa exclaimed.

"The moose acted as though it knew we were there watching it, but the critter just kept on eating because it didn't feel threatened by us," Paul added.

Lisa enjoyed staying in her pajamas for a while this morning, but eventually decided that they both needed to get dressed and go out into the cold. She initially considered staying in the cabin all day and not even attempting to go out, but after seeing the moose in the yard, Lisa wanted to drive up to the souvenir shop that Dave told Paul about off the highway, just up the road from the lake entrance. She wanted to see if they could find any moose souvenirs to take home with them, perhaps in an effort to somehow preserve the excitement they shared when they saw the animal up close, and forever remember their encounter. As they got dressed, she talked more about the moose and tossed out ideas for souvenirs that she hoped to buy at that shop.

"Maybe they'll have a moose on a picture frame with white birch trees on the sides of the frame, and we can put one of your photos in it," Paul suggested, and Lisa nodded in agreement.

"How about a moose trash can, or a moose lamp shade," but Lisa just looked up, frowned at him, and shook her head.

Lisa said, "I wonder if a magazine might publish some of these photos, if they turn out as good as I hope, taken at such a close distance." She hadn't seen many photographs of a moose in the snow, so Lisa realized how blessed she was to be there at that moment and not scare off that amazing animal while she snapped the pictures. After a while, she felt a chill and glanced up at the silent fireplace.

"Are you ready? The fire has run it's course."

Paul looked longingly into the fireplace and reluctantly agreed it was time to venture out into the cold. "OK, I guess this is as good a time as any."

Once they bundled up for the trek down the road, Paul opened the cabin's back door near the SUV and Lisa realized she was not as ready as she thought she was for the arctic blast that hit them. Lisa squealed, her reaction at how cold the wind felt, and ran to the passenger side of the SUV while Paul shivered noticeably as he locked the cabin door. They both had thick jackets, gloves, extra socks, long underwear, and hats that covered their ears, but the drastic change from the warmth of the fireplace to the outside wind took Lisa by surprise.

"Hurry up, Paul, unlock the doors. It's freezing out here."

"Oh really? I didn't notice."

He ran to the SUV and unlocked her door, but once inside, Lisa realized that it didn't feel that much warmer there either. They were out of the wind now, but it was probably still cold enough inside the SUV to freeze a cup of water.

Paul said through chattering teeth, "I think we got used to the warmth of the fire a little too much this morning, because it feels so much colder now."

Lisa just looked at Paul up close with her eyes wide open, chattered her teeth for a few seconds for him to see and hear, and finally busted out laughing as Paul quickly tried to get the heat going in the SUV. Paul couldn't help but smile at his freezing wife, and he leaned over and gave her a kiss on her cold lips. To her surprise, he pretended that his lips were frozen to hers, and put his hands on her ears to pretend to try and pull her head away from his. She laughed so hard as Paul, his eyes wide open, pulled his head back repeatedly to see if he could get their lips 'unstuck', but his hands held her head close to his so it actually seemed as though he wasn't kidding around. Just then, Paul made a loud 'Pop' sound with his lips and he pulled his head back, successfully freeing up their lips again. Paul put his hands on the steering wheel, looked behind the SUV, and winked at his wife as she watched him. She held her hands up to the vents, but the air coming out was still cold.

He pulled out of the driveway, headed around the lake to the highway stop sign, and soon turned onto the road into town. It wasn't very far to the souvenir shop, so by the time the heater started warming up, they were already there at the entrance to the little store. Paul waited for one lone car to drive by, coming from town, going in the direction toward the lake.

"I can see how we missed this shop when we first drove by with Jake. That casino across the street is huge," Paul said, as he pointed over at the building across the highway. Lisa looked over at the casino, following the direction of his finger.

It was a massive stone structure with tall windows overlooking the highway, and looked like it would have been beautifully landscaped in the summer, with a lot of places for flowers. Mostly covered by snow now, the bushes ran along a frozen man-made stream that once flowed to the base of a now immovable waterwheel, oozing with tranquility. The windows tried to overlook the lake, past the trees across the road that were in the way, but Lisa figured they would still be happy with the pleasant view. Instead of a nice forest around the casino, however, was a never-ending parking lot, with several busses waiting for their disappointed passengers to come out of the building and climb back inside for the trip back to whatever hotel they came from.

There wasn't much traffic on the road today, and not many cars were in the parking lot of the souvenir shop, so Paul had an easy time turning in to the place and finding a spot to park in up close to the front doors. This little parking lot was quite a contrast to the one across the street with dozens of cars already there before the lunch crowd.

"How busy can a souvenir shop be in Upper Michigan in the winter?" he asked Lisa.

"Well, this is certainly not the tourist season."

When the engine shut off, he looked at her and said, "Ready... get set... go."

They quickly opened their doors, jumped out into the cold, shut the doors, and raced to the shop. Lisa squealed again as the cold air hit her, but Paul just kept quiet, laughed, and moved quickly around the SUV toward the entrance. She got to the door first, but waited for Paul to open it for her since her hands were too cold to take out of her pockets. She looked up at him as she waited with a big pleading smile on her face. Paul yanked opened the door for her, and she rushed in saying, "Brrrr," shivering and laughing at the same time. It occurred to Lisa that if people had been watching them, they probably would have thought Paul and Lisa were a little strange, but she didn't mind. This had been an incredible morning, and she was having a lot of fun with her wonderful husband. They were on vacation and it really didn't matter what the townspeople here thought of them. Lisa figured she would probably never see any of these people again anyway.

Chapter Fourteen

ONCE INSIDE THE SOUVENIR shop, Paul realized that there were a few people in the shop, and each one of them stared at him. He looked sheepishly at Lisa for a second, and then turned toward the register at the front of the shop.

Paul said, "Hi" and waved as he shook off snow from his jacket and took off his hat.

A friendly gentleman behind the counter smiled and said, "Hi folks."

Lisa walked down one of the aisles toward the pictures on the back wall, and Paul followed a little ways behind her. She headed for several white birch tree picture frames, as well as some with black bears, wolves, and moose carvings on the frames. Paul stopped and made faces when he saw a few tacky tourist-trap items, like real moose droppings in a bag with potpourri, chocolate moose droppings, which he assumed were not real, and many other similar items that Lisa just walked on past as if there was nothing there. For a brief moment, he considered buying Lisa a pack of chocolate moose droppings, but came to his senses immediately. Even though she loved chocolate, he didn't think these would go over well with her. As he looked around, Paul didn't realize just how big moose droppings really were, so he was truly surprised.

"Wow! I guess I should have figured that moose droppings would be huge based on how large a moose actually is," but he noticed that Lisa just ignored his comments.

There were some interesting themed room decorations, many of them with black bears, and Paul walked over to peruse that section of the shop. As he looked around, the gentleman from behind the counter walked over toward Paul. He was intimidating as he kept getting larger and larger with each step toward Paul, but this bear of a man, with long straight black hair, broke into a smile in the last few steps and looked down on Paul, standing almost a head taller and outweighing him by possibly a hundred pounds.

"Hi, I'm Michael Dufresne. Is there anything specific you're looking for?"

Paul looked up at him and shook his enormous hand, saying, "Well, we saw a moose this morning eating breakfast outside of the cabin we're renting, so my wife and I are looking for a couple of moose souvenirs to take with us back home." Michael was solid, with more muscle showing through his tight long sleeve shirt than Paul expected on an older man. Although he appeared to be friendly, this was one person he wouldn't want to be enemies with. It occurred to him that Michael was the only person he had met in this town who could have actually lifted up someone like Little Frank.

Michael responded, "I have heard of a moose wandering around Kisinaw Lake recently, so that is probably the one you saw. Is that where you're staying?"

"Yes, that's the place," Paul responded and Michael pointed over to where Lisa stood.

"There are nice nice frames with moose on them where your little lady is standing, and we have a few pocket knives with moose carved into the handle by some of the local Ojibwa men."

"Where are the knives?" Paul asked with great interest.

Michael walked him over to the counter where there

were dozens of knives to look through. Paul commented "Wow, if these are hand carved, someone is very talented," and Michael smiled.

"Yes, these are hand carved and thank you for the compliment. I am one of those locals who do the carving."

Paul looked up at him and asked, "Are you Ojibwa then?" and Michael nodded. "I'm impressed, because this is just as good as any machine could do."

"Better than any machine because we put our hearts into our work," and they both laughed.

******

Just then, Lisa walked up and Paul introduced her to Michael, who gently shook her petite hand and said, "It is a pleasure to meet you, Lisa."

Lisa asked, "So you're familiar with Kisinaw Lake?"

"Oh yes, I have explored around here all of my life, and that is a very long time."

Lisa studied his eyes and guessed that he might have been over sixty years old, probably a little older than the locals who had been found dead in the lake. Life was very harsh around here, so he may have only looked older than he really was. She was impressed with his handshake, in that he was obviously a caring person to softly take her tiny hand in his catcher's mitt, and make her feel welcome with his tender face and twinkling eyes.

"Do you know anything about the men that have been found frozen in the lake recently?" Lisa continued without hesitation. Paul cringed at the question, but knew he wouldn't be able to take Lisa's mind off of these events.

Michael looked deep into her eyes for a few seconds before glancing away across the shop, folded his arms across his chest, and nodded his head. Lisa read into his sad expression, and anxiously awaited his explanation. His frame was as big as a grizzly bear, but she could somehow tell it was actually a teddy bear behind all of that muscle, height, and intimidation.

"Unfortunately, I knew both of the men who are now dead, but we were honestly not good friends. Actually we were not friends at all. They were both very prejudiced all of their lives, and never had anything good to say about my family or acquaintances."

Lisa looked at Paul, and then back at Michael as he continued.

"There are people here, including those two men who are no more, who do not like the Ojibwa and have always tried to make it difficult for us. We have accepted it as a part of life, and have tried hard to be good workers, good friends, and good citizens in order to show everyone how wrong these men were in their assessment of the Ojibwa."

Lisa asked, "Has it always been like that here?" and Michael nodded.

"Yes, as far as I can remember, there have been people in this area who do not like us, but you will find that most of the people here are very nice to be with. Most people around the lake, and the people in Manitow, are good people who will go out of their way to help another person. It is just a small group of people who spoil it for everyone else."

"If you've been here all of your life, do you remember a young couple about twenty years ago who were found frozen in the lake?" She noticed from the corner of her eye that Paul just looked away and shook his head.

Michael raised his eyebrows and said, "I thought you were just visiting this area. I am surprised you would have heard about something like that from years ago." He paused, and Lisa was about to respond, when Michael continued. "Yes, I remember the story you mention, and I remember hearing that those two people were also victims of prejudice.

They were not Ojibwa, but they were good, honest and devout religious people from a good family who had lived in the area for many years. Some people treated them the way they treat the Ojibwa, and I have heard stories that say the deaths of these two were not accidents. There are secrets in the ice that have not been revealed even to this day."

Lisa said, "Some people say that the two recent deaths are somehow related to the deaths of that couple twenty years ago, and that their ghosts are getting revenge on a few of the townspeople who made their lives difficult all those years ago."

Michael smiled, looked at Paul, who shook his head again and looked away at that last question, and responded, "I have heard about the ghosts, but I don't think that theory would be taken seriously in a court of law. Still, it is an interesting aspect to consider." He looked at Lisa again and continued, "Are you a detective or a ghost hunter?"

Paul quickly cut in and said, "No, she's neither, but we've just been in the middle of several interesting discussions with some superstitious people lately. A few locals have been throwing out all kinds of ideas."

Michael said, "I didn't mean to make you feel cornered or anything. I just thought that she would be very good at either one, since she is confident and seems to be a go-getter."

Michael's face broke into a big grin.

Paul said, "Oh yes, she's certainly all that," and she elbowed him playfully with a smirky smile.

Lisa liked Michael's face, and somehow was drawn to him in a very positive way. She believed he was an honorable man, and realized from the few moments when their eyes met, that he had a good heart. She wanted to ask Paul if he felt it too, since he appeared to have enjoyed being with Michael this morning, but she would wait until they were alone to discuss it with him. The other customers in the shop said their goodbyes to Michael, and he waved to them as they left the relative warmth of the store. Lisa wondered what kinds of secrets could be buried in that lake over the years as she waited patiently for the opportunity to question Michael some more.

Chapter Fifteen

MICHAEL SAID, "IF YOU WOULD like to talk more about this, let's sit down and discuss it over hot soup. Would you join me in the next room? We have a delicious cream of mushroom soup that is thick and tasty."

Lisa noticed that the gift shop area went back a long way and saw a section where Michael sold food on the right side of the shop.

"We'd like that," Lisa responded with a pleasant smile, without waiting for Paul to say anything, and they all walked over toward one of the tables.

Behind the cash register was a large window that looked out across the highway, and she saw the massive casino on the other side of the road. Michael poured three bowls of soup, while Lisa admired the large window in the back, with a nice view of the woods between the highway and the lake. She and Paul sat facing that back window, and when Michael returned with their soup, he sat across from them, facing the front window.

Michael asked, "Have you been to the casino across the road?"

"No, we saw it on our way in to town, but haven't stopped. We're not much into gambling," Paul responded, and Michael smiled.

"Some people say that the casino is the Ojibwa revenge against the atrocities of the white man from generations past. You can see by the impressive size of the building that it is doing very well, and so their revenge must be doing well too. Others say that the people in this area are very generous, since they are faithful to 'donate' their paychecks to the Ojibwa at the casino every week."

Paul and Lisa both smiled at these comments, and Michael continued.

"The Ojibwa run the casino and make a good living on the money spent by the townspeople and visitors, but it is sad to see so many people hoping to win big only to be disillusioned at losing so much. One good thing is that the Ojibwa do put a lot of the money from the casinos back into the community. We don't brag about this, so a lot of people do not even realize it, but we know it and that is important to us. Anyway, how is the soup?"

They both responded at the same time, "Excellent!" and Michael started again.

"Unfortunately, there has been hatred and jealousy in this town for generations, and we hope it will be coming to an end someday. The two men who died this week were two of the hateful ones, and I am not sorry to see them go. I am saddened that they will spend an eternity in Hell, but that was their choice."

"So do you believe their deaths were accidental?" Paul asked, while Lisa tried to read Michael's expressions.

"It is rare to see two men freeze to death under the same ice within one week, especially on the lake where they had spent their entire lives," Michael replied without hesitation.

"Good point," Paul commented.

"No, it would not seem accidental," said Michael, "but I am curious as to why you would say that ghosts have come back now, over twenty years later, to get their revenge. Why would they have not done this many years ago?"

Paul held up his hand and interrupted, "We don't believe in ghosts, so we're not saying that this was done by ghosts out of revenge."

Michael nodded, then tasted his own soup, and it was obvious to Lisa that he enjoyed it.

After a brief hesitation, Paul continued, "Do you really think there's some kind of connection between the old murders and the recent deaths of these two men?" Michael paused for another sip on his hot soup, and responded.

"When the young couple died years ago, their deaths were left unsolved, perhaps an accident. They should have been investigated further, but it wasn't. I have heard whispers that the incident was covered up by people who didn't like their family, never to be mentioned again. Now with these two recent deaths, the same people who covered it up twenty years ago may be determined to point the finger at someone who didn't get along with Little Frank or Eddie. Based on that, I would certainly be a suspect. Unfortunately, I never had the chance to get to know the couple that was murdered years ago, but from what I was told, I would have liked them very much."

Suddenly, Lisa lit up with excitement, but had her mouth full, when a deer walked by the large window in the back of the shop. Michael turned around when she pointed it out.

"Yeah, she comes out here once in a while looking for food just outside of the woods. She is almost like a tourist attraction herself, since many of the visitors get so excited when they see her walk by that window."

He looked over at Lisa, and she appreciated his friendly smile.

"Sometimes she comes here with a young fawn, and the little deer are very funny to watch when they play. They will dance around as though they are performing for an audience."

Lisa asked, "Can't she see us here? I would think if she saw people here, she would be scared away."

"I believe she can see us, but as long as we do not make sudden movements or walk around the back of the shop and appear threatening to her, she is not afraid of us."

She then wandered back into the woods, and Lisa commented, "Well, she sure is a beautiful animal," and Michael smiled at Lisa and nodded.

"You have a gentle heart, Lisa, and it makes you a very special person. Paul is fortunate to have found you."

Lisa blushed with embarrassment as Paul softly squeezed her hand in his.

Paul came back to the original subject. "Who else would have a motive? I met a man who says he believes that a local policeman, Officer Haley, has been acting suspicious."

Michael held up his hand and said, "The policeman is still new here, and is trying to fit in with the townspeople. He has not taken sides with the prejudice, but he has not yet stood his ground to stop it either. I honestly do not think he would cover up for one of the locals. We need to give him a chance. He is being tested here, so we need to wait and see what he will choose."

Paul nodded, a little surprised at Michael's defensive response, and ate more of the soup, while Lisa stared curiously at Michael, wondering what he meant by that.

Michael added, "Officer Haley has seen the way many of the older townspeople treat the Ojibwa and newcomers to the lake, and I am disappointed that he has not done more to change people's attitudes. However, he cannot work miracles. Some of the hatred runs generations deep."

Lisa asked, "I haven't seen you at the pub on the lake. Do you ever go there?"

"No, the Ojibwa have not been welcome there, so we stay

away from it. I believe you would see shouting and fighting if I walked in the front door there," Michael replied with a laugh. Lisa didn't, since she had never seen this kind of prejudice before, and she just sipped her soup in silence.

Michael said, "Now, tell me about this moose you saw. Were you able to take any pictures of it?" Paul immediately gave him the details of their experience that morning, while Lisa just gazed out the back window, deep in thought.

Chapter Sixteen

AFTER THEY LEFT THE SOUVENIR shop, Paul said, "Let's go see the shoreline of Lake Superior. I've heard how amazing it looks in the winter, and I think you'd like to get pictures of it."

Lisa nodded her head and replied, "Sounds good," as they turned left onto the highway toward the town.

They passed a few old farms and some old houses that were probably built over a century ago, and Paul enjoyed the peaceful scenery the short drive provided for them. It didn't take long to find the first road that led to the giant lake, so they turned off and followed it to the shore. The bumpy road took them through thick forest areas, and when they came out into the clearing, Paul noticed that Lisa appeared to be awestruck with the massive ice boulders and huge shards of ice that looked like broken sheets of glass.

Paul couldn't take his eyes off of Lisa, who just stared at the scene in front of them, and he parked the SUV. He had seen pictures of Lake Superior in the winter, but he didn't think she had a clue about what to expect. Based on her reaction, he was right. Lisa quickly got her camera and they both stepped out into the cold wind again for a walk along the shoreline. Even after his experience this morning with the cold, Paul underestimated how frigid the wind would be coming off of the massive lake, and in no time, his eyes were watering.

Interestingly enough, the clouds seemed to have cleared just for them, and they were treated with a beautiful, blue-sky background for the photographs for the first time this week. Paul climbed with caution up onto one of the large snow-covered boulders, and looked out over the lake. Ice covered the water for a long ways out, and Lisa snapped several pictures in every direction. She got a few of Paul hamming it up as a strongman with a giant snowball, making silly faces behind a large ice shard that he had picked up and looked through, and captured some unique winter scenery of the Lake Superior shoreline that many people are not even aware of.

Paul asked, "Do you mind if I take a few pictures?" to which Lisa shook her head and handed him the camera. Now that he was in a few of the pictures of the icy shoreline, he wanted to make sure he took several with his gorgeous bride too. She had such a playful attitude and was naturally photogenic, so every picture he took of her was a classic. He liked to think it was his skill as a photographer, but he knew that his wife was the key to how great his pictures turned out. As he snapped picture after picture, Lisa climbed on chunks of ice, posing, moving in front of the ice shards, smiling, and Paul just followed her lead.

One of the most impressive things about Lisa was that even though she was the most attractive girl Paul had ever met, she didn't think she was beautiful. She figured she was average, and was content with that. As long as Paul was happy with her looks, she was happy. She loved life and made everything around her more fun because she was there. This was very evident in the pictures Paul took, because some of them were very funny with Lisa often clowning it up with the great backgrounds in each picture.

Eventually, Paul said, "I have to thaw out my fingers, so

let me put my gloves back on for a while."

He decided they should walk around on the beach with their gloves on, hand-in-hand, and explored the shoreline together. Many of the ice chunks were taller than Paul, as they stood next to a few of the larger ones. They walked up to where the waves would have normally been rolling on the shore in the summer, but instead it was eerily silent now. The water was still, as though it hibernated, just waiting to come crashing through the ice again with the roar it was accustomed to providing for those on the beach. It would still be at least several weeks before the ice thawed, so Paul and Lisa had come at the perfect time.

"As this all melts over the next month or so, it would be nice to come here regularly to take pictures, since the scenery will be changing every day."

Lisa puffed out cold air and replied, "I'd like that. I really do want to come back again and see what this area is like in the other seasons."

Paul looked over at Lisa and noticed her pink cheeks, cold from the Lake Superior wind.

"Should we head back to the SUV?"

She looked at him and replied, "I am getting cold. It's so beautiful here though, I hate to leave."

They walked back to the parking lot, and Paul saw someone walking a big dog where they were at earlier. As they made their way closer, he realized that it was Michael Dufresne, and they both waved to him. Michael waved back as they walked toward each other.

Paul said, "We saw someone who looks just like you back at a souvenir shop up the highway. Do you have a twin brother?"

Michael smiled and said, "I watched the sky clear up from my window, and I could not resist bringing my dog for a walk along the shore. She enjoys coming out here. I closed up the store and took the afternoon off."

Paul replied, "I guess that's one of the benefits of being your own boss."

"Your dog is beautiful. What's her name?" Lisa asked.

Michael glowed as he talked about his pet. "Yes, she is beautiful. Her full name is Miikawaadizi, which actually means 'She is Beautiful.' I usually just call her Miikawa. I raised her from a pup, and she has been a good friend for many years."

Lisa knelt down to pet her, and asked, "Is she part German Shepherd?"

"No, she is pure wolf. Her parents were killed near here, and she is the only pup from the litter that I was able to save. She is a strong one, and is full of love. I have never had a dog quite like her."

"I didn't think wolves made good pets. Is it safe for Lisa to be so close to her face like that?" Paul asked.

"Miikawa can tell that Lisa has a good heart, so Lisa is very safe. I believe Miikawa would protect her if anyone ever tried to hurt Lisa. I would not recommend trying to raise a wolf, but I believe Miikawa and I were meant to be together. We share a very special bond that I cannot explain. I have a tremendous respect for the wolf, as do all of the Ojibwa, so it is an honor for me to protect her and be her friend."

Paul knew that he was fortunate to meet Michael on this vacation, and wished he could get to know him more. There was something so honest and wholesome about him that Paul wondered what it would have been like to be raised by the Ojibwa. Michael was indeed a fascinating character, just like Dave had mentioned, and Paul was glad that they met him again on the shore of Lake Superior.

"Paul, your bride is looking very cold, so you should get her out of the wind," and Paul agreed.

"It was good seeing you again so soon Michael, and

thanks for introducing us to your friend."

Lisa petted Miikawa one more time, and then stood up and said, "Yes, bye Michael. We'll stop by and see you again before we leave."

They parted ways, and Michael walked along the frozen shoreline with Miikawa. Paul and Lisa marched back to their SUV and cranked up the heater on high.

"I brought a surprise for us," Lisa said. Fortunately, she had packed hot chocolate in a thermos, so they warmed their insides up with that while they warmed their hands in front of the SUV's heater vents.

Chapter Seventeen

WHEN PAUL AND LISA STRODE INTO the lakeside pub that evening, Paul immediately felt like he was walking in a dream. It was that strange feeling where he thought he moved in slow motion, and all eyes were on him. He wanted to step back outside to see if the feeling went away, but he kept moving forward toward the table. He looked around the room and felt an angry, hostile stare at him from every corner, although Lisa kept walking with apparently no such feelings. It seemed as though he heard angry voices, slurring with a dreamlike quality, while some people pounded their fists into the tables. In reality, nobody stared at him, gave angry looks, or spoke with anger, but that's what Paul thought had happened. Then he heard laughter and the usual discussions in the crowd, and everything appeared to be back to normal again. They both sat down, and Paul felt compelled to let Lisa in on these episodes.

"Lisa, have you been having strange feelings of paranoia on this vacation?"

Lisa looked at her husband, and Paul held in a smile when he saw her confused look.

"Uhhh, yes Paul. I think everyone here is out to get me, especially you," and she smiled. Paul could tell she believed he was joking about something.

"No, I'm serious. Have you walked into a room and then felt that everything moved way too slow, angry people stared at you, or anything unusual like that?"

"Are you feeling sick?" Lisa asked.

"Listen, I've had this happen more than once here, and I can't explain it at all. When it happens, I feel like I am being stared at, like there is so much hatred coming at me that I feel like I'm going to pass out. At first I thought maybe I was getting sick, or needed some food in my stomach, but I'm fine once that initial feeling goes away. What do you think?"

Lisa looked at him and said, "When did it last happen?"

"Just now as we walked into the pub."

Lisa frowned and said, "But I looked over at you as we walked in, and you looked fine."

"Yeah, but I wasn't. I felt as though I was in a dream, walking from the front door to the table, and I just felt hatred engulfing me the whole way in."

Lisa held his hands and said, "That's a little strange. Let me know the next time it happens, while it's happening, OK?"

"I will." He then asked, "Do you know what you want to eat?"

A bubbly waitress came up at that moment and said, "Our special today is the Whitefish sandwich, and it's awesome. Would you like to give it a try?"

Lisa nodded at Paul, who told the waitress, "That sounds great to me, so we'll each have one, with two root beers."

"I'll put the order in and be right back with your drinks," and within a minute she had the drinks on their table.

"You know, I don't like what Dave said about not trusting Officer Haley. Do you think Jake could really be a suspect?"

Paul replied, "I have no reason to doubt what Dave said about Jake, but it's strange that a police officer would have covered up potential evidence, and jumped to the conclusion right there on the scene that it was an accident. It was interesting to see Michael defend Jake so quickly, wasn't it?"

Just then, Officer Haley walked up to their table and the conversation shifted immediately.

"Hi Jake. I didn't even see you when we came in. We were just talking about this great pub. What do you know about it?"

"Hi Paul, Lisa. Well, I've been told the same family has owned and operated this place for many years, and up until just recently, the cottages along the shore right outside here were always booked for months in advance."

Jake took a sip from his drink, sat down at their table, and continued.

"People from all around used to come here for fishing, boating, and camping, but with the economy the way it is, and for whatever other reasons, business isn't what it used to be."

"You can't imagine how much I appreciate the beautiful wood décor inside," Paul responded. "I've always wanted to be skilled enough to build things, especially with an old antique theme, but I confess that I just don't have the knack for it. I am a good 'gofer' and can help someone else build things, but I'm certainly not a handyman."

"He's tried to do a few simple things around the house, but usually ends up having to get an expert to finish the work or bail him out and fix whatever he's messed up. He works hard at it, but it just doesn't come naturally to him."

Paul glared at Lisa, who was a little too quick to agree as she gave him a nod and a smile.

They all had a good-natured laugh at that, and Paul sadly acknowledged, "Yeah, she's right about that."

The waitress brought their plates, and Lisa asked, "Do you want anything, Jake?"

"No, thanks anyway. I just finished eating."

Paul sampled his sandwich, and said, "Wow, this is excellent."

"Yeah, the whitefish is very good," replied Jake.

Lisa then asked, "Jake, do you believe in ghosts?" which took Paul by surprise.

He had hoped that Lisa wouldn't bring up ghosts to anyone else, but now that it was out, there wasn't much he could do about it except try to change the subject.

Before Paul could interrupt and talk about the Detroit Tigers baseball team's chances for the coming season, Jake responded, "I've never had any reason to believe in ghosts, and I don't think there is any kind of ghost involved in the deaths of these two men, if that is what you're asking. However, we have had a couple of Sasquatch sightings near the lake in recent years."

In the middle of a drink when Jake said that, Paul couldn't help but spray it out all over the floor next to him when he heard it.

He coughed and laughed so hard that Lisa and Jake both started laughing, and Paul, who still gasped for breath, apologetically told him, "I wasn't prepared for that response."

Jake said, "Actually I'm not kidding. There have indeed been several Sasquatch sightings off of the highway near the lake a few years ago and one just down the road from Old Deerfield less than a year ago. Ghosts I have to scoff at, but Sasquatch sightings around here are a little more believable."

Paul still had a difficult time taking this in, but he realized that Jake was serious.

"I wasn't in town when either of them happened, but I've since talked to the people who claim they saw a large animal walking upright like a human and it wasn't a bear, and I believe they did see something unusual. We have bear up here all the time, and these people know a bear when they see one. What they saw was definitely not a bear, and definitely not a human."

Paul just studied Jake's face for a moment, and didn't say anything right away.

"Did anyone ever find out what the animal was?" Lisa asked.

"Well, both cases were just listed as a Sasquatch with no further questions asked. It may be surprising to you city folk, but it's not so unusual to have Sasquatch sightings in the forests of the UP."

Lisa then said, "Hmmm. Back to the ghost story and what someone told us about these two recent deaths being related to an old murder from over twenty years ago," and Jake nodded. He looked a bit nervous, and Paul just studied his reactions.

"What's your interest? You're on vacation, aren't you?"

Lisa responded, "It's a fascinating story, and since I'm the one that found the second victim, it makes the story a little more personal for me. Plus, if the two guys that died this week are somehow intertwined with two mysterious deaths from a generation ago, it becomes that much more intriguing."

"Fair enough. This twenty-year-old drowning case was news to me until yesterday, so I haven't gathered all of the facts about it yet. I'm definitely looking into it, since this could bring in an element of revenge. However, just because I believe that Big Foot might be real doesn't mean I've bought into this story about the ghosts of a dead couple coming back to kill some of the older locals. There has to be a logical explanation, and I'll keep investigating. You should focus on enjoying your vacation."

Paul was happy with that response, and Lisa nodded her head. He looked at her and saw that she still thought there was something more about this ghost story, but he would talk with her about it later when they were alone. They talked and laughed more while Paul and Lisa finished eating, and several people slowly cleared out of the pub.

Lisa said, "Paul, I'm getting tired and need to get back to the cabin for some sleep," so Paul got his jacket and went up to pay the bill at the bar. Lisa and Jake stood up to put their jackets on, and Tim happened to reach for his his at the same time.

Tim said "Excuse me, please go ahead" and he let Lisa get her jacket first, while she smiled at him, just giving him a passing glance.

"Good evening, Tim," Jake said, as Tim nodded.

When she stepped out the front door, Lisa asked, "Has a Sasquatch ever been seen in winter up here?"

"I really can't remember reading about a winter sighting. I just knew of the few sightings that were both in the early summer," Jake replied.

Jake and Lisa stepped out into the cold evening, with Tim following close behind, still zipping up his jacket, and their boots crunching in the snow outside the restaurant. Lisa moved out of the walkway to wait for Paul, and stood next to the corner of the pub where snow had been piled up over seven feet high. Something stepped out of the snowdrift and walked toward them moaning with its arms reaching forward, and Lisa screamed, jumping back into Tim. It appeared to be all white, covered with snow, but apparently Lisa hadn't noticed that it looked like Paul's purple ski jacket under the snow. Jake brushed off the snow from its face and shoulders to reveal Paul wearing a big grin, and the men had a good laugh. Lisa, however, didn't seem very happy and slapped the snow off of Paul's jacket in a not-so-friendly manner.

"I just couldn't resist slipping in behind the snowdrift and stepping out at the right time when you walked by," and he finally got a smile out of Lisa as he tried to get her to hug him.

"With all of the talk about ghosts and Sasquatches, this seemed like the perfect thing to do, if you catch my drift."

At this, Tim smiled too, and Jake said to him, "I'd like you to meet some friends of mine from the Lansing area. This is Paul and Lisa."

They all shook hands, and Tim added, "I've seen you come in to Old Deerfield a couple of times, but I'm glad to finally meet you both. I'm Tim."

Lisa looked up into his blue eyes and apologized, "I'm sorry I bumped into you just now. I looked up and thought you were Paul for a second while he pretended to be a Yeti," as she turned and gave her husband a scowl.

They all bid each other goodnight, while Paul and Lisa got in their SUV for the quick trip back to their cabin. Paul still couldn't help but laugh, as Lisa just smirked at Paul out of the corner of her eye, shaking her head.

Chapter Eighteen

PAUL AND **L**ISA DROVE IN TO TOWN Sunday morning so they could attend the old Lutheran church Lisa had found, and see what the inside of the building looked like. Lisa was impressed with the look and feel of the church and since both of their backgrounds were Lutheran, due to their Swedish ancestry, Paul 'decided', and Lisa agreed, that this was the church they would attend this week. They turned onto Main Street from the highway, and she saw the white tower.

"I don't think the exterior has changed much in over a hundred years, and I'll bet the interior is the same. I can't wait to get inside to see it," commented Lisa.

As they turned onto Walnut street, she looked at the old steeple up close through the window, and guessed that it was probably the original bell in the tower. Except for a few electrical lines nearby and several modern cars that were not horse and buggies, Lisa could easily picture it being 1890.

"The trees in the front yards of those houses near the church are much bigger now than they were in the photos I saw of the church from a hundred years ago, but you can still tell that everything else looks unchanged," Lisa added.

Paul parked his SUV, and they walked along side the historic building. Lisa smiled as she held Paul's arm, and they puffed out cold air with every breath. As they stepped on the sidewalk that ran along the entire side of the church, Lisa slipped on the ice and Paul gracefully caught her so she didn't fall.

"Good save," Lisa said, a little out of breath.

She steadied herself as they continued along next to the old building.

"I don't know how you stay balanced on high heel shoes anyway, even without the ice," added Paul.

"It's a natural feminine talent that I hope you'll never understand, my handsome hubby."

Snow concealed the grass around the sidewalk, and they were cautious of ice as they walked carefully in their dress shoes up to the front entrance. It wasn't very crowded this morning, but it looked like a good turnout from the small town.

"You look absolutely stunning, of course, in your dress and heels," he said.

"Thank you my dear. You look snazzy with a jacket and casual pullover shirt. I don't like wearing stockings, but today I wish I had since the air is so chilly and this dress just barely covers my knees. I hope you're happy, since I'm only doing this for you. My calves are freezing. I should go get my overcoat from the SUV."

"We're not dressed up extremely formal, but we're not overly casual either. I figured this would be acceptable just about anywhere, and we shouldn't stand out too much. Besides, your calves drive me wild."

"Hmmm. Yeah and if you notice, everyone else here is wearing long skirts with boots or they're wearing pants, so I do stand out here as the only woman showing off her calves in the middle of winter. I think you owe me."

Paul cleared his throat and tried to change the subject, immediately shaking hands with someone from the church as they all walked up to the entrance.

"Hi, we're visiting from out of town for a week or two. My name's Paul and this is my beautiful wife, Lisa. She really likes the architecture here."

One of the elderly gentlemen introduced himself, "Good morning. I'm John. Let me take you inside the church and I'll show you around so you can see some of our real treasures."

Lisa smiled at Paul as they walked around and John pointed out a couple of exquisitely carved benches, antique paintings, stained glass windows, and more. This was exactly what Lisa had expected to see, and she was very pleased with what the elderly gentleman showed them.

"Often, an old church can be like walking around in an impressive museum, and this is no exception," said Lisa.

John nodded and showed them a painted, wooden statue hanging on the side wall of the church.

"This was originally brought over from Sweden by the founders of the town."

"It's certainly a museum piece," Lisa replied.

"Yes ma'am. Well, I need to get ready for the service, since I'm in the choir. It's good to meet you both," said John, as he shook their hands. As he left them, he pointed back over the entrance to the massive pipe organ upstairs.

"That's over one hundred years old too," and then waved at them.

Lisa looked around at the upstairs seating and at the massive pipe organ in the back, and was pleasantly surprised when she noticed a few familiar faces coming in the front doors below the organ. Martha and Abigail walked toward them with big smiles, and came up to shake hands with them both. She was again impressed with Martha's taste in clothes, especially being a librarian in a town of less than a thousand people, and noticed that Abigail was also better dressed than she would have expected. She wondered if Martha and Abigail shopped at the same place, then realized there may only be one clothing store in the entire town.

"You both look great," Lisa commented.

"Thanks. Are you Lutheran, or did you just like the looks of this old church and stopped by to investigate?" Martha asked.

"Yes to both. Paul and I were both brought up Lutheran, plus after I left the library a couple of days ago, I was captivated by the old architecture of this church."

Abigail commented with a wry smile, "When I saw you here, I figured you must have been following a clue on your murder mystery."

Lisa laughed out loud and said to her husband, "This is Abigail from the library, and this is Martha, also from the library," and she introduced him to her new acquaintances, "This is my husband, Paul."

"So you must be Lutheran too?" Paul asked Martha, to which Martha and Abigail both nodded, and Paul continued, "It's interesting that some of the few people that we've met in town are also Lutheran."

"It's even more interesting that two visitors from out of town would be Lutheran when most of this area is Methodist," Martha commented, and then Abigail looked at them both and agreed.

"I just live a couple of blocks away," Abigail mentioned. "When I was younger, and Martha was very little, we all used to walk to church since it was so close. My husband passed away a few years ago, but Martha has always been a big help to me."

Paul looked at Martha and asked, "Dave Bramwell is the person who told us about you and the library, but where is he?"

"I'm not sure," Martha responded, and Lisa recognized her disappointment. "Dave was supposed to be here by now, but we haven't seen him yet. We waited out front for a little while, but gave up and came inside to get warm. Hopefully he'll make it on time. It's not like him to be late."

Lisa noticed that Martha seemed a little frustrated Dave wasn't there yet.

Martha mentioned, "Dave and I have been dating for over a year now, and it took me a while to get him to start going to church regularly. This is the first time he's not been here at the beginning of the service since he began coming with us."

Abigail selected a row and they all sat down, as people started getting ready for the service.

"I forgot to invite you to church the day before, but I'm glad to see that you both came even without my invitation," said Martha.

"I think the church is beautiful, and the people we have met so far are very friendly. We feel right at home," and Paul nodded.

"How long have you been going to this church?" Paul asked Abigail.

"Only about twenty odd years. My parents used to take me to the Methodist church down near the lake when I was in school, but I stopped going for a while. Once I was married and started raising a family, I knew that I needed to get back involved with the church, and so I chose to attend this one. I wanted a positive church influence on my kids from the start, and I liked the families that went to this church back then, many of whom are still here today." She added, "Martha has been a member here all of her life, and was baptized here as a child," and Lisa noticed Abigail looked at Martha with pride.

Just then the music got louder and several people walked up to the front of the church to speak. The service was about to start, so the place quickly quieted down. Paul looked at Lisa when he heard the powerful sounds of the church organ start.

"Wow! The sounds coming out of that church organ are incredible."

She raised her eyebrows and nodded in agreement, while they both looked back to see it again. With that, the crowd hushed and the service began.

Chapter Nineteen

AFTER THE SERVICE ENDED, LISA saw Dave waiting for them outside the old church and he waved.

"What happened this morning?" Martha asked him, disappointment clearly visible in her voice. "You missed the whole service, and look who else you missed."

"I'm sorry, but I had an unexpected call this morning and had to help Mr. Wilson fix his pump. It was something that just couldn't wait with the weather being so cold still. I'm sorry I missed being seen with you today. You look exceptionally elegant."

Martha blushed at the positive attention she received in front of everyone, when her eyes caught Lisa's and they both smiled. Dave was right, though, Martha's appearance was fabulous today. She wondered what it was about Martha that stood out, and noticed that her facial structure was striking. She had prominent cheek bones that complemented her smile, with a cute nose in the middle, all framed in by an adorable shoulder-length haircut. For a moment, Lisa realized she actually felt a little jealous, but quickly got that out of her mind. She knew Paul loved her exactly as she was, and that's all she needed.

Abigail said, "Hi Dave. I need to get home for a nap, so would you and Martha walk with me back to my house?"

"We sure will," Dave replied and offered his arm for her to hold.

"It was good meeting you Abigail," Paul commented, and then looking at Martha and Dave, he added, "Hey, Lisa has told me a lot about the downtown area. We're going to take a walk down Main street now. Would you want to join us for lunch in a little bit at that café Lisa told me about? The one near the antique store?"

"That sounds good to me. We'll join you in about thirty minutes," Martha replied, and they all waved and went their separate ways.

Lisa insisted on getting her overcoat because her legs were numb from the wind, so they walked to the SUV and he helped her put it on. He looked disappointed that her skin was almost all covered up now, but he had all morning to enjoy her calves. It was her turn now to get what she wanted.

She enjoyed walking arm in arm with Paul, showing him the shops and stopping to stare at the old pictures in a few of the store windows. She pointed out the original wood floors and brick walls, and they went inside a couple of the stores to walk around and warm up occasionally. Lisa took him to the antique store and an old book store, and she was glad Paul seemed content looking around at the ancient relics. Paul didn't mention it, but Lisa knew he wasn't much of a shopper. He usually identified what he wanted before he went shopping, and then while he's at the store, he would go straight there, pick it out, and would be ready to leave.

She figured he owed it to her to walk around and do some window shopping with her as he was the one who talked her into wearing this short dress on such a cold day. Since Paul didn't complain about it, she knew that he let her do this as his payment for that request. She didn't feel guilty at all and just made the most of this time with her husband. Sometimes marriage involved a little bit of compromising to make both parties happy.

Soon enough, they walked up to the café Lisa wanted to try, and they saw familiar faces heading their way.

"You picked out a great little place, Lisa. I think you'll enjoy it here," Martha said as they all went into the front entrance.

While they sat down at one of the tables, Lisa took out a packet of photographs that she had gotten printed and picked up the day before.

"Martha, would you like to see the pictures we've taken around the lake and around town?"

"Of course. Did they turn out as well as you hoped?"

Lisa showed the excitement in her eyes and said, "Yes, most of them are great."

They all gathered around to see the photos, which were of Paul and/or Lisa playing around on the ice, with snow-covered trees or the cabin in the background. The moose photos were still in the camera so they weren't part of this pack.

As they flipped through the pictures, Dave said, "Wait, what's the white streak on that last picture?"

Lisa went back to it, and looked more closely. "I'm not sure. It may be a sun streak, if I took the picture too far toward the sun."

"No, this one has the sun behind the camera," Martha replied. "That's strange. Is it on any other pictures?"

Lisa skimmed through quickly, but said, "No, it looks like it is only on this one that has Old Deerfield in the background."

"You know that the Nelson's cabin is just a couple of lots down from Old Deerfield," Martha added.

"What are you implying?" Paul responded dryly.

Lisa sat back in her chair and replied, "Some people believe that streaks like this are from the presence of ghosts," and she saw Paul give Dave a frustrated look.

Dave laughed, as the waitress came over to their table to take their orders, and Paul put a finger up to his mouth. Lisa knew it was to tell them all to not talk about ghosts in front of the waitress.

After the waitress went back to the kitchen, Lisa finally asked, "Martha, have you thought any more about the two murders on the lake twenty something years ago and how they could be related to the recent deaths?"

Lisa realized this question took Paul by surprise, since he turned to look at his wife.

Martha replied and Lisa saw the excitement in her eyes, "Yes, and I think you're right about the connection. I don't know for certain how this couple who died in the lake more than two decades ago could be intertwined with these two ruffians from around Kisinaw Lake, but there sure seems to be something going on between them."

This 'ghost story' was the main interest Lisa had this afternoon, and so all of her conversations tended to move toward that topic. Even when Dave or Paul tried to change the subject to their ice fishing expedition, Lisa strategically steered it back to the ghost story being told around town. The waitress stopped by to bring them their drinks, and Lisa realized that she had been listening intently to their conversation. Again Paul changed the subject to the different types of fish in the lake by the cabin he and Lisa rented, and Dave took the bait, responding perfectly with a good discussion on his favorite fish, the Walleye. The waitress walked around the table and took their orders. Lisa knew that Paul hoped if they talked enough about fishing, the waitress would go away without hearing any more talk about ghosts. It worked, and she walked back to the kitchen.

"Lisa, I never realized how fascinated you would be in a supernatural tale. You know I don't believe in ghosts at all,"

Paul commented.

"Yeah, I have to admit that I just don't think there's any such thing as ghosts," added Dave.

"Wait Paul, you know I don't believe in ghosts either," Lisa replied.

"I wish my mother didn't," added Martha.

They all looked at her, and Lisa asked, "Why?"

"For some unknown reason, my mother believes she'll be the murderer's next victim."

Lisa saw Paul's puzzled expression, and then Martha told them, "Maybe you didn't realize it, but Abigail is my mother."

Lisa smiled at Paul with a surprised look on her face and said, "I should have known. I thought the way Abigail looked at you at church was like a proud mother, but I just figured you'd been family friends for many years."

The waitress brought out their meals to an interesting silence, while the four of them waited for her to disappear again. She smiled and stepped through the kitchen door again.

Martha then mentioned, "My mother finally admitted this morning that she knew something about the couple found in the lake twenty-four years ago." That got Lisa's attention as she looked directly at Martha and leaned in closer. Martha continued, "She called it a murder rather than an accident, but wouldn't give any more details."

Lisa exclaimed, "That partially explains why Abigail looked like she had seen a ghost when she saw the photograph of the murdered couple in the library a couple of days ago."

Martha nodded, while she took another bite from her salad.

This really captivated Lisa even more, and she stayed silent at this point, thinking again about Abigail's expressions when she saw the old newspaper articles. She wanted to follow up with Martha on this subject, but decided to wait until the men weren't around. They all went on eating, as Lisa let Paul change the subject again. It had been awkward having two separate conversations at the table, so Lisa allowed Paul and Dave take over for a while as they brought up their confrontation with Daniel Boone.

The waitress came to their table with their bill, and said, "I couldn't help but overhear some of the comments you all made about ghosts." Paul rolled his eyes at Dave, who stifled a laugh, while Paul put the money down for the bill. She continued, "I think that picture with the white smudge or streak on it is proof that you have a ghost in the picture. I've seen studies and for many of those photographs, there are no other explanations for those streaks. Also, the building here where this restaurant now stands is believed to be haunted," and the two couples stared at each other and at the waitress in silence for a few seconds.

Lisa didn't know what to say, and didn't want to be rude to the waitress, so she asked, "Do you think it's true?"

"Yes," said the waitress nodding her head, and Lisa could tell she was excited. "We've had employees complain about hearing noises, lights going out, a couple of the waitresses have mentioned seeing a man in unusual, old fashioned clothes standing in the doorway one second, but disappearing right away. Another waitress actually quit on the spot last weekend when she saw this herself."

Lisa knew they were all pretending to be interested, when Dave finally said, "Well, thanks for the delicious lunch. We need to get going, but we'll stop by again real soon."

He got up from the table, while the others followed his lead, and the waitress smiled as she bid her farewell to the group.

Once they stepped outside, they all laughed out loud on the way to their cars and Dave said, "People have already picked us out to be ghost hunters or something. My reputation will be ruined."

Paul said, "You won't believe this but last night at dinner, we heard about Big Foot sightings here near the lake, so now all we need is for someone to talk about their UFO sighting and our vacation will be complete."

Dave snickered again, but said, "Laugh now, Paul, but I do believe there's something to the Sasquatch stories. I'm just not so sure about ghosts."

Martha asked, "Hey, what about that photograph I took of the UFO over the lake a few months ago?"

There was silence for a few seconds, and then everyone busted out laughing again.

Paul said, "You've got to be kidding," but Martha shook her head.

"No, as far as we know, there have been no explanations, and it was in the news as far down as Lower Michigan, across this part of the UP, Wisconsin, and into Ontario. It was the strangest thing I've ever seen, and several photographs were sent in to the newspapers from people between Lake Michigan and Lake Superior that day."

Dave added, "Yeah, this was a strange one. It just sat there in the sky for the longest time, almost thirty minutes, with its lights on, just sitting there above the lake as the sun went down. All possibilities were ruled out, and it was just left as an Unidentified Flying Object. I'm thinking it was some kind of military experiment the government doesn't want us to know about."

Lisa watched Paul as he shook his head, and she wondered what he thought. She knew he had a difficult time believing this, but coming from Martha, she figured there had to be something to her story.

Dave added, "I don't want people to think I'm not playing with a full deck, so we don't really mention this to people, ay? I'd appreciate it if you didn't tell anyone."

"I'd really be interested in seeing the photograph some-day if you don't mind showing it," Lisa commented.

"Sure. I want to see what you think it could have been."

Dave finally said, "I apologize for having to leave you so soon, especially with the prospects of having more of these fascinating ghost story conversations, but I need to get back to work. I have a job on another lake nearby."

Lisa noticed that Martha was disappointed he missed church and now had to leave again, and she watched her and Dave discuss his plans. Martha didn't look very happy, but Dave gave her a kiss on the cheek, waved to everyone, went to his truck and drove off.

Martha shrugged her shoulders and asked Lisa, "Would you like to go to the cemetery where the drowned couple was buried twenty-four years ago?"

"Yes," said Lisa excitedly without even consulting Paul.

He looked at his wife, smiled and said, "I'm just along for the ride."

Lisa heard him comment under his breath, "I should have gone with Dave and maybe learned something useful."

"What was that honey?" Lisa asked sarcastically.

"Oh, nothing, sweetie. Hey Martha, do you want to ride over there with us?"

"Sure, thanks."

"Just tell me where I need to turn off the road."

They all walked back to the church, and once everyone climbed into Paul's SUV, they pulled out of the church parking lot. Lisa was a little anxious about going to the cemetery, but was also filled with eager anticipation, since she suspected they would find something of interest there. She sensed it, and the feeling was so strong it gave her butterflies in her stomach.

Chapter Twenty

PAUL DROVE **L**ISA AND **M**ARTHA TO the local cemetery, only a few minutes from the downtown area, and they slowly pulled into the parking lot. Paul had never cared for cemeteries, but couldn't remember having any traumatic experience as a kid that would give him a fear of them. It was just not a place where he felt at ease walking around, whether it was day or night. Lisa and Martha got out of the SUV, but Paul made no effort to join them.

"Are you alright?" Lisa asked Paul.

Rather than make a scene, he replied, "Sure," and opened the door to follow the girls.

He looked up at the old sign over the entrance, and it didn't make him feel welcome. It appeared to be a quiet, peaceful place in the daylight, but he still knew this was a place where hundreds, maybe thousands of dead bodies were laid to rest, and it wasn't a comforting thought for him to take in. He pushed it out of his mind and walked through the gate behind Lisa and Martha, glancing up cautiously as he walked under the imposing sign.

Together, they all started looking for the gravestone of the couple that was 'murdered' twenty-four years ago, at least according to Abigail. The ground was covered with a few inches of snow, which made the task more challenging with the flat headstones. Paul looked up to take in the entire scene, and saw that the cemetery bordered a row of tall pine trees on the left, followed some hills down, then up, then down again, and went way back to another row of tall pine trees in the back. Then on the right side, it looked like a large open field with no graves, which was probably reserved for future growth.

"That's comforting," he mumbled to himself. "This area here is for all of the people who have already died in this town, and that area over there is saved for the rest of the people still living in the town."

******

Paul and Martha then wandered off along a man-made path, each in a different direction, while Lisa slowly stepped on patches of grass reaching up through the snow, making her own path between the graves. Lisa looked over and saw Paul and Martha talking together, thankful that she met Martha and glad they all got along so well. Snow froze her feet at it covered her shoes with each step, but she tried to ignore it, questioning her decision to not wear hosiery today. She was still in heels, but she gave no indication of minding a walk through the snow.

A cemetery could be a scary place for some people, even during the day, but to Lisa that was not the case here. She was so impressed with the beauty of the cemetery with the snow on the ground all over the hills, and she followed deer footprints for a little while without saying anything. The tracks looked like two medium-sized deer, and ended up leading out of the cemetery into the forest.

She marveled at how the clouds seemed to be sitting on top of the hill, although she knew that couldn't be the case. Lisa smiled to herself as she thought about going up there to touch a cloud, something she had always wanted to do as a child. She enjoyed hearing the Chick-a-dees making chirping noises in the nearby trees, and wondered how recently the deer had been through here. The tracks looked so fresh that she guessed they must have only been here not much more than an hour ago. They might even be standing in the woods watching her now. After walking for a couple of minutes, Lisa was curious that for such a small town, this seemed like a very large cemetery. She slowly turned to take in the full size of the place. It looked as though everyone who had ever come through this town must be buried here.

Is this the only cemetery in town, and could all of these people have lived here at some time or another?

Lisa looked at the stones, read the names and dates, and it tore her apart when she saw the markers that showed a person who was only a few years old.

"Wow, how sad. Only two years old."

Martha had circled around and was now only a couple of rows away from her, and read a gravestone that looked like it was for a child.

"Lisa, this little baby was only a couple of days old. There must have been an incredible amount of sadness as these children were taken away from their families so young."

"I couldn't imagine going through something so difficult," Lisa responded and Martha nodded.

Lisa said, "Look at this. There are fresh flowers on a grave, with snow around them. It would have made a beautiful photograph, the colorful flowers against the snowy background, but I just don't feel like taking a picture at this moment."

Just then she realized she stood next to the Nelson's gravestone, and took a couple of steps over to read the information on the stone. There were fresh flowers on this grave too, and it reminded Lisa of the beauty of spring, despite the snow all around the flowers. For some reason, her heart fluttered while she stood there, maybe because she felt as though they were about to find another clue to the mystery they wanted to unravel.

"What secrets were buried with you, Mr. And Mrs. Nelson?" she said out loud to herself. "It was only the previous day that Martha found out you were here at this cemetery, and now we've found your headstone."

Lisa still stood in front of their grave as Martha stepped up beside her to read it. Lisa leaned over to brush some of the snow from the stone, and thought about how cold the ground was. A chill ran up her spine as she considered what it would be like to lay in this cold ground forever.

Martha exclaimed, "Fortunately, these people aren't really laying here under the cold earth and snow, but they're in Heaven."

Lisa looked at her and nodded as she considered Martha's comment, which almost sounded like a response to her thoughts.

The Nelsons, previously unknown to any of them, seemed to come out of nowhere; presented their story in an obituary at the library, and now they lay right in front of them with a potentially unsolved murder. Lisa thought about that for a second and, just like Martha had commented, she realized that the Nelsons were not actually there now, just their bones, and that their spirits were most likely in Heaven with God. She remembered hearing that they were religious, and for some reason, she believed that they were not just 'religious' but were actually good people who had a real relationship with God. Lisa didn't know what made her think that, but it was just a feeling that came over her as she stood there.

Lisa didn't know what they might possibly find at the cemetery, but since Martha had suggested looking for their graves this afternoon, she couldn't resist.

When Paul joined them, they all stood there at the Nelson's grave site and he said, "Look at the dates. When they died, they weren't much older than we are now." He paused for that to sink in, and then added, "How sad it is the way they died. Nobody in town seems to want to talk about the circumstances. I wonder if they were really murdered or if it was just an accident."

Martha added, "Dying so young, regardless of the circumstances, is such a tragedy," and they all nodded. She continued, "The people left behind miss being with them and wonder what things would have been like if they hadn't died then."

Paul read the names and dates over again out loud to himself, and didn't even seem to notice that Martha had been doing the same thing. Lisa stood between the two of them, and smiled as she looked at each of them. She stared at the gravestone for a few seconds, then squeezed Paul's arm thinking about how young they were, and Paul looked over at her. She put herself in that couple's place; contemplating how much life this couple must have thought they had ahead of them. They were probably only recently married a few years before, and since Lisa was a romantic, their tragic deaths tore at her. Lisa had a way of feeling another person's pain or joy by imagining herself as that person, and Paul stared at Lisa's tears as she imagined what it would have been like to know this couple, then find out that they had died so tragically.

******

Paul looked over at Martha as Lisa wiped away her tears,

and without a word, they all walked away, trudging through the snow back to the parking lot. As they headed toward the SUV, Paul and Lisa walked quietly together, arm in arm. Martha, who was a little ways behind them, noticed someone drive up and park in another section of the cemetery parking lot, away from Paul's SUV. She didn't recognize the man, since she hadn't seen him at the library before, and didn't think anything of it. He was just another visitor to this big cemetery. For a second, she wondered who he would be visiting here, but realized that it could be any one of the thousands of graves. The man didn't seem to notice the three of them coming out of the cemetery either. He just stayed in his truck for a few minutes, reading the newspaper, as Lisa and Martha finally got in Paul's SUV and drove off.

Chapter Twenty-One

MARTHA SUGGESTED, "WHY don't we open up the library and do some research on our own? The library is closed on Sunday so nobody would come in to interrupt us."

"That's a great idea," said Lisa. "I've got more ideas that we could look up there."

Paul said, "How about if I drop you off, then come back and get you in a little while?"

To his surprise, Lisa didn't complain and simply replied, "OK, that sounds good."

Paul glanced at Lisa for a moment, and then continued driving down the highway. Within about ten minutes, he turned into the library parking lot. Paul stopped in front, then kissed his wife as she and Martha stepped out into the wind and walked to the library door.

"I'll be back and pick you up before it gets dark," Paul told her as they both waved back at him, and then he headed down the road toward the cabin.

As he drove, he said, "Oh great. If I go all the way back to the cabin and return right away, it'll probably be dark by the time I get back to the library since it starts getting dusky early in the winter here. Lisa and Martha may not even realize how late it is, since they'll be inside with the library lights and would be so focused on their investigative work."

Paul soon thought about visiting the souvenir shop instead to talk with Michael Dufresne about the recent deaths in the lake, and was happy when he saw a car outside the shop. This was a little closer than driving all the way back to the cabin, so he figured he would save some daylight and stop here instead. He noticed that the casino parking lot across the street was packed with cars, and smiled when he remembered that Michael said the townspeople were 'donating their paychecks' to the Ojibwa Indians over there. He parked by the souvenir shop, and went inside to look around.

Greeted with, "Hi Paul, did you see another moose?" he knew right away it was Michael.

Paul replied, "No, but I did hear a story about a recent Sasquatch sighting in town here," and they both laughed.

Michael came up to shake hands and he told Paul, "You will hear things about the Sasquatch around here, since it has been seen here for many generations. I believe I have heard one and smelled one several times when I have been in the woods, but I have never seen it. I am sure it watched me, but it never made me feel threatened. The creature is here, but he is very elusive."

Paul shook his head in disbelief, but said, "It is a different realm up here. What I really wanted to talk to you about are the two guys that were pulled out of Kisinaw Lake recently. Do you have a few minutes?"

Michael looked around at the empty store and said, "For you? I think I can take a break now. Let's sit down over here."

Paul followed him to a table and sat down with Michael.

Without hesitating, Paul said, "So who do you believe are the suspects if it was indeed foul-play?"

"Who do you hear as suspects?" Michael responded.

"Dave Bramwell suspects Officer Haley, and most of the town seems to suspect me and Lisa since we arrived right when the first man was found dead."

Michael reminded him, "Don't forget that I am a suspect in the eyes of the older locals, and some people believe it was the work of ghosts."

At this, they both smiled, and Paul said, "OK, so that makes four sets of potential suspects, if you count the ghosts."

Michael continued, "I believe that Eddie and Little Frank made many enemies during their lifetimes, so it will be a challenge to pinpoint just one who would want to see them dead. I can't remember them working together, though. I just know that they were both difficult to get along with over the years, each in their own ways."

Paul asked, "So you don't think they worked together on anything that could have gone wrong and gotten them into trouble?"

Michael thought for a moment, but said, "It is possible, but I just can't remember anything they did together. If they did, it may have been many, many years ago when they were very young. Would you like some hot, wild rice soup? It is one of our specialties up here."

Paul contemplated that for a second, and said, "Sure, I'd like to try it."

He really wanted to focus on the questions he had for Michael, but he remembered from his last visit here that Michael liked to have soup while he talked. If that's what it took to get a few details out of him, then it would be worth it to have soup with him. Besides, the last bowl he served them was delicious.

Michael said, "I'll be right back with two bowls and spoons. Would you also like some hot tea or coffee with the soup?"

Paul responded, "Well, since you twisted my arm, I'll take hot tea with a little bit of your local honey if you don't mind."

Michael walked over to the counter to get everything, while Paul turned and looked out at the casino through the front window. He saw the full parking lot again. He then turned to look out the back window, almost expecting to see the deer nibbling on a branch, but she wasn't there this time.

Michael returned with a tray full of hot, steaming bowls and cups, and Paul said, "Mmmmmmm, that smells awesome."

"I told you that you would like it. I saw you looking out the back window for the deer. She was out there again this morning, so your little lady missed her today. She mostly likes to come out after dawn and at dusk, so she may be back for her dinner time in a little bit. You should have known the deer would have only been there now if Lisa was here with you."

"Yeah, she has a way with animals, and can see things that most people wouldn't even notice."

"Where is Lisa?"

"She's at the library with our friend, Martha," Paul replied.

"On a Sunday?" Michael questioned.

"Yes, Martha opened up for her and Lisa to do some special researching while nobody else is there."

Michael nodded, as Paul leaned over to smell the wild rice soup.

"Honestly, I believe you and Lisa can be taken off the suspect list, and I really do not believe that I had anything to do with the recent deaths."

Paul laughed and said, "I'm glad we got that straightened out," which made Michael laugh as well. "So that leaves Officer Haley and the ghosts," Paul continued.

"Officer Haley is a man of the law, and since he is new in town, it is not in his best interest to be involved with something like this. As much as the older locals have harassed him, I do not think he would stoop to such action to get them back. I also don't think he would be so angry at these men that he would actually take their lives. He appears to be very levelheaded and in control of his emotions."

Paul considered that for a few seconds while he poured the honey into his tea and stirred it slowly.

"So that leaves the ghosts, from our initial suspect list," which caused Paul to glance up with a look that said, "You must be kidding." Michael held up a finger and continued, "Now I am not saying that it must be spirits that are involved, but I believe you should consider the revenge aspect from the initial murder over twenty years ago as a real possibility, maybe not in the form of ghosts, but from that same point of view. Who could be out for revenge over a murder that happened many years ago? It is the only thing that makes sense to me."

Paul nodded as he tasted the soup, and he said, "This is very good soup, Michael. Lisa will want to try this."

Michael smiled and tasted his, replying, "Yes, indeed it is."

Paul asked, "Who were the murdered couple's friends and family, and who would still be in this area twenty years later? Plus, why now after all this time?"

"The friends and family were all good people who would probably never even consider murder, but there is always the possibility that someone has allowed an evil spirit to take control of his thoughts and actions. Identify all of those from the past who could even have any interest in these old locals, and talk to each of them. You may find something."

Paul nodded, and finished off the rest of his soup. They talked for a little while more, and both had another cup of tea.

Paul looked outside, realizing it was darker now, and said, "I'd better go pick up Lisa from the library. Thanks again for the soup and conversation."

"Stop by anytime. Those are my specialties."

"Now you mentioned evil spirits. I am probably going to regret this, but maybe we need to talk about that a little more the next time we see you."

"Yes, I think you will be interested in my explanation," Michael replied, his eyes locking in with Paul's.

Paul started to get out his wallet to pay, but Michael said, "Soup and tea is on the house today."

"I appreciate it, Michael. Talk to you later."

He headed outside into the cold again, and drove back toward the town, trying to remember what he had learned about evil spirits while growing up. Although he didn't want to dwell on it too much, he recalled that whenever evil spirits were involved with something, bad things always seemed to follow like an ominous dark shadow.

Chapter Twenty-Two

THE LIBRARY WAS EMPTY THIS AF-
ternoon, since it was Sunday, so the echo of the door slamming shut behind them seemed different from the other day when the library was full of people and other sounds. Her first thought was that of a tomb closing with finality, but she hoped it would be more like a tomb opening up and revealing its secrets.

Martha called Abigail from the library and Lisa listened to the conversation. She now knew that Abigail was Martha's mother, so it changed things somewhat in Lisa's eyes.

"Mom, would you be willing to meet Lisa and me at the library to talk about the Nelsons?"

There was a long silence from the other end, but Abigail finally answered.

"I know I'll have to tell you what I remember about the Nelsons sometime or another, so it may as well be now."

Lisa felt relieved when Martha smiled with a nod, and replied to her mother, "Great. Thanks mom. We're there now starting to look up old records. Can you meet us in a few minutes?"

"OK, I'll be right over there. See you soon," said Abigail.

"Alright. Thanks Mom. We'll be waiting for you."

Martha hung up and looked at Lisa, "It sounded as though she wants to get something out in the open, so I'll bet she knows a lot more than we think she knows."

******

"Hi Mom. Come on in and get warmed up," said Martha once her mother had walked into the library.

They all sat at one of the tables in front of the librarian's desk. Martha had already set out hot tea on the table for each of them, and they sipped it right away to start warming up their frozen hands and lips. Martha had also placed a small space heater under the table, so she and Lisa both kicked off their heels and warmed their feet at the same time.

Lisa had one topic she wanted to address, and she jumped right in to start the conversation.

"Abigail, why did you say that you thought you would be the next to die in the lake?"

"Straight to the point, I see. Well, years ago I was rebellious and dated a troublemaker, called Big Frank, and at the time, Big Frank didn't like the Nelsons at all. He told everyone that they were religious fanatics, and he would threaten them occasionally for no reason, other than just to be mean."

Lisa interrupted, "Why was he called 'Big Frank' rather than just 'Frank'?

Abigail smiled and responded, "There was another guy on the lake named Frank, and they were about the same age."

Martha nodded and said, "So to differentiate them, one must have been called 'Big Frank' and the other was 'Little Frank.'"

Lisa mentioned, "One of the people found in the lake was called 'Little Frank', but he was very tall and over 300 pounds. He couldn't have been the same 'Little Frank', could he?"

Abigail laughed and said, "Big Frank was actually about 5'6" and 120 pounds, but he was considered the brains of his gang of friends, which says a lot about these guys. Because of his 'importance as the leader', he insisted that everyone call him 'Big Frank' and our friend who was tall and over 300 pounds was 'Little Frank'. It should have been no surprise to me, but I found out that Big Frank wasn't the brightest guy in the area, despite what he wanted people to believe." She looked at Lisa, nodded her head, and said, "The person found frozen in the lake this week was indeed the same 'Little Frank' that I knew so many years ago."

Abigail continued, "I didn't date Big Frank again after that first 'mistake' but living in a small town I still occasionally went to the pub and into town as part of the group, so I still saw him once in a while. The Nelsons and their family had been on the lake longer than Big Frank's family, and he probably resented that. For some reason, there are men on the lake who think it's so important to be the oldest families to have settled in the area, and they look down on those who have been there for a fewer number of years than them. It doesn't make sense to me, but I still see it today. I even moved into town after the Nelsons died, farther away from the lake, but I've heard about that new policeman being treated like dirt from those same old-timers. It's just not right.

Anyway, the Nelsons had just as much right to be there as he did, but Big Frank would get drunk and make all kinds of threatening comments about them. I don't know why I even went anywhere with him and his 'gang', except they were just about the only people close to my age on the lake at that time, and that I was afraid of him if I did anything to make him angry. He hadn't always been mean when we were kids, but once he discovered beer after he dropped out of high school, he changed for the worse.

One winter night, Big Frank was at the pub with some of his friends. Unfortunately, I was one of them, and they all had too much to drink. They decided to leave, and he wanted me to come along for a drive along the shore of the frozen lake. I told them I needed to get home, which was the other direction, so I walked to my house alone while Big Frank grumbled. What I figured is that they must have driven by the Nelson's cabin, just one lot past Old Deerfield, and the Nelsons were outside heading toward their cabin after a leisurely walk along the road. Big Frank ran over them both, whether on purpose or the result of his drunkenness I don't know, and his gang all got out of the car and argued about what to do with their bodies.

I heard the commotion, but I just continued walking up the road to my house rather than turn around to see what was happening. I guessed it was just a drunken fight between Frank and his friends, and it occurred to me that he might have crashed into a telephone pole. I actually laughed at that. It was very dark that night, as a lot of winter nights are here when the clouds cover up the stars, and I was tired. I regret that I didn't investigate, but looking back, I don't think I could have done anything to help the Nelsons with the four of them drunk. My guess is that the Nelsons were already dead by the time the boys started arguing.

Apparently the boys must have finally agreed on hiding the bodies. Someone dragged them both out onto the lake, broke a hole in the ice, and put the Nelsons into the freezing water. Even if the crash didn't kill them, they never came out of that hole alive, and the boys all kicked snow over the place where the accident happened, to hide their tracks.

When I spoke with Frank the next day, I should have known something bad went on the night before, but they all covered it up and pretended nothing happened. He threatened me, and told me that I'd better not say anything about that night, and didn't believe me when I told them I hadn't a clue what he was talking about. To me, it was just immature, young men playing around on the lakeshore after a few drinks. I didn't know what had gone on that night. I didn't think they could have really done something so bad, and figured they must have just been behaving mischievously, as usual. That's all. Later that day, when I heard the news, I was in tears, ran home, and never spoke to that Frank again. I've kept quiet all these years."

"What happened to those guys?" Lisa asked.

"My old buddy, Big Frank, was killed on the lake that same year, supposedly the result of a drunken boating accident, which didn't surprise me. Two of those 'guys' were found dead in the lake in the past week, and the other one, named Robert Vallee, keeps to himself on the other side of the lake. Only he and I remain from the group that was there that night, so that's why I believe one of us is next to die in the lake."

Martha added, "It sure seems like the Nelsons are finally getting their revenge."

"We need to find that man, Robert Vallee," Lisa commented, so Martha looked up his address.

Lisa glanced up at the small windows that ran along the ceiling, about six feet off the ground, and noticed that it looked dark outside already. Her heart raced as she wondered when Paul would be there.

"I know he's on the same lake where you and Paul are staying, but I don't know which cabin," Abigail said as Martha fumbled through the phone book.

"Knowing him, he probably has an unlisted number so he won't be bothered," Abigail added.

"No, here he is Lisa. His cabin is number 808 on the Kisinaw Lake road."

Just then, Paul came in the front door to pick up Lisa and before he could say anything, she jumped up, blurting out, "You're just in time, Paul. We need to get over to the Vallee cabin and make sure he's OK."

"Hi Lisa, I'm glad to see you too."

Paul looked around with a confused expression and asked, "What are you talking about, Lisa?"

"Vallee had been part of the gang that killed the Nelsons, and is the only one still alive, except for Abigail."

"Wow, that's news to me," Paul responded as Lisa marched passed him on the way to the front door. "It was nice seeing you all again. I guess we're leaving now," and he waved to Abigail.

Martha followed them outside the library and said, "I'm going to take my mother home now. After what she told us, I'm really concerned for her safety now. You know, it's going to be dark in another hour, so maybe you should do this in the morning."

"If this man is really in danger, then we need to warn him as soon as possible," Lisa commented. "Tomorrow may be too late. Besides, it'll only take us fifteen minutes to get to his house, right?"

Martha nodded, but Lisa noticed she didn't look reassured.

On the way out to the SUV, Paul stopped and mentioned to Lisa, "Remember that I said Robert wasn't the friendliest person on the lake? Why don't you go with Martha and Abigail, and I'll pick you up after I talk to Mr. Vallee?"

Martha said, "Yes, that's a good idea," however, Lisa shook her head.

"No, I'm going with you, Paul."

"You know that this man threatened Dave and I with a gun, and he'll not be too happy to see one of the trespassers again," but he saw that Lisa had made up her mind and was determined.

Although he wasn't too happy to involve Lisa in this social visit, he smiled.

"You know, I've always loved this stubborn trait in you," but Lisa was unusually quiet.

"Please be careful, both of you," Martha said.

"We will," Paul told her, and they drove off toward what might prove to be another unpleasant confrontation.

Chapter Twenty-Three

AFTER THINKING ABOUT HIS EXPE-rience with this hermit only a few days earlier, Paul pulled off of the highway into a roadside park just past the downtown area.

"I know you're adamant about checking up on this guy now, but based on what I saw of him already, I'd rather get the police involved."

"I agree Paul. I thought the same thing exactly, and hoped you'd say something about it. I don't like the idea of this guy coming out to greet us with a shotgun, but I just don't want to wait until tomorrow, in case it's too late."

Paul went directly to Officer Haley to let him know their concerns about Robert Vallee. The police station was on their way back toward the lake, and to their relief, Jake just happened to be in his office at that time.

"Well, what brings the romantic tourists to my humble place of employment at this time of day?" Jake asked as he motioned them toward his office with a friendly smile and a wave of his arm.

Lisa mentioned, "You know that we looked up old news-papers and found some details on a case where a young couple was found dead in Kisinaw Lake, and we believe this couple was murdered twenty-four years ago. None of us think it was an accidental drowning."

She paused for a moment.

"Someone is out for revenge," Paul and Lisa both exclaimed at the same time, as Paul looked at Lisa with surprise and smiled briefly.

Lisa explained, "The two people who were discovered dead in the lake this past week were somehow involved with the murder of the Nelsons, and everyone from Big Frank's gang back then is at risk of this retaliation now."

"I've asked around since our last discussion at the pub," said Jake, "but I haven't found any leads to go on. I'm still a little skeptical about the revenge aspect, since it's been over twenty years since the initial murder," although, to Paul's satisfaction, he added "However, I agree that it couldn't be the work of ghosts, as was initially suggested." Jake continued, "You two are only here on vacation. Why are you so determined this old case was a murder?"

"One of the librarians, Abigail, knew the Nelsons, Eddie, Little Frank, Robert Vallee, and the other man called 'Big Frank'. One night, they left Old Deerfield in Big Frank's car after having a little too much to drink, and she walked home. She heard shouting but didn't go back to see what was going on. Big Frank and his friends drove home drunk, apparently ran over the Nelsons coming home from a moonlight walk along the road that circles the lake, and Big Frank's gang ended up putting the Nelson's into the freezing water under the ice. Abigail didn't think it was anything more than a drunken fight between Big Frank's friends so she didn't pay any attention to the arguing. The next day, she found out that the Nelsons were dead. She's convinced that these men murdered the Nelsons, and of the original group that knew about this, only she and Robert Vallee are still alive today."

Lisa noticed that Jake's expression changed once he heard this, and gave him a minute to think about this new information.

Jake finally replied, "I've never heard anything about these grouchy old men being involved in something like this. I've tried to find a connection between Little Frank and Eddie, and it sounds like this could be it. If any of this is true, though, Vallee may be in real trouble. Listen, I'm not saying that this is all factual, since its information that was never presented in the original case, but if it is true, then it's the lead that I've been looking for. I'll drive over to Mr. Vallee's house as a precaution to make sure the old guy is OK. Do you want to come?"

"I appreciate you following up on this," said Paul. "It'll sure make us feel a little better."

To make the situation more challenging, however, once they all got outside, Paul noticed it was really getting dark and felt much colder out now. They all drove out to Vallee's house in Jake's car right away.

On the way there, Paul asked, "That guy named Tim that we met at the pub. He seems like a nice guy. What do you know about him?"

"Yeah, Tim's a good guy," replied Jake. "He's only been in town a little longer than I have, but he's made a good impression on people. He helps with repairs and things, and doesn't charge these people an arm and a leg. I've talked to some of the older folks who say that Tim didn't even charge them a thing for emergency fixes they needed for the winter. That's the kind of person you want to have in town, don't you think?"

Paul nodded and asked, "What do the older locals think about him?"

Jake shook his head with a short laugh, "There are people that just hate everyone, even the person who would give the shirt off his back. No matter what Tim does, or how good his work is, those guys don't even acknowledge him and say derogatory things about him behind his back. That's the way some of those people are, unfortunately. He even fixed up a part of Old Deerfield that rotted away quite a bit around the front door and one of the windows, and did a great job of it last month. The owners were ecstatic, yet the old locals don't want to think about that down there. They walk through that door every week, and sit by that window, but won't acknowledge how good of a job Tim did with it all."

Lisa added, "That's too bad. He seems like a good person."

Jake replied, "Yep."

"You know," Jake started slowly, "that night we talked at the pub I said I hadn't heard of any ghosts around here, but later that night I was reminded of a strange experience I had several months ago after I first moved up here."

Lisa sat in the front seat and turned back to Paul with a look that said, "See, I told you so."

It was all Paul could do to keep from busting out laughing at her expression and interrupting Jake's story. Lisa just smiled as she listened to Jake.

"I received a call to check out an old abandoned house one evening, maybe around 9:30 PM, before it got dark. You know it stays light up here pretty late in the summers. Apparently there was a report of kids and potential criminal mischief, so I drove out with another officer, Brad Feula. We drove down the old road, now covered with grass, and saw the old house. It had two stories, plus an attic window, and looked like it hadn't been painted in over a hundred years. It must have been a beautiful house at one time, with ornate decorations over the windows and doors.

There was no way to get inside without finding something to stand on, since the steps to the doors were gone, and the house set up off the ground quite a bit. We looked around the house, shined the flashlights into each of the windows, and saw no signs of mischief anywhere. We walked out in what was once the old yard, but still nothing suspicious. Brad said that it must have been a false alarm, so we headed back to the car. As we piled into the car though, I froze when I looked up into one of the second floor windows, and pointed it out to Brad. There was a candle burning, and a fresh red rose sitting next to it."

"But you had already shined the lights into each of the windows. Didn't you see it before?" asked Lisa.

"Both Brad and I were certain we looked into that same window only minutes before and there was nothing there. We then went up to the house thinking that someone had to be in there, but it took us several minutes to find blocks we could stand on to get up to the door. Once high enough, we found that the door had been nailed shut, and was not an easy thing to get open. Brad looked for a way kids might have climbed into a window, but all of the first floor windows were shut and there was nothing but small bushes under each window. None of the windows had been broken either. I finally got the door opened, and we both climbed in, announcing out loud who we were to whoever was in the house. At this point, however, we had serious doubts that anyone had been in this house for decades."

"But you know that wasn't true since somebody had just lit the candle upstairs, right?" asked Paul.

"What first gave me a creepy feeling was the dust that blanketed everything, including the floors, and there were no disturbances anywhere, except the footprints left by Brad and myself by the front door. We pulled out our guns at the same time, looked at each other with surprise, and walked quietly toward the stairs. The creaks in the floorboards gave me chills with each step, and I was overcome with a fear that I've never felt before or since. When I made it to the top of the stairs, I looked down and saw our trail through the dust from the front door to where we now stood. It was obvious that no-body had been in this house for many years.

I found the bedroom with that window and stood there trembling as Brad walked into the room behind me, both of us speechless. The entire room, covered in dust, showed no signs of anyone coming in for years, yet there was a recently lit candle and a freshly picked rose in a vase with water, sitting on the window sill.

I blew out the candle and touched the rose to make sure it was real, and Brad said, "Let's get out of here!"

We quickly made our way through the rest of the house, only to find no signs of life in any room, and we hastily left much faster than when we initially came in. I tried to talk with Brad on the way back to the station about what we saw, but he won't talk about it even to this day. I can't explain it, and if it was some teenagers playing a trick on two cops, they sure did a great job."

"That's an incredible story, Jake," Lisa finally said. "I don't know what to say."

Paul didn't say anything, and it stayed quiet for a few minutes.

Just then, Jake pulled off the road and said, "Here's the Vallee driveway."

This surprised Paul, because it only looked like a path for snowmobiles. It was almost impossible to tell that someone lived back here, since the forest was so thick and overgrown.

Jake told them, "This is how Robert likes it, and he hopes it keeps people from coming back here and bothering him." They continued driving up the path to the house, and Paul noticed an old structure that hadn't changed in many years. "The place needs repair, but Robert doesn't want anyone out to work on his house. He's too old to do some things himself, so the big repairs have been left undone for several years."

Jake stopped the police car, so everyone got out and headed toward the house.

"Paul and Lisa. I'd really appreciate it if you didn't mention the story about the old house, the candle, and the rose to anyone, OK? It's just not something that I want spread around, and I'm sure Brad would appreciate a little discretion as well."

"Of course," replied Lisa, and Paul nodded in agreement. They walked for a few minutes in silence up the path to the house.

"In case you haven't heard, Robert Vallee can be a little grumpy when people get too nosy," Jake warned them.

"Yeah, Dave Bramwell and I already saw just how grumpy he can get," Paul explained.

Jake stopped walking, turned around to look at Paul and Lisa, and stared at Paul for a second, which startled Paul.

Jake puffed cold breath near Paul's face, and told him, "Dave has a tendency to rub some of the locals the wrong way. It would be better to not let Dave get too pushy with these people, since not very many of them like him much." Paul hadn't heard this before and looked at Lisa in disbelief. Jake mentioned, "It's a good thing that we didn't bring Dave with us here to Robert's house, since it may have been a very unpleasant meeting if we had."

Paul told Jake, "Dave and I came out near here ice fishing, and this guy came out and chased us away with a shotgun." That got Jake's attention, and Paul continued. "I figured that he was just an angry old hermit that was as unfriendly as an ornery wolverine. Although it did surprise me that Dave would even argue with him when this guy had a shotgun in his hand," and Jake just looked at Paul for a minute or so without saying anything.

Jake breathed in deep and exhaled, and then told Paul, "I really can't discuss details on this case, so what I am about to say is just off the record. You should be cautious about what you say around Dave, since he's currently one of the few plausible suspects we have for this case."

Paul was taken aback even more at this revelation, and stared into Lisa's pretty eyes for a few seconds. Lisa gave him a worried expression, so he held her hand.

Paul commented, "Dave doesn't seem the kind of person who could kill anyone," but Jake held up his hand and interrupted.

"You two have only been here a few days, and you don't know what all has gone on between Dave and several of the locals here over the years. There's more to him than you realize. I don't want to discuss this any further, but I want to remind you both that you should just be cautious."

They all turned and walked up toward the house again in silence.

To Paul's disappointment and relief, they couldn't find Robert at his house, or on his property, but Jake said, "He may still be in town picking up things he needed."

Jake left a note on Robert's door to call the police station when he returned home, then they all walked quietly back to the car and returned to the station.

"I'll give him a call later this evening once he gets home to see how Vallee is doing," said Jake without looking at either of them.

Paul thought Jake was trying to show his confidence to him and Lisa that Robert Vallee would be back soon, but Paul could tell that Jake wasn't so sure himself.

Chapter Twenty-Four

SUNLIGHT STREAKED DOWN through the clear water, alternating shadows with the morning's rays. Several of the lake's plants reached up over eight feet from the bottom of the lake, and provided great hiding places for many of the smaller fish swimming through and around the tall weeds. A good-sized small mouth bass came by as the smaller fish moved out of its way.

Tim watched a large pike slowly move past a few of the weeds, and he was reminded of a barracuda prowling around for its next meal. The sunlight shimmered off of the fish's scales and created a striking display of light in all directions. Tim could tell the smaller fish knew that this impressive hunter was not something to stick around and stare at, but many of them stayed close by as it made its way through the water like it was the king of the lake. Perhaps it truly was. The other fish appeared cautious, but seemed mesmerized by this ruthless giant as they wisely cleared a path for it.

It was so peaceful down there, with more splendor than most people could ever imagine. The average person might think this was just a muddy lake with weeds and rocks, but Tim realized that this was another world worth considering. There were spectacular places on the land, but this was something else. As Tim took it all in and saw how much light surrounded him, he looked up and saw the underneath of the frozen surface, along with an eighteen inch, circular hole in the ice. It sure seemed much lighter up there than he expected in the winter, since it was most often overcast this time of year, but was amazed at the spectacular view from this side of the ice. The silent shadow and sunlight show danced in front of him, occasionally reflecting off of a fish, while the underwater current caused the tall weeds to slowly sway back and forth. The weeds were like a supporting cast to the underwater sunlight that was the star of the show.

Tim enjoyed what he witnessed, and he slowly looked around to his left to see more.

This was really not a bad place to spend a lifetime.

Everything appeared to be in slow motion, but he figured that was normal for anything moving underwater. Out of the corner of his eye, he thought he saw something that seemed out of place, so he tried to look in that direction to see what it was. He saw it clearly now, but it was not part of the peaceful scene that he was getting used to here. It was a dead body, wrapped up by weeds, and stuck near the sandy bottom of the lake! Was this real? He moved his eyes to his right, then slowly looked back to make sure he did in fact see a body. Sure enough, it was still there, just floating with the motion of the weeds in the gentle current.

He wanted to move closer to get a better look, but just stayed in place, staring at the face. He didn't recognize the person, since the water and fish had damaged so much flesh. He wondered why the flesh would have started rotting with the water being so cold, since this temperature should have preserved the body. He then realized that the water didn't feel cold at all, and thought maybe he was just disoriented because it was freezing down here. But was it cold? He didn't feel numb or uncomfortable.

Wait a minute... why would he be under the water in

winter? He would die from hypothermia within fifteen or twenty minutes. His heart beat faster as he realized something was seriously wrong here. He moved his eyes up toward the surface again, and could tell that the hole in the ice that he saw before was now smaller.

"Why am I here? Did someone knock me out and put me under the ice, where I'm going to die within minutes?" He gave a panicked look over at the dead body in the weeds again, and it was still there.

Who would this be? Could it be another murder victim that had not yet been found?

Tim now faced the realization that he would die soon if he didn't get to the surface, but what made him panic more was the fact that he didn't even try to get out of the water. His arms weren't moving and his legs wouldn't kick. He just floated there near the sandy bottom, not doing anything. He looked up at the surface again, and saw that the hole was almost completely frozen over, but he still made no effort to swim for the surface.

"Am I already dead? Is my mind still active with my body no longer alive?" Tim wondered, and he just moved his eyes around more.

"I need air, but I don't seem to be running out of breath yet. I should be panicking by now."

"What was that? Another body to my right, also stuck in the weeds?"

Yes, it looked like it might be another person off in the distance, but still visible in the surprisingly clear water. He was also entangled in the weeds, and rotting beyond recognition. Tim felt his heart beat wildly with fear, as he considered that he was definitely not dead.

"If my heart's pounding in my chest, then I'm still alive. I need to get out of here!"

He just floated aimlessly in the slow current, and made

no effort to swim up for air.

"How can I be so alive and panicking with a need to get to the surface, but my body won't respond?" His eyes were opened wide, and would have been filled with tears if he wasn't underwater, but he still just drifted. He tried to scream, but his mouth never even moved. He had no problem moving his eyes in every direction, which he did in a panic mode, but it seemed as though his body was paralyzed as the current carried him wherever it pleased. He wanted to flail his arms and legs and get to the surface immediately, but he still just floated with the current near the bottom of the lake. Then a rotted face floated next to his as he bumped into one of the dead bodies.

Tim woke up with a scream finally, and sat up immediately. Petrified with fear, his heart indeed pounded so hard he feared it would break through his chest. He breathed so fast, thankful to be getting some air finally, and was drenched with sweat. Or was it from being in the lake?

"No, it was just a bad dream," he tried to reassure himself. It was still dark outside, and although the room was cold, Tim burned up as his body felt as though he had just run a marathon. He lay back down on his left side, put his hand over his eyes, and the tears finally came. He couldn't take this much more.

"Is this where I'm going to end up, at the bottom of the lake, another victim? Or are there really ghosts that are out for revenge? I need to get out of this house."

Chapter Twenty-Five

THE NEXT MORNING, PAUL WOKE up early and got dressed in his 'mountain man' clothes that Lisa set out for him. She had bought flannel shirts and hiking boots, and wanted him to wear them today. He already felt like a local, and couldn't wait to get outside and try out the new winter hat she picked up for him as well. Paul got a nice fire going and was proud of his accomplishment. He noticed Lisa step into the doorway, wearing her long underwear and thick socks, and he smiled.

As she stood by the kitchen, Lisa said, "I'm just standing here admiring my 'mountain man', savoring some hot chocolate," and Paul tried to hold in his laughter.

Still sitting in front of the fireplace, prodding the wood, he asked Lisa, "So how do you like this fire? It's feeling pretty warm already, and it's burning just perfectly. Wouldn't you like to join me next to it?"

She made a face at his comment, and said, "Yes, it sure is quite a fire there, Paul. I'm so proud of you." She walked over to the couch, where Paul was about to sit down, and she joined him there. She commented, "You know, it is a little concerning that Dave missed church Sunday, had to leave soon after church, and hasn't been available a few times when Martha had expected him. Martha said that's definitely not like him."

Paul said, "I don't know how he usually behaves, but if a person has a job offer to work on something around the lake or outside of town, it's a good idea to take the offer. He should explain it to Martha better so she's not left in the dark, but I don't think it's anything for her, or for you, to be concerned about."

Lisa tasted her hot chocolate, and then replied, "You're probably right, but he should let her know about his plans a little better than he has. Martha's worried about him."

"To make it even more interesting, Officer Haley suspects Dave of being involved with the two recent deaths, so Dave had better be a little clearer about what he's doing and where he's doing it. He doesn't need people accusing him of murder."

Lisa questioned Paul, "Do you think Dave has been acting suspicious lately?"

Paul looked at her for a few seconds, and then replied; "I guess I could see how someone might suspect him of doing something fishy, based on his behavior Sunday. I have to admit that I was shocked Dave confronted that hermit on the lake, even when he had a gun pointed at him. He certainly has a motive to do bad things to these older locals that give him a hard time, but then again, so do several other people around here."

Paul turned a little on the couch so he could look at his wife better as she enjoyed her hot chocolate.

"You look great in this outfit, and your hair looks wild."

Lisa just gave him a weird look and replied, "You like my hair, which hasn't even been brushed yet today?"

"You're exceptionally beautiful this morning, hair and all."

Just then a knock came at the back door, and Lisa scampered back to the bedroom. Paul went to find out who was there, and was surprised to see Officer Haley at the door.

"Well, it's nice to have an honored guest stop by to visit us at our humble rental cabin. Please come on in."

Jake replied with a smile, "Hi Paul. I hope this isn't a bad time to come over."

Paul opened the door and said, "No, this is just fine. Lisa's getting dressed and should be able to join us in a minute. Do you want any coffee or hot chocolate? I've been drinking coffee and Lisa's drinking hot chocolate."

Jake came in and said, "I'm just here on police business to ask routine questions, but if you have coffee already made, I could sure use a cup."

Paul poured some into a mug and handed it to him as he nodded his thanks. They both went in to the living room where the fire crackled, and sat down across from each other.

"I know you're just visiting this area, and I apologize for a few of the unpleasant things that have happened while you've been here. This is certainly not a typical week in Manitow or on Kisinaw Lake."

He paused for a moment, as Lisa came out and joined them. She wore a shirt that matched Paul's flannel shirt, but a different color, and had the same kind of hiking boots too.

Jake stood up and commented, "Wow, you look great this morning, Lisa,"

"Hey, you didn't tell me that, and I'm wearing the same thing as her."

Jake slowly turned his head to Paul, scowled at him and said, "She looks a lot better in it than you do," and they all laughed. All three of them sat down as Jake went on, "I'm intrigued by your story about the couple from around the lake twenty something years ago, and would like to know more. Can you tell me again where you got this information?"

Lisa said, "We found out information from the old newspapers at the library on microfilm, but heard the details of the actual events from the older librarian, Abigail. She's scared that she or the hermit is going to be next."

Jake nodded, and then said, "I'm going to stop by Robert Vallee's place later today, and hopefully will be able to talk to him about this a little more."

Paul asked, "Is it possible that he's fled the area because he figured out someone knows what happened to the Nelsons, or would he have killed Eddie and Little Frank for one reason or another and skipped town?"

Jake held up his hand, "Now all of these ideas are good theories, and we need to consider each one, but remember that they're just theories. I have no proof that this librarian's story is indeed factual, if Vallee was ever involved with Eddie or Little Frank when they were younger, or if the Nelson's deaths were even mysterious. I intend to follow up with the librarian today, just to hear it from her, and I'll talk to Vallee and a couple of the other locals to see what kind of connection there may have been. Do you think the library would be open now?"

Paul said, "Yes, I believe both Martha and Abigail would be there now."

Lisa asked, "Jake, what do you think about the idea that someone is out for revenge for the deaths of the Nelsons?"

Jake started to get up and replied, "I can tell you that I still don't believe their ghosts have come back to kill off these guys one by one, twenty-five years later, if that's what you're asking." He smiled at Paul, who shook his head, and continued, "I'll head into town and talk to Abigail now. Thanks for the coffee. Sorry to bother you," and he went out to his car.

******

On his way to the library, Jake received an anonymous call from someone with a rough voice. It could have been anyone trying to disguise his voice.

"Michael Dufresne knows more about Eddie and Little Frank than he's told anyone."

"Good morning. To whom am I speaking?" Jake questioned.

"Dufresne was at the lake where Little Frank was found just one night before, and he was seen snooping around Robert Vallee's house two days ago."

Jake pulled off the highway, and asked, "Can I meet you now so we can discuss this?" but the caller hung up the phone.

Jake wasn't too happy to hear this news, but looked around to see if he had passed the casino. As it turned out, he had only passed it a couple of minutes ago, so he turned his car around and headed back toward the lake. He figured while he was here, he would stop in the souvenir shop across from the casino, and visit Michael Dufresne for a few minutes. When he walked into the shop, Michael greeted him with a smile.

"What can I do for you today, Officer Haley?"

Jake shook hands with him, and said, "Unfortunately, I am investigating the deaths of two of the older locals here, and just need to ask a few questions."

Michael nodded, and asked, "Would you like to talk while tasting delicious hot soup and tea?"

"No thanks. I am kind of in a hurry, and need to be somewhere else as soon as you and I finish talking. Were you acquainted with Eddie Larson?"

"Yes I knew both Eddie and Little Frank, but they really were not very friendly with me over the years."

"Actually, from what I hear they weren't very friendly with anyone over the years," Jake replied and then asked, "Do you know Robert Vallee?"

Jake noticed Michael trying to put a face to the name, then asked, "Is that the older gentleman who lives by himself at the north end of the lake?" Jake nodded, then Michael said, "I know who he is, but I don't think I ever had a conversation with him. From what I hear, he is about as friendly as Eddie or Little Frank, maybe even worse."

"Have you seen him recently?" Jake asked, but Michael shook his head.

"No, not for several months, possibly not even in the past year."

Jake thought briefly, and then asked, "Do you think Eddie and Little Frank were killed, or do you think it was accidental?"

"Those men have lived here all their lives, so for them to both accidentally fall through the ice within a week is highly unlikely."

Jake looked into his eyes, and nodded. "Mr. Dufresne, were you anywhere on Kisinaw Lake last week?"

"I like that lake very much, but there are people there who don't like me. I haven't been over there for many months, not since I took my canoe there back in October."

Jake smiled and said, "OK Michael, thanks for your time."

"Stop by anytime when we can sit down to talk, and I'll have you try some of my soup."

"Thank you. I'd like that," Jake replied, and he stepped out into the cold air again.

Chapter Twenty-Six

MARTHA CALLED LISA FROM THE library later that morning, and Lisa noticed she could hardly contain her excitement.

"Apparently, the house that was built by their immigrant ancestor from Sweden is still standing just off of the highway between the lake and town," Martha said, "and it's only about ten minutes away from the library. I've already called up the people who own it now, and they've graciously invited us to stop by and visit."

Martha continued, "This is a chance to see some of the history of Manitow, since the house was built in 1903 when the town was still very new. Plus, the 'murdered' Nelsons probably visited the house when they were younger, at least Mr. Nelson, since his grandfather built it. He probably took his wife there to visit his grandparents. Can you meet me there now? Just turn off the highway at the big barn on the right side and wait for me."

Lisa was already hooked and replied before checking with Paul, "We'll be there in about ten minutes. Thanks Martha."

Paul drove Lisa to Nelson road off of the highway, just past a large barn with a dozen or more horses in the nearby pasture, and waited for Martha. They parked and looked for her beside the road, and didn't have to wait long.

Lisa knew that Paul didn't see how this visit would be beneficial, but he followed Martha's finger as she pointed down the road toward the old Nelson family home.

From the highway, Lisa noticed the white house standing near a few old trees in the back forty acres, and they were all silent as they followed Nelson road, Martha leading the way. It was paved, but a little bumpy, and Lisa took in what she saw as they moved toward the old place. Two stories tall and shaped like a barn, it looked more unique than the other houses in the area, with old rustic windows observing its surroundings from every side.

It didn't take long to reach the Nelson's farmhouse, and they each drove up into the circular driveway. It was just gravel covered with snow, and Paul stopped the SUV along side the front porch of the house, parking behind Martha's little car. The historic white house was actually in excellent shape for being built at the turn of the century, and Lisa could just imagine what it would have been like back then. There were apple trees all over the place, plus an old root cellar and a very rustic-looking barn that wasn't far from collapsing. She pictured the Nelson's children running around here, with no cars at the time, just horse drawn carts.

Lisa ran up to Martha and said, "It's beautiful. Thanks for bringing us along to see it."

"Someone else in 1898 bought the front forty acres nearest the highway, but Carl Nelson bought the back forty acres," Martha added. "The logging company in town had been advertising in Sweden to entice people to come overseas and settle in this area, and the bait used was 'free land'. They said that if a person cleared the forty acres and gave the lumber to the logging company, then that person could keep the land. Carl and his new wife, Selma, worked together to clear hundreds of trees, and they built this house soon after arriving from Sweden."

"Think of how romantic it would be for the husband and his new bride to build their lives up together like that," replied Lisa.

"Yes, but think about how much harder it would have been to live here back then with no indoor plumbing, no central air and heat, etc," Martha added.

Paul finally climbed out of the SUV and walked up toward the front door where Martha headed, while Lisa stayed in the driveway and looked up at the upstairs windows. She imagined seeing the faces of the children looking out at visitors in their front yard. Just then, an elderly lady answered the door, and Lisa heard Martha explain who they all were. She then introduced them to Mrs. Carlson, who welcomed them all inside with a smile, and Lisa was glad to be given the opportunity to see the interior.

The first thing Lisa noticed was the fireplace, which she knew had been used thousands of times over many generations. They stood in the living room talking for a few minutes, and another woman about the same age joined the elderly woman who met them at the door.

She introduced herself as Mrs. Nilsson, and asked, "Would anyone like something to drink?" but everyone politely declined.

Lisa asked, "Did you say you're name is Nelson?" but the older woman smiled and corrected her.

"No, my name is Nilsson, but it sounds a lot like Nelson. We were all friendly neighbors here years ago, the Nilssons, Nelsons, Olsons, and Carlsons." She then asked, "Would you like to have a look around?" to which Martha and Lisa both glanced at each other.

"We'd love to."

The house was small so it wouldn't take long to see it, but what they did see made Lisa feel as though she had stepped back in time. The kitchen contained a magnificent iron stove that had not been moved since it was installed when the house was first built, and was yet another working museum piece.

Mrs. Carlson mentioned, "A lot of the little knickknacks around the kitchen had belonged to Carl and Selma Nelson, and they just stayed with the house through multiple owners."

They followed the older ladies into the master bedroom on the first floor, and Lisa knew that Carl and Selma had owned the bed and dresser as well. Paul looked closely at the wallpaper in the open closet while they talked about these antiques, and Mrs. Carlson noticed.

"The original builders also put up the wallpaper too."

"This is definitely a unique old design," Paul said with obvious fascination. "You just don't see patterns like this anymore."

Lisa smiled at him, glad he finally appeared to be interested. She felt a joy that couldn't be explained, and began feeling warm and peaceful all over. She wondered what it would be like to have her own children and just visualized them all playing on the bed, climbing up and waking their sleepy parents. She didn't know why she saw her own kids from somewhere in the future playing on the old Nelson's bed from the distant past, but she didn't want the feelings or the vision to go away.

They all filed out of the bedroom and went to the stairs by the kitchen, which were thin and winding, just like in an old building. They almost looked hidden since she hadn't noticed them when they first walked by. The steps were stone, yet there were worn spots on each step where generations of this family walked up and down every day.

Upstairs, Mrs. Carlson said, "Carl and Selma had a lot of children, and they all stayed in this one big room upstairs, boys on one side, girls on the other, separated by a sheet that didn't even reach the ceiling."

Martha and Paul immediately went to the windows and gazed out at the view from each. Lisa watched them and smiled since they both appeared to have had the same idea at the same time. She wondered if she and Martha were on the girl's side and if Paul stood on the boy's side, and thought about how many children would have looked out these windows over the years. The sheet was no longer here, and there were only two beds in the room now, but Lisa knew how it must have looked when the room was filled with kids.

While Mrs. Carlson talked to Paul and Martha, Lisa imagined the playful sounds and laughter of the children all together in the one room. She wondered if the room was bursting with happiness most of the time or if they argued and fought a lot. She smiled, closed her eyes with her arms crossed, and felt the love that had enveloped this room for generations. She didn't hear Paul come up to her, but when he put his arm around her, she realized that there were tears in her eyes. He hugged her and kissed her on the cheek without saying a word, and Lisa saw one of the older ladies smiling at them both. Paul, Lisa, and Martha walked down the narrow staircase and went back to the kitchen,

Mrs. Nilsson said, "I insist that you have some hot tea made from Selma Nelson's teapot."

Lisa couldn't resist such an offer this time, especially since it was from the original Nelson teapot, and replied, "We would love to have a cup."

They all sat down at the table while she made the tea, and Mrs. Carlson shared a bit of the Nelson family details while they waited.

"Their grandchildren would enjoy walking the cows down the road out to the pasture in the mornings when they visited, and there was a hidden lake on their property. They would also bring the cows back in at sunset, although the cows could do it all by themselves. They just let the children have their fun thinking they were leading the cows."

One of the grandsons would have been the man who was found dead with his wife in Kisinaw Lake down the road twenty-four years ago near the pub.

Mrs. Carlson continued, "Carl Nelson not only cleared forty acres, but also made a deal with the logging company to clear and take ownership of the next forty acres behind his first forty, so he actually owned eighty acres here. However, there was a catch: if the buyer couldn't pay the taxes on the property, the land went back to the logging company. Unfortunately, there were many immigrants who came over from Sweden, built a house, and cleared the land, only to find out they couldn't pay the taxes and lost their homes. Carl Nelson somehow came up with the money for the taxes on the first forty acres and kept his land with this house on it. He wasn't so fortunate with the rest of the taxes and ended up losing the second forty acres."

Lisa commented, "That's so sad that the logging company took advantage of these families and took their land after all of that hard work."

Mrs. Carlson nodded and added, "Carl found the lake on the first forty-acre lot, and the family used it for fishing for many years. It had a thick mud-bottom, so they never swam in this lake. I've heard stories of deer getting trapped in the mud near the shore and dying, while the family had to struggle to pull the dead animal out. It was dangerous and the kids knew to be very careful around it. Their favorite lake, of course, was Kisinaw Lake, where the family spent a lot of time swimming, boating, and fishing. You two are staying at Kisinaw Lake, and that's eventually where one of Carl's grandsons built a cabin."

Lisa noticed that Mrs. Carlson looked sad, and she stopped talking at that moment, while Mrs. Nilsson took that opportunity to bring over the tea and started pouring it.

She explained, "The teacups and plates had belonged to Selma Nelson too."

Martha commented, "I like how beautiful the old designs are."

"Paul is probably most interested in the woodwork, since he's the opposite of a handyman, and likes to see good, quality craftsmanship," Lisa explained.

"Yeah, that's true. I'm so impressed with the molding, the trim, and many of the little things that many people take for granted."

Both of the older ladies smiled and Mrs. Nilsson added, "The Nelson men had always been very talented carpenters, as you can all see from Carl Nelson's work."

Chapter Twenty-Seven

THERE WAS A KNOCK ON THE door, so Mrs. Carlson excused herself, and then walked to the door to answer it.

Mrs. Nilsson explained, "We found rotted wood in parts of the house, and a carpenter from around the lake had been recommended to repair it. He's been coming out over the past few months to fix these spots, and has done an excellent job with each repair."

Just then, the older lady walked into the kitchen with Tim, who had brought his toolbox, and Paul immediately got up and shook his hand.

"Lisa and I have informally met Tim at the pub on the lake this week, but Martha may not have met him yet."

Martha reached over to shake his hand, "Hi Tim. I work at the library in town. I don't get out to the pub much,"

"Well, I don't get to the library much either," Tim confessed. They all laughed, and Tim asked, "How do you all like this old house?"

Lisa told him, "We absolutely adore it."

"I'm fascinated by some of the details in the wood," added Paul.

Tim said to Paul and Lisa, "It's good to see you two in a proper light, since the pub is so dark most of the time, and I'm glad to meet you, Martha." Tim then asked, "Paul, do you want to see the parts of this house that I like the most?"

Paul excitedly replied "Of course." While the two men talked, the two elderly ladies took turns telling Martha and Lisa about the things Tim had done for them, and Paul overheard how happy they were to have found someone who was nice, reliable, and could do their repair work too.

"Tim doesn't even charge half of what other carpenters charge for this kind of work," whispered Mrs. Carlson.

"He does a better job than anyone we've worked with in the area," added Mrs. Nilsson.

"I'm curious about how you two came to own this house," Martha asked.

"Our parents were friends with Carl and Selma Nelson, and just lived up the road a little further," Mrs. Nilsson replied.

"Are you two sisters?" Martha interrupted.

"Yes, we're sisters. I remember the Nelsons coming to our parents' house to talk and snack," replied Mrs. Carlson, "and they always spoke Swedish and had old Swedish recipes for each other to try. Unfortunately, they didn't teach their kids Swedish, because they were so determined to fit in here in their new country, but they did talk Swedish among themselves and their neighbors sometimes. Most of the Nelson's children moved down to Chicago or one of the other Swedish towns in Upper Michigan or Minnesota, and when Carl Nelson passed away, Selma moved down to live with one of their children. She sold the house to our father, who then passed it to me and my husband as a wedding gift. My sister here married soon after and lived up the road at the house near the highway, and when our husbands passed away within a year of each other, she moved in with me here."

"Do you know of any Nelson family members in the area?" Lisa asked.

"There aren't any around, except in the cemetery," replied

Mrs. Carlson. "Carl and Selma had a son who stayed in the area and built a lot of the houses along the highway and in the neighborhoods around the library, and he had a son who lived out on the lake for several years. Unfortunately, they've all passed away in the last thirty years or so, and as far as we know, there's no family members left anymore."

Paul and Tim came back in to the kitchen, and Paul said, "If it's OK with these two nice ladies, Tim offered to take us over to his cabin on Kisinaw Lake to see some of the restoration work he's done there."

Mrs. Carlson replied, "That's fine. We're not going anywhere."

Lisa and Martha looked at each other and both said, "OK."

"I'll be back in less than an hour," Tim told the ladies.

Paul, Lisa, and Martha thanked the two ladies for inviting them in and sharing their house with them for the morning, and they all left in Paul's SUV.

It was only a short drive to the lake and on the way there Tim said, "I'm glad to be able to have a few guests at my cabin. Not many people stop by."

Outside it looked similar to the cabin that Paul and Lisa stayed at, with the same beautiful view of the lake. Paul saw the dark stained log siding, and noticed that it had a dark green metal roof.

"Do you like the metal roof better than a shingled roof?"

"I was told it would heat up and help the snow slide off easier than with shingles, and I think that's probably true. I didn't have to climb up on the roof at all this winter to shovel the snow. It's a little noisier during a rainstorm though, and I do have problems with cell phone reception inside the cabin."

Tim showed them some of the areas that had rotted near the kitchen window and under the back door.

"I just need to seal them and stain them now that these

areas have been repaired."

Except for the lack of a natural wood stain in those spots, the new wood looked as though it had always been part of the cabin, and Paul couldn't believe how good Tim was at his repair work. Tim led them inside the back door.

"Why do you call this the back door? I assumed this side of the cabin that faced the road would be the front," Lisa asked.

"The part of the cabin that faces the lake is always considered to be the front. It's as simple as that," Tim explained.

The kitchen looked like a typical functional kitchen with a lot of wood shelves and cabinets from floor to ceiling, but when they stepped into the living room, it was very rustic with log siding that ran along the wall to the fireplace.

"I built the bookcases on each side of the fireplace, since I had so many books and the space was perfect for bookcases. There's storage at the bottom of each for games or whatever, and you can sit there next to the fireplace."

"This is the room where I would want to spend the most time if I lived here," Martha commented, and everyone agreed. "It feels so relaxed, with a great view of the lake through the front porch."

"I like this area so much that I just bought this cabin and will be staying here permanently," Tim added.

"Wow, that's great news. I'm jealous because you've really made this cabin feel like a home," said Paul.

"I've also done the wood flooring on the porch, since it had been damaged over the years," Tim continued, and Paul just shook his head in awe as examined at it.

"I wish I had the skills to do this kind of work," Paul said to Tim, and Lisa held his arm with a smile.

"Paul tries his best, but he just doesn't always have the best results," and they all laughed.

Tim looked Paul in the eyes and told him, "Keep trying

because it takes time and practice. I guarantee that if you keep working at it, especially with a person who has experience, you'll be able to do it someday."

Paul felt the confidence coming from Tim's words and replied, "Thanks for that. I appreciate it." He looked at his watch and added, "Shouldn't we get you back to the Nelson's old farmhouse?"

Tim nodded and responded, "Yeah, thanks for stopping by. It's nice to have visitors who are interested in cabin life. I hope you'll come over again when we have more time to talk."

They all headed outside back to the SUV and Paul, Lisa, and Martha drove Tim back to the old farmhouse.

Lisa said, "Thanks again for showing us around today and giving us a tour. We really enjoyed it."

Tim waved, as he turned and walked up to the front door.

Martha strolled over to her car, and said, "I'm so glad you could come over here with me today. There was something special about being inside this house. I think I'd like to come back and talk to these ladies again."

Lisa replied, "There's a lot of history in that house and in those two sisters. I wouldn't mind coming up here again either."

"Yeah Martha, thanks for inviting us. It really was worthwhile. I wasn't so thrilled about it at first, but it was like going back in time. And seeing Tim's handiwork was a real treat for me. I'm glad we came too. Have a safe drive back into town."

Martha waved as she pulled away from the house, and drove up the road.

Paul drove out of the circular driveway, following Martha back onto Nelson road, and headed toward the highway. It was only a few minutes back to the cabin from here.

"When Tim told me he knew I could do carpentry work, I felt as though I actually could," commented Paul.

******

Lisa looked over at him and said, "I think you should give it a try with something small, and I'll bet he's right. You would do a great job if you put your mind to it." Paul nodded as he turned onto the road to the lake. Lisa asked, "Would you like me to make us lunch today?"

"Yeah, that would be great. I'm going to look through the woods next door to see if I can find a few pieces of wood to practice carving something."

At the cabin, Lisa went inside to make them both lunch, while Paul walked up to the lake and stood there for a few minutes. He saw Old Deerfield across the lake, and could barely make out Tim's cabin just to the right of it. While looking at the lake just thirty feet to his left, Paul was awe-struck at the number of white birch and cedar trees that leaned over the ice and provided a stunning sight with snow on their branches. A few days ago, Dave told him that ice was so destructive to the shoreline of the lake each winter that even large trees would get uprooted and pushed out over the lake, eventually falling all the way down into the water. Paul marveled at the natural beauty of these fallen trees, almost laying on the frozen surface of the lake, and then walked down the path by the shore.

He saw dozens of these trees lying down in the woods, several of them more than twelve inches in diameter, many of them covered up with a thin layer of snow. He didn't have to walk far before he found what he had been looking for, and he squatted down to examine a small fallen cedar tree. It was no more than two inches in diameter, and he wondered what caused this fine young tree to be knocked over and uprooted this way. The larger trees looked so powerful, and to imagine something strong enough to force them to bow down to the ground or completely push them over so their roots came up out of the soft earth was beyond him.

As he knelt down, Paul felt as though someone or something watched him. He casually looked around while still brushing the ground at the base of the tree, but didn't see anything unusual. Yet the feeling remained, as the hair on the back of his neck stood up. He knew there might be bears or wolves here, plus there had been two people killed in the lake this past week, so he was a little nervous. Scanning the woods around him revealed nothing, and the feeling of being watched eventually went away as quickly as it had come upon him. He was relieved, but his heart still raced.

Paul picked up one end of the small tree, and saw it was still barely connected at the roots.

"If only I had bought that knife at the souvenir shop," he said out loud. He twisted the tree at the roots, and it easily came loose. He then snapped off a few of the small branches, as well as the top of the tree, where it was too small to do much with. Hitting the tree on the ground a couple of times knocked off any remaining snow on the tree, and Paul happily carried his prize back to the cabin, just in time for lunch. As he walked toward the path along the shore, he glanced back into the thick forest, wondering who or what had stalked him.

Chapter Twenty-Eight

PAUL AND LISA DROVE IN TO TOWN for groceries, then met with Martha and Abigail again after lunch. They all sat at the big table in the library, and Abigail set out snacks and hot tea for everyone. It was a cold afternoon, maybe a little windier than usual, with a wind chill factor below zero, so Paul was certainly glad to feel the warmth of the tea. He noticed the dismal grey skies through the old library windows, and figured that this was one of those days it was best to just stay inside and read a book.

Paul told everyone, "There's something about Tim that makes him a very likeable person. He gets along with the older people in town, is very talented at what he does with woodworking, and is the kind of person I'd like to have as a neighbor."

Lisa looked at him, raising her eyebrows, and he added, "Lisa, I think I'd like to look into buying one of the cabins on Kisinaw Lake over the next few years so we can come here for vacations. Tim has the right idea, and I know he'll do well here. I like the people we met this past week, and would enjoy coming back regularly."

Martha smiled at that idea and commented, "That would be great. I've really enjoyed getting to know you both this past week."

Lisa added, "I have to say that I agree. This is a beautiful area, and I'd like to come back in the summer to spend more time in the water, but not like Eddie or Little Frank." Everyone was silent as they all drank some of their tea at the same time.

Paul added, "The only thing I don't like is the way the locals at the pub kind of ignore Tim when he comes in and sits at the bar. Not all of them do, but I can see the ones that treat him differently."

Abigail looked at Paul and said, "Those people are from the older generation, and they won't always be here. Once they're all gone, the lake will be a wonderful place to live and the pub will be much nicer to visit."

Martha commented, "Yes, and if the ghosts keep killing all of those older locals, then it'll be sooner than you think," to which they all looked at her and laughed.

Paul saw Abigail gave her a motherly smile and then she shook her head at her daughter's comment.

Lisa told Martha and Abigail what they had learned from Officer Haley, but Paul noticed she didn't mention the negative things that were said about Dave. He wasn't sure how they could talk to Martha about that yet, so it would have to wait for a better moment.

Lisa said, "Right now, I'd like to know who would be out for revenge if it wasn't a ghost, since both of the Nelsons are dead and they don't appear to have any other family."

Abigail still went on about the two recent murders in the lake being done by the Nelson's ghosts, but Paul tried to politely get her to consider other possibilities.

"Who else might be alive today that would know what really happened to the Nelsons, and why would they have been quiet all these years until now?"

Abigail looked around at each person's face, and slowly said, "When the Nelsons died twenty-four years ago, they had very young children, all under the age of five I believe, who were quickly and quietly put up for adoption or put in the orphanage in Marquette, the largest town nearby."

Martha looked up quickly at her mother, and asked, "Are you sure? You never mentioned this before."

The older woman had tears in her eyes, and looked into her daughter's eyes.

"Soon after the murders, I married an older man who had been working near the lake, but lived a few miles west of town. In a way, the marriage was to get away from Big Frank and the other guys around the lake, and we lived near the downtown area. I had thought about adoption, and when I found that the murdered couple had a little baby girl that was still at the orphanage over in the big city, I felt it was my obligation to raise that child as my own. My husband, being the kind and understanding man that he was, agreed and so we became parents right away after we married. There was no delay in the adoption process, so we had a family sooner than the usual nine months' wait that most couples have to endure. I never told my husband what I knew about this child's parents, and I never told anyone else, until now. We both loved the little girl with all of our heart, and she grew up to be the best daughter we could have ever imagined."

Her daughter, Martha, had tears in her eyes now too.

She said, "I've known that I was adopted but I didn't know anything about my biological parents. You've been the best mother to me, Mom."

They hugged for several seconds, while Paul looked on with surprise.

Lisa immediately blurted out, "You mentioned that there were other children too."

"The two boys had already been adopted and their families moved away from the area or already lived somewhere else."

Paul looked over at Lisa in silence for quite a bit of time, thinking seriously about something related to Abigail's story, but Martha and Abigail didn't notice because they appeared to be deep in thought themselves over the news Abigail had just shared with her daughter. This certainly put a new spin on the situation. Paul's mind already raced through all of the new possibilities, and had several leads that he now wanted to follow up on.

Lisa mentioned, "Now there are potentially a few real suspects who might be out for revenge, but how can we find out about these kids who were adopted so many years ago? They would be two young men in their mid to late twenties, but they'd have different last names since they were adopted by different families. This won't be easy."

Abigail added, "You know, there used to be several photographs of the Nelsons at Old Deerfield, but since Big Frank didn't like them, he insisted that those pictures be taken down. It's a shame, because over the years, I've heard what a nice couple they were. Even now, there are photos of Big Frank and his circle of idiots, but they certainly don't deserve a place on the wall there. Not even in an outhouse."

Paul thought about that for a second, and then added, "Now that most of them have died, maybe things will be different over there. I know Michael Dufresne said that he never felt welcome at Old Deerfield, but hopefully things will change for the better with some of the hatred being buried with Little Frank and Eddie."

Lisa asked, "Abigail, do you remember anything about Michael Dufresne when you were growing up?"

Abigail looked at her and thought for a few seconds, then replied, looking from Paul to Martha and to Lisa while she talked, "I really don't remember much about him. He didn't interact with us at all back then. I guess he stayed to himself. The things I heard about him when I was younger were always negative, just like Big Frank's hatred toward the Nelson family. Someone in town once said that Mr. Dufresne was probably responsible for the Nelson's deaths, but I knew that wasn't true. Just the typical lies spread by those prejudiced people from around the lake. But over the years, I've heard how he helps a lot of elderly people in the area, takes care of wild animals when they're injured, volunteers at the animal shelter, and I believe the negative stories were all just because he's an Ojibwa Indian. I know that he found a young wolf pup years ago whose parents were killed by one of the locals, and he raised the pup as his pet. He may still have it even today. A couple of the older locals are prejudiced against the Ojibwa, and Mr. Dufresne has had to deal with that for many years. I believe he's an honest man and is good for the town. I also think that you can tell a lot about a person by seeing how he treats animals."

Martha and Lisa both nodded.

Although many of the townspeople still considered this to be a ghost story relating an old 'accidental death' case to two new 'accidental death' cases, not as three unrelated, isolated accidents, Abigail's revelation had changed everything for Paul.

Chapter Twenty-Nine

PAUL SAID, "LISA, WE NEED TO get going if we want to stop by the souvenir shop on the way back to the cabin," and Lisa agreed.

"Abigail, thank you so much for the information you shared with us today. You're indeed a special person, and Martha is blessed to have you as her mother."

She hugged Abigail, then Martha, and left the library with Paul. They braved the cold wind and ran to the SUV hand-in-hand, and he quickly opened the door for his wife. They drove down the highway for a few minutes.

"I'd like to talk to Michael about one of the carved knives he showed me the last time I was there," Paul mentioned casually.

"After what we just learned, you can sit there and talk about buying a souvenir?" Lisa questioned sternly.

Paul didn't know what to say, and tried to recover, "I... well, I meant to say that while we talked to Michael about the possible suspects, I could look at the knife. The main point of the visit is to try to learn something new, but it's a perfect opportunity to pick up a souvenir too. After all, it is a souvenir shop."

Lisa just shook her head as Paul made a face out the driver's side window while squeezing the steering wheel, and they turned off of the highway into the parking lot.

******

Shortly after Paul and Lisa left the library, Officer Haley stopped in to talk to Abigail. There weren't many cars in the parking lot this afternoon, and he figured that would be a good thing since he didn't want to draw unwanted attention to the librarians. He walked into the building and saw them sitting near the front desk. They had never formally met, so he politely introduced himself.

"Good afternoon ladies, I'm Officer Jacob Haley from the Manitow Police Department, but everyone calls me Jake. I hoped that I could ask you a few questions."

Martha stood up and shook hands with him, and Jake noticed that her mother looked a little nervous. Martha's smile caught his attention, and when he realized that he was staring at her, he quickly looked away.

"We've seen you around town," Martha said, "but have never been in a situation where we would be in the same room to talk. I guess that's a good thing though, right?"

Jake responded with his pleasant smile, "No, you don't need to do anything wrong to talk to me. I try to meet and greet the people around town and around the lake, and I know most of them even though they never committed a crime. I just don't get to the library very often, and I guess you two don't get out very much."

Martha asked, "Plus, since we haven't seen you on Sunday mornings, I guess you don't get to church much here either?"

Jake paused and laughed, "No, I guess I don't."

Abigail finally stood and asked, "Would you like a cup of hot tea Officer Haley?"

He looked at her and said, "Yes please, if you have some already made, and please call me Jake."

She smiled at him and said, "Of course. Have a seat then,

and let's see what we can do for you."

He and Martha sat down while Abigail poured another cup of tea and handed it to him. Jake took it and smelled the pleasant aroma coming out of the cup in a ghostly wisp.

******

Paul and Lisa walked into the souvenir shop, and were greeted with a friendly "Aanii Boozhoo."

They looked up and saw Michael Dufresne walking toward them with a smile.

"Gesundheit," said Paul.

"What did you say?" Lisa asked inquisitively.

Michael repeated with his easily recognizable deep voice, "Aanii Boozhoo. It is an Ojibwa greeting."

"Aanii Boozhoo to you too," Lisa said with a twinkle in her eyes.

He looked at her and said, "It is good to see you again Lisa. So what brings you two back to this part of town? Aren't you worried that you might be seen with a murder suspect?"

Paul started to speak, but Lisa interrupted with an attitude, "Paul wants to look at one of your carved knives."

Paul stammered and said, "That's not the main reason we came by, but since she brought it up, there is one knife that I would like to see again, if you don't mind." Lisa scowled playfully at him, and he quickly added, "But first we would like to talk to you a little more about the two men who were found in the lake."

They walked toward the cash register, and Dave Bramwell surprised them with his thick 'Yooper' accent.

"Well, if it ain't our newest ice fisherman and his beautiful amateur detective wife."

Paul said, "Hi Dave. What would you be doing in a souvenir shop in your hometown?"

He smiled and responded, "I can surely tell you that I'm

NOT buying souvenirs, don'cha know. Michael had an electrical problem that he wanted help with, so I stopped by to see what I could do. I'm no expert, ay, but I was able to figure it out."

Lisa asked, "So how long have you two known each other?"

"Oh, I've known him since I was a little boy. A lot of the locals don't like Michael because he's Ojibwa, but my parents weren't prejudiced and encouraged me to listen to him. He has a lot of truly fascinating stories, and I still enjoy hearing them today."

"How about if we all sit down and enjoy a bowl of hot soup? I think we can take a break from the winter crowd here," Michael said with a hint of a smile. They all looked around at the empty shop, laughed, and sat down while he went to pour four bowls of soup.

******

Officer Haley said, "I'm investigating the recent deaths of two men who lived around Kisinaw Lake, and have been told that you might have information that could be useful in the investigation." Jake noticed that Abigail looked away, and he continued, "Abigail, if you have any information on these men, it might prevent someone else from dying."

She nodded, and responded, "I know, but I'm not sure what you can do about it. Three of the men who were involved with the murder of the Nelsons have already been killed, while Mr. Vallee and I can only wait our turn."

That got Jake's interest, but Martha shook her head and said, "Mom, that's nonsense. There are no such things as ghosts, and you're not going to be next."

Abigail calmly said, "No, Robert may be next, but I am certainly next in line after him."

"Abigail, why do you say that? Some people believe that

both of the recent deaths were just accidents, and there's no evidence of foul play as far as anyone can tell."

Abigail sat back and took a sip of her tea. "Let me tell you what I should have told the police twenty-four years ago," and she proceeded to repeat her story to Jake.

******

As Michael brought bowls of soup to Lisa and Paul, he said, "Kisinaw Lake has also been known as 'Kisnanibuin' for many generations, and has only been called Kisinaw Lake for the past sixty years or so. I remember being scared of the lake as a boy because of that name. I only grew to love the lake as I grew older and saw the beauty of it over the years."

Lisa asked, "What does 'Kisna whatever' mean?" Michael brought two more bowls of soup to the table, set one down in front of Dave and one in front of his own seat.

"Today we have a delicious broccoli and cheddar soup. I think you will like it. Kisnanibuin sounds like a loose translation from the old Ojibwa language that could mean 'Cold Death.'"

Paul and Lisa looked up at him with their mouths open, both about to taste the soup, then at each other.

Michael didn't even look up, but continued, "The story goes that there were mysterious deaths in the lake many generations ago, several in the winter where the bodies were found under the ice. Even the name of the nearby town, Manitow, is taken from an old Ojibwa phrase 'Gitchi Manito.'"

He stopped to taste a bit of his soup.

Dave added, "That means Great Mystery, and it was called that because this area used to be considered a place of healing for the soul, don'cha know. Over the years, however, people have changed the meaning to somehow be related to the mysterious deaths that happened in Kisinaw Lake many generations ago."

Michael interrupted, "So how is your soup?"

******

When Abigail finished telling Officer Haley about the four young men and their involvement in the deaths of the Nelson couple, he said, "Abigail, you should have gone to the police as soon as you heard that the Nelsons had been found dead. You could have brought closure to the family and to the town with what you saw and what you suspected."

"I know, and I've regretted it for so many years. I thought of moving away from here to try to forget about it, but I felt obligated to stay and raise my family in this town. Now I'm prepared to face the consequences of my silence all those years ago."

Jake said, "Other than what you're feeling inside, I don't think there are any consequences that you'll need to face. You weren't involved, and you broke away from that group right away. Let me tell you something else. It's very possible that Robert Vallee may have been involved in the deaths of Eddie and Little Frank." Both Abigail and Martha looked at Jake with confused expressions, so Jake continued, "After the bodies were pulled out of the lake, I went to talk to Robert, but it looks like he may have skipped town. He hasn't returned to his house, and nobody has seen him. He's now one of the most likely suspects at this point in time."

Chapter Thirty

AFTER TAKING ANOTHER SPOON-ful of soup, Paul asked, "What do you know about the cabin closest to Old Deerfield, where Tim is staying?"

"I've worked with Tim on a few jobs, and he's a great guy. He does excellent work, probably the best in this area. That cabin where he's staying now was just getting run down when he came to town last year, and he's fixed it up nicely."

Lisa added, "Some people say it is haunted," and Paul choked on his soup.

Michael laughed, but that statement obviously bothered Paul.

Dave looked at Paul, started laughing too, and responded, "Lisa, you need to stop this obsession with ghosts, or you'll have a bad reputation around here."

Paul looked intently at Dave and added, "I think she already has a bad reputation around here," and he circled his finger around his ear as a sign of craziness. Lisa saw this out of the corner of her eye, and without looking at him, gently kicked him under the table with a smile. Paul grunted, while Dave continued.

"There are no such things as ghosts, Lisa, and the cabin is not haunted."

Michael replied, "Apparently something very bad happened there years ago, and there could be evil spirits still in that place. However, I don't believe in ghosts coming back for revenge."

Lisa asked, "So are evil spirits different from ghosts?" and Michael nodded.

"Oh yes. When a person dies, his spirit goes to Heaven or to Hell, one place or the other. That is like what a lot of people call our 'ghost'. It does not stay around here on Earth to wander around aimlessly or haunt a specific location. But spirits are all around us here on the Earth, some good, some very bad. They are not the ghosts of dead people, but are beings that have been around for a long time. Many people call them angels and demons. I believe that evil spirits have been at work in this town for many years, probably even generations, and there appears to be spiritual involvement around the lake even now. I also believe that evil spirits can influence people to do terrible things."

Paul looked at Michael, and thought about what he had just said. Silence took over for a minute or so, as everyone else took another spoonful of their soup. He then glanced over at Dave to see what his response would be to Michael's comments about evil spirits, but was surprised that Dave didn't have a smart comeback. Dave was usually the most outspoken about talk of ghosts, but maybe he believed that evil spirits and ghosts were two different things. Maybe he agreed with Michael's theory.

Paul and Lisa finished their soup, and then Lisa looked at Paul asking, "Shouldn't you get your souvenir now?"

Paul smiled, and replied, "If you insist, I guess I should," and he asked Michael, "Could I go ahead and buy that knife I've been admiring?" They both walked over to the display case, while Lisa and Dave stayed in their seats. Michael unlocked the case and handed the knife to Paul, who looked at it with pride and traded Michael money for the knife. Paul asked, "So this is one that you carved?" and he noticed that Michael nodded with a proud smile.

Just then, someone else came in from the cold, and everyone looked to the door. It was difficult to tell, underneath all of the cold weather gear, but when he pulled back the hood on his jacket, Paul recognized the man from the lighthouse.

Dave said, "It's about time, don'cha know. I just finished fixing it, and don't need it now."

Larry replied, "Sorry about that. It took longer than I expected to get out of the lighthouse today, but here are the tools I borrowed from you last week." Larry looked up and saw Paul standing with Michael, and then saw Lisa sitting with Dave. He said, "Hi folks. I see you found the souvenir shop."

Lisa said, "Hi Larry. It's good to see you again. We were just talking about the possibility of Lake Kisinaw being haunted, or maybe just one of the cabins on the lake."

Paul winced and made a face at Michael, who laughed, and then Paul whispered, "I thought we were leaving."

Larry's eyes brightened up when he heard Lisa's comment and said, "Now that you mention it, there are a lot of old legends about that lake and several of the mysterious deaths that have happened there, but none of them are documented in recorded history. If you look at the records, there have only been three deaths on the lake in the past century or so, except for the two recent ones, but legend has it that there have been many more over the past few hundred years. There are more secrets in the ice there than people realize, if you know what I mean."

Lisa added, "That's what Michael said too."

"Despite what everyone says, Michael is a pretty smart fellow." Everyone laughed, even Michael, while Larry continued. "I know the guy who's staying at the old Nelson cabin now says that he thinks the cabin is haunted, because he's had terrible nightmares since he's been there – the kind that will scare the life out of you. He says something very, very bad must have happened there, and he's absolutely convinced there are ghosts still around."

Michael added, "Now I just told these nice folks here that I don't believe in ghosts, Larry, and .."

"Oh, I know that, and I was only going to mention the Native American legends say that evil spirits have been in this area for many generations. That makes more sense than the ghost stories that I've heard."

Paul asked, "OK, so evil spirits are different from ghosts, and it is perfectly sane to believe in evil spirits, but not in ghosts. Is that correct?"

Dave added with a straight face, "Also remember that it's OK to believe in Bigfoot, but not in UFO's," which brought a smile to Paul's face.

Lisa asked, "But Dave, didn't Martha say she took a picture of a UFO over the lake recently?"

Paul just stared in disbelief at his wife, while Larry ignored the last comment and replied to Paul.

"Yes, there have been unusual things happening around Kisinaw Lake for a lot longer than the past twenty-odd years when that couple had been found dead, so their ghosts obviously had nothing to do with the old legends. However, evil spirits that have been around for generations could have been involved with the Nelson's deaths by influencing the people who killed them."

Lisa chimed in, "Plus, now that there have been new deaths on the lake, those same evil spirits might be responsible."

Larry replied, "Exactly."

Michael nodded and added, "It is a possibility."

"It's good to see you all again, but I have to get back to work. I just needed to drop these off for Dave. Talk to you later," said Larry with a wink.

"Thanks Larry. See yah around, ay?" and Larry walked across the room with a wave of his hand, and out the door. It was quiet for a minute or so as Paul pondered what they just discussed.

Paul asked, "So Dave, what do you think about evil spirits?" and he noticed Dave's hesitation.

"Well, I certainly don't believe in ghosts, if that's what you mean, but I have to admit there have been times when I've felt an evil that I couldn't explain, ay? I've explored a few of the old abandoned houses around here that are supposed to be haunted, and with a few of them, there are certainly some strange things that you just can't explain, especially the creepy feeling you get. A couple of times I've felt an overwhelming despair or hatred that almost smothered me and I just had to get away from it."

Paul looked over at Lisa, who stood fixed on Dave's expression, obviously thinking about what Officer Haley had told them a couple of days ago. He recalled his own experience recently when he heard voices early one morning but found nobody in the cabin, but chose not to bring it up for discussion. He also remembered the odd episodes at Old Deerfield, but didn't bring them up either.

Dave continued, "I've never really been able to understand how hateful a few of the people around the lake are, and if an evil spirit can influence a person in a negative way, then that would be one possible explanation. Another possibility is that these people are just plain stupid and self-centered. I'm not saying that evil spirits are the only explanation, but I can't rule it out."

As Paul and Lisa got ready to leave, Dave added, "Remember, the one who I think is the most suspicious around here is Jake Haley. My money is on him. I don't trust him, and I think he's capable of covering his tracks, if you know what I mean."

Michael heard this and interrupted, "Dave, please do not talk about Mr. Haley behind his back like this. If you have a problem with him, it is best to talk to him about it rather than spreading that kind of information to other people."

Dave held up his hands and apologized, "I'm sorry. You're right. My bad."

Michael added, "You may find that Officer Haley had good reasons to do what he has done, so talk it over with him in private instead. Otherwise, you just add to the hatred and division that already exists in this town."

They all shook hands, and then Paul and Lisa headed out the door into the colder air. Paul couldn't get it out of his mind that the police officer was actually still a plausible suspect in Dave's eyes, and he pondered the possibilities as he helped his wife get into the SUV.

Chapter Thirty-One

ANOTHER DAY HAD PASSED, AND the old hermit hadn't come home. Jake stopped by his house twice, each time only to find the note was tacked to his door, apparently unread. From the look of the undisturbed snow on the front porch and the lack of human footprints in the front yard near Robert Vallee's old truck, it was obvious that nobody had been there for a few days. Something was wrong, but Jake didn't want to think about what Paul and Lisa had told him.

Was Robert being tied in with an old murder, and was he really a target for revenge? If anyone in this town was a killer, surely it had to be this guy.

Jake was still bothered about Paul telling him that Dave got into an argument with Robert just before the old hermit seemed to disappear, and he was still suspicious about Dave from other run-ins he and a couple of the locals had in the past with him. It was a little concerning that Robert had actually confronted Dave and Paul with a gun, then the next day or so Robert was nowhere to be found. Jake didn't really suspect that Paul had anything to do with the hermit's disappearance, but it didn't look good for Dave. Jake wanted to remain optimistic, and continued to ask the various townspeople when they had seen Robert last. It was no surprise that it had been days since anyone had seen him, since he stayed to himself most of the time, so Jake found that he was really getting nowhere. One other theory that Jake came up with was that Robert had some kind of disagreement with Eddie and Little Frank, Robert 'took care of them both,' and then left town. If Robert had done something like this, though, he would most likely have taken his truck, which still sat in his driveway covered in snow.

Jake stood on the porch and stared at the hermit's truck for a minute wondering, "Would he have left the truck there to throw people off so they wouldn't suspect him? If so, did he have another way to get out of town?" Jake didn't know Robert well enough to understand what kind of thoughts would have gone through his head, but he knew that Robert was a mean and angry man who could certainly hurt a person without thinking twice about it. If he was a friend of Eddie and Little Frank, like Abigail said they once were, Jake hadn't seen any sign of such a friendship since he had been in the town.

The policeman decided to stop by Tim's cabin to ask him routine questions, and was glad to see Tim's truck in the driveway. Jake sat in his car for a minute or two, admiring the woodwork on the cabin, and had to agree with the rest of the townspeople about the quality of his work. Tim was a personable guy, so all of the people he worked with said positive things about him. Jake liked him, and talked with him quite a bit at the pub on the weekends and evenings. He figured that since Tim wasn't a local either, he would have a lot more in common with him than he would with any of the other townsfolk, and Tim didn't seem to mind the company either. Several of the people at the pub and around the lake treated Jake like a second-class citizen, and he had seen them give Tim the same kind of treatment. That's probably one of the reasons Jake liked to talk to Tim, since they both faced the same kind of hostile treatment from the older locals. Jake didn't like it, but no matter how hard he tried to fit in with these locals, they wouldn't let him in their 'circle'.

Tim had invited Jake to go fishing this past fall, soon after he moved up here and started working at the police station, but he hadn't taken him up on it. Jake wished that he had, since Tim was really the person he enjoyed talking with the most in this town. He finally made his mind up to get out of the car and walked slowly up the path to the back door.

Tim appeared to be glad to see Jake when he came to the door, and invited him in right away.

"What a pleasant surprise," Tim said with a genuine smile.

They walked in, and Jake immediately eyed the fireplace.

"I've always liked this cabin, especially the beautiful stone fireplace in the living room."

He stared with interest for a few seconds, and then sat down.

"Do you want anything to drink, Jake?"

"No, I'm on official police business, so this really isn't a social call."

Tim sat across from him and made himself comfortable, as Jake looked out the window and saw the frozen lake. The new fallen snow on the surface of the ice made it look like a large open field as far as he could see.

"Tim, this is a beautiful view out the window," Jake said with a bit of envy in his voice.

Tim turned and looked out the window too, and added, "I like to just sit here or on the front porch in the summer, watching the water, the animals, and the impressive storms that come out across the lake. A few months ago from my dock, I watched a large beaver swim back and forth from the creek over to the left here, all the way to the southwest corner of the lake, near the park. I mentioned this at the pub, but people said that I should shoot it before it floods the access road to the highway."

Jake laughed, "Did you shoot it?"

"No, he never caused any problems. I don't know if I could shoot such an amazing animal anyway. I never realized how big a full-grown beaver really was. He was like a medium sized dog. I enjoyed watching him swim close to me when I sat on the dock around sunset every night for weeks. He didn't seem to mind me being there, but eventually he must have moved on somewhere else or was relocated by the Fish and Wildlife crew."

They talked more about the cabin Tim had been staying at for a little while, discussed the history of the cabin as Jake had heard it, and they both laughed a bit more about the ghosts getting revenge on the two older locals. Jake noticed that Tim's laugh seemed to be a nervous laugh.

Tim got serious and said, "Let me first just say that I've never believed in ghosts, but I've had terrible nightmares in the past couple of weeks that make me wonder if there really is some kind of connection. You know I just bought it, and the closing is this week. I hope it was the right decision. I like this cabin, but there's definitely something spooky about it."

Jake replied, "It must just be your nerves, with everything that's going on around the lake. Speaking of that, have you seen Robert Vallee recently? He is the old hermit that lives on the north end of the lake near the rocky section."

Tim looked concerned and said, "No, I haven't seen him in quite a while. I know who he is, but he doesn't come over to the pub much at all. Certainly not recently. Do you think something has happened to him too?"

Jake confided, "Well, nothing concrete yet, but I have been told that he may have been involved with the Nelson's death on this lake years ago, and it brings out an aspect of revenge. I don't know who would be after him, since the Nelsons are dead, but when I went to talk to him, it looked as though nobody had been at his house for days. I checked on him again this morning, and found the same thing. Nobody has seen him at all, and his truck is still there, buried under almost a foot of snow."

Tim leaned forward and suggested, "Why don't you go check inside his house to see if he's fallen or had a heart attack? He's an older man, and may be stuck inside the house. Seriously, I'll go with you now if you want me to."

Jake replied, "Thanks for the offer. I thought about that, and have talked one of the paramedics into meeting me there in about an hour. It is difficult to get volunteers, since Robert is such an ornery critter."

Tim nodded, and then asked Jake "What do you really think about the two recent deaths?"

"I'm not prepared to talk about them to anyone yet. They both seem to be accidental, but we're still investigating. The autopsy on Eddie didn't give us any clues, except that he drowned in freezing water, and I'm expecting the same from Little Frank's."

Tim nodded, as Jake stood up and they shook hands.

"Thanks for letting me stop by and chat. It's good to be able to relax a bit and slow down. I really want to take you up on that offer to go fishing, so don't let me put it off like I did over the summer. I'll see you at the pub."

"You're welcome here anytime," said Tim as the policeman got into his car to move on around the lake to the next cabin.

Chapter Thirty-Two

SINCE THE MEETING WITH ABIGAIL, Paul, and Lisa, the young librarian had done some research on the Nelsons and their children, but Martha wasn't able to find many answers. She figured she had exhausted all she could find from the library records at this point in time, most likely just needing a change, and felt like she had to start looking elsewhere for leads. She decided to spend more time on the phone this morning with the orphanage, which was a couple of hours away, and planned to use leverage about a murder investigation in order to gather additional details. The person at the orphanage answered the phone.

"Hello, this is Carrie at St. Mary's Orphanage. How can I help you?"

Martha responded, "Hi, Carrie. I'm investigating a murder here in Manitow, and need to find out information on the family that adopted the children of Stephen and Laura Nelson."

Martha certainly didn't have any legal authority to obtain this information, but since she sounded official, the person on the phone was apparently impressed about there being a local murder investigation and was more than willing to help.

Carrie exclaimed, "Oh my gosh! Who was murdered?"

Martha replied, "I can't reveal much about the case, since

it is still in progress, but we do need to find out who adopted the couple's children. The Nelsons were killed over twenty years ago, and due to at least two recent deaths and how they tie in to the Nelsons' murder case, we're concerned that their children may be in danger now."

Carrie asked, "Let's see, so their names were Stephen and Laura Nelson and they died about twenty years ago?"

"Yes, that's correct," and then there was silence on the phone.

Martha asked, "So Carrie, can you help me identify the names of the families that adopted the Nelson's children?"

Carrie responded, "Wow, I've never worked on a murder investigation. That's pretty exciting. Usually we can't give out this kind of information, but I think for something like this, it should be OK, right?"

Martha said, "We really appreciate your cooperation," and wondered if Carrie was even eighteen years old.

She sounded very young, and Martha thought that Carrie's inexperience might help her get the elusive information. However, Martha hoped that this wouldn't get Carrie into any kind of trouble.

After a brief pause, Carrie said, "It looks like a family named Parsons adopted the murdered couple's oldest boy and moved down south soon after the adoption was complete, but that's about all I can see on the Parsons family."

Martha had been holding her breath in anticipation, and finally exhaled with relief at her good fortune. She had a name now – the Parsons. At this point, however, Martha heard someone question Carrie about giving out information like this over the phone, and Martha realized her little private investigation had probably come to an end.

She heard Carrie meekly try to explain, "Um, there's a murder investigation going on, and ..."

Immediately a gruff sounding woman came onto the

phone and questioned Martha.

"Who are you working for and what's your name?"

Martha simply replied, "Thank you for your time," and hung the phone up quickly.

It wasn't a total loss, since she did find out something about a family called 'the Parsons' being involved with the adoption of one of the children. What a stroke of luck.

She sat back and smiled at her success, and said out loud, "Thank you Carrie."

However, she wasn't able to find out anything about the other boy this time. She would still keep digging. Now she was convinced, however, that the information was indeed out there, just waiting to be found and brought to light. With the help of her new friends, Paul and Lisa, along with clues from her mother, Martha felt determined to find the answers.

"Maybe it would be worth bringing this information to the police to see if Officer Haley could go through an official process to get more details out of the orphanage."

She stared at the name she had written on the page for a minute or so, deep in thought.

"I wonder if my brothers are still alive. What are they like? Do they look like me at all? Do we have any of the same interests, even though we didn't grow up together? Could one or both of them be the murderers of these two older gentlemen, or do they even know anything about our parents' deaths?"

After the revelation from her mother, Martha now knew that she was the murdered couple's youngest child, the Nelson's baby daughter, and she had thought a lot about her biological parents being killed by several of the townspeople. These were people who lived in the same small community where she grew up, and were people who she ran into occasionally in town. This in itself was a disturbing reality, and it bothered her more than she realized it would.

She never really cared for many of these people, since

they were usually the ones arguing about stupid things at the grocery store, or complaining to a waitress at one of the restaurants in the downtown area. Martha did remember both Little Frank and Eddie from those kinds of incidents, but fortunately never had to deal with them in person. She thought back over the years, but couldn't picture one time when her mother came into contact with any of these men.

It may be that they knew Abigail spent a lot of time at the library, so they avoided going there completely. It could be that they weren't even able to read, so maybe that's why they never came to the library. She knew that wasn't entirely true, but it made her laugh.

Martha wondered how she would have reacted over the years if she knew back then what she now knew about these men.

"Would I have tried to do something to Little Frank or Eddie, or would I have kept in so much hatred for these men that it would have eaten at me all my life?"

She actually had feelings of revenge, and struggled to get those kinds of thoughts out of her mind. It made her realize that the revenge aspect made more sense than the involvement of ghosts, but she wondered if the other adopted children knew anything about the killing of their parents, were interested in their small town, or were even still alive all these years later.

To make it more confusing, her adoptive mother, Abigail, almost witnessed the murder of Martha's biological parents and had been threatened about revealing any information. Abigail even believed that someone, either a ghost or a real person, was out to kill her for being there that night over twenty years ago. She wondered if the killer would really think that Abigail had anything to do with the murder and would consider her an accomplice, since Abigail had walked away from Big Frank and the boys about the time the deed was done. She would never have been part of such a crime of prejudice. Martha didn't like to think this way, since she wasn't sure she believed in ghosts herself.

Yet she remembered that Abigail had told her several times, "It is most likely the ghosts of the Nelsons who are getting their revenge. I should have turned those boys in that night when I heard them fighting or the next day when I found out what had really happened."

Martha tried to rationalize with herself that the Nelsons didn't know Abigail back then, since she never formally met them or talked to them. Even though it was a small town, they were in different circles, due to Abigail's involvement with Big Frank and the others, and the Nelsons being involved with the church. But as far as the Nelsons were concerned, she could just as easily have been part of the crime, especially by covering it up and not reporting what she knew about the actions of that evening outside the Nelson's cabin. Martha did agree that Abigail's silence was the worst thing anyone could have done, and that one issue made her realize the killer may still be after her for not coming forward years ago. By not saying anything, the real murderers had been walking freely in town for all this time with no retribution for their actions. Abigail truly was guilty as an accomplice and could legitimately be a target for revenge just like Eddie and Little Frank, and Martha didn't like these kinds of thoughts.

Anyway, to get her mind off of the potential danger that her mother was in, Martha spent the rest of the morning at the library tracking down the oldest Nelson boy's adoptive parents with this new information, and she soon found out to where they moved. By looking up useful resources like old phone books, tax records, land records, etc, Martha was able to develop a trail that showed where the Parsons went and when they moved away from this area. Coincidentally, right after the death of the Nelson couple, the Parsons moved down near the Upper Michigan border, and they had been there ever since.

"Wait a minute," she soon exclaimed out loud. "I've heard this name before, and very recently. This adoptive parents' name still remained around the lake, but I can't place where I've heard it. They must have come back up here at some point in time for one reason or another. I know I've seen something recently about the Parsons family here in town. I need to ask around a little more."

Chapter Thirty-Three

WONDERFUL AROMAS SPREAD all throughout the cabin this morning as Lisa made her delicious Swedish pancakes for breakfast. That was one of the nice things about a small cabin, since the aromas easily filled up each of the rooms in a short amount of time and everyone in the cabin could enjoy them.

Paul breathed it in while he dressed in the bedroom and spoke to the mirror, "I'm a lucky man to have a wife who can cook as well as Lisa, who also enjoys doing it." He walked in to the kitchen, still tucking in the back of his shirt, and suggested, "I think I'd like to go talk to Michael Dufresne at the souvenir shop today. Would you mind stopping by to ask him a few questions after we eat?" Before she could answer, he walked up behind her and kissed her on the cheek, and she turned to look at him.

"Today is kind of a lazy day for us, except for getting whatever we need for our trip tomorrow. Remember we're driving out to the falls in the morning."

Lisa had planned out a nice day trip to do a bit sightseeing, and Paul looked forward to seeing a frozen waterfall. She turned her attention back to the griddle, and flipped a couple of pancakes over to cook a little bit more on the other side. Paul gazed out the window and saw a winter wonderland scene in the back yard.

"Yeah, I know. On our way into town to fill up the gas tank and pick up snacks, we could stop in and spend a few minutes with Michael."

Lisa reminded him, "Remember that he likes to eat while he talks, and I won't be hungry for a while after eating these pancakes. What if we stop by the shop after we pickup the snacks and fill up the tank?"

Paul considered that and agreed, "You're right. Michael does like to eat when we talk with him, and I'm not sure if he would talk to us if we didn't eat something with him." Lisa smiled, as Paul continued, "His soups have been so tasty that I'd want to make sure we try whatever he offers us. Let's plan on visiting him a little later, on our way back to the cabin."

Lisa turned around with a plate full of Swedish pancakes, and Paul noticed her apron for the first time. It said, 'Kiss the cook', so he gave her a kiss on the lips.

"Where did you get that apron?"

Lisa told him with a Southern accent, "Oh, this ol' thang? Ah jus' put it on when Ah don' care what Ah look like."

Paul cracked up and she added, "I just picked it up in one of those shops downtown. Do you like it?"

She curtsied and held the apron out with one hand for him to see it all. Paul took the plate from her, sat it down on the table, and gave his wife a big hug with another kiss. Only this one lasted for a few seconds.

"I guess that means you like it?" she asked.

"Oh yes," he responded.

Then Paul sat down to enjoy a taste of her cooking, and added his favorite, Lingonberries, on top of the pancakes, with a little bit of powdered sugar.

After breakfast, Paul offered to clean up the kitchen, but Lisa said, "No, why don't you work on your woodcarving for a half hour, and I'll clean up the kitchen."

"Sounds good," Paul responded. "Are you sure you don't want me to help you though?" and Lisa gave him a kiss.

"No, go see what you can do with your new toy."

So Paul hugged his wife, and went outside to cut up the small tree he found. He had an idea for what he wanted to do, and planned out how he should use each part of this small tree. This was a small project, but would be a good test to see if he enjoyed trying to make something out of it or if it frustrated him so much that he couldn't stand it. He took out the knife from his inside jacket pocket, and looked at it for a few seconds. He used it to cut off a couple of small branches that he didn't need, and then scraped off bark from another part of the tree.

He cut several small straight pieces thicker than a pencil; about two inches long each with a notch in the middle, and fit them together two at a time to create several X's. He then sliced a section of the small tree like a carrot, and had several O's. After cutting four thin branches the same length, carving two notches in each one, he laid two sticks down horizontally a couple of inches apart. He then laid the other two sticks vertically on top of the first two, also a couple of inches apart, and he had a little Tic-Tac-Toe game. He took it all in to show Lisa his masterpiece.

"It's not much, but I think our kids may want to use it to play games with us someday."

"I am proud of you Paul. It's a wonderful souvenir to bring home with us."

******

As they drove back to the cabin after picking up supplies, Lisa looked over at the casino and saw that the parking lot had filled with cars again.

Lisa commented, "The locals must be donating a little more of their paychecks to the Ojibwa today. What a charitable town this is."

Paul turned in to the souvenir shop parking lot, but noticed a police car was in the spot closest to the door.

"I wonder if Jake might be here trying a bowl of Michael's famous soup today," said Paul as he found a spot and parked the SUV.

They both stepped out into the cold again, and quickly made it into the shop. It surprised Lisa when she heard Officer Haley's stern voice.

"Sorry folks. The store is going to be closed for the rest of the day, so you'll have to leave."

She looked up to see that Jake had handcuffed Michael Dufresne, and walked him toward them.

"What's going on here, Jake?" asked Paul.

"Paul, this is official police business. We're investigating a possible homicide, and you're on vacation. Let us handle this, you two just go on your merry way and relax, have a good time, etc."

Lisa saw this infuriated Paul, and he said, "So you're arresting Michael for the murder of those two old guys found in the lake? Are you kidding me? This is ridiculous. It's prejudice because he's a Native American and someone in this town doesn't like Native Americans."

Lisa was upset, but she also became a little concerned that Paul felt so angry. She didn't expect to see him confront a police officer in this way, especially one that they were getting to know. She held his arm and put a hand on his shoulder.

"Paul, I think..." she started to say when Jake interrupted.

"He's being brought in for questioning, and it would be in your best interests if you stayed out of it."

Michael tried to reassure Paul, "Don't worry my friend. I have done nothing wrong, so nothing will happen," but Lisa wasn't so sure that nothing would happen.

"What evidence do you have to even suspect him, Jake?" Jake stepped right up in Paul's face.

"You've been here about a week. How well do you know this man? Hmmm? How well do you know him?"

Paul hesitated, and looked into Michael's eyes. In a softer voice, Paul said, "Jake, you know this man had nothing to do with those two deaths."

Jake looked at Lisa, then at Paul, and responded, "There have been accusations from people in town that have to be investigated, so I .."

Paul interrupted, "These are false accusations from people you know are not trustworthy. These are people who are angry that they lose money week after week, gambling in a casino owned by the Ojibwa, and they don't like anyone who is different from themselves."

Lisa tried to calm her husband, but she felt the same kind of anger that he experienced.

******

"Paul, let me follow up with this investigation, and we may find that you're 100% correct. I just have to check things out with him to see if any of the claims against him can be substantiated."

Paul gritted his teeth and looked away, trying not to say anything more in anger.

Michael calmly added, "Officer Haley is a good man, Paul. Let him do his job, and see what comes out of this."

Paul looked into Michael's eyes again, and then looked intently at Jake.

"This is pure prejudice, and you know it. You need to stand up against these people and not let them get away with walking all over the kinds of people they don't like – the good people in this town." Paul hesitated for a moment, and then continued, "There are people who believe you may have covered up evidence at one of the crime scenes, Jake. This is going to look like you're trying to frame Michael to take attention off of you."

Paul noticed that Jake was taken aback, and he asked, "What are you talking about? What evidence? That's so ridiculous I hope you can't possibly believe something like that."

Jake looked back into Paul's eyes for a few seconds, and then when Paul turned abruptly, he followed Paul and Lisa as they walked out the door. Lisa silently hugged Paul as they stood by their SUV and watched as Officer Haley put Michael into the back of the police car and drove away. Paul felt things slow down again, as the police car carefully pulled out onto the highway, and he noticed that the sounds around him were muffled.

It struck him as odd that his head felt light and only turned very slowly. This didn't seem real. How could time slow down like this? The car's brake lights left a trail of red, like in a time-release photograph, and they both realized that a group of people watched from the casino parking lot. Paul wondered if one or more of them had put Jake up to this.

Lisa spoke and broke Paul's trance, "Maybe you should call Dave and let him know what happened."

Paul hesitated, seeing that things were back to normal again, and then tried to call him, but Dave didn't answer his cell phone. He called him several more times that afternoon with no success, as he and Lisa got things ready at the cabin for their day trip the next day.

"Why doesn't Dave answer his phone?" asked Paul.

******

After spending over an hour talking and filling out paperwork at the police station, Jake said, "I apologize for all of the drama of the handcuffs and having to take you away from the shop, Michael. I'm getting so much pressure from the town to show that we're making progress in the investigation, and someone called in a tip that outright accused you of being involved."

Michael looked him in the eyes and said, "Officer Haley, I do not have a problem with you doing your job. I can see that these deaths are tearing away at you, and I feel sorry for you. Remember that there is a great deal of hatred in this town still, and you are right in the middle of it all. Do not give in and let it take hold in your life."

Jake just stared at him for a few seconds, surprised at Michael's candor, and then nodded. He smiled and shook hands with Michael, saying, "Here, let me give you a ride back to the souvenir shop now. I do apologize for the inconvenience." He wondered what the world was coming to if he had to question the honesty of a man like this. He was angry at himself for using handcuffs and even considering Michael as a suspect. Jake knew that Paul was right, and he ached inside for what he had done.

Chapter Thirty-Four

MARTHA WAS STILL AT THE LI-brary, looking up old newspapers, tax records, etc from after the murder twenty-four years ago, but was still unable to find anything useful about the orphaned boys, her two biological brothers. Through sheer luck, she had found out the name of the family that adopted the oldest boy, and discovered that they moved down near the Upper Michigan border after the adoption. She decided to ask her mother to tell her more about what she knew on that family, since Abigail seemed to know everyone who had been through the town for decades, and she always remembered exactly what happened to each one of them.

Martha stopped by Abigail's desk to chat, and Abigail shook her head, obviously suspecting it was something to do with the recent drownings in the lake. That seemed to be all Martha talked about now, along with wanting to find out more about her biological parents. Abigail had already set up hot tea for herself, and went back to get another cup for her inquisitive daughter. They joked around about her new obsession, and eventually got to the questions Martha wanted to ask.

"Martha, I think you should go into detective work with your new friend Lisa. You would make a great team."

They both laughed, and Martha said, "I do like Lisa a lot.

She and I are very much alike in many ways."

Abigail began, "I remember Mr. and Mrs. Parsons, but I don't remember that the Parsons had any children at all," which surprised Martha because she figured her mother would have remembered the oldest boy being adopted by the Parsons.

"It's possible that they couldn't have children, and had gotten to know the oldest Nelson boy from their time spent with the Nelson family. The Parsons didn't have a lot of money, like most of us, and times were hard for a lot of people, just like they are now. Once the Nelsons were dead, the Parsons may have determined that they could adopt one child, but were unable to adopt the other two because of their financial situation. That thought probably broke their heart, knowing that they'd be separating the children, but for one reason or another they must have felt that they couldn't take all three. That was a blessing for me, because it meant that I would be able to raise you."

She smiled, touched Martha's hand and continued. "Anyway, I never knew that the Parsons had any children of their own or from adoption, so what you found out is news to me. I heard that they moved down south a little ways about the same time of the Nelson's deaths, and at the time I thought it was strange to just get up and leave without much notice. Usually, word would get around town that a family was having a hard time and planned to move to another town to see if they might do any better, but the Parsons were just gone with no explanation.

I do know that they were close friends with the Nelsons, and that the Parsons didn't like my old friend, Big Frank, at all. They may have got along OK for a while, but something happened and they didn't talk with each other after that. Of course, a few of the locals, mostly Big Frank's buddies, speculated that the Parsons must have been involved with the deaths of the Nelsons, but everyone that knew them all were certain that the Parsons would never have done anything cruel like that. They were all good friends, and they all went to the same Lutheran church down the road, where we've been going for many years.

Because it was the Nelson's church, and your church when you were a baby, that's why I chose to change churches and raise you in the Lutheran Church. That church had been there since the early 1900's, maybe the 1890's, and both the Nelson's grandparents and the Parsons' grandparents helped to build it back then. Both families had been prominent in the early stages of Manitow, and for some unknown reason, Big Frank resented that."

Martha shook her head at the pettiness, and Abigail went on, "It is very possible that Big Frank may have scared the Parsons away with his threats, but that's just my own speculation. Maybe Big Frank thought that if he got rid of the Nelsons, then he could intimidate the Parsons so much that they would leave and that would give him more 'seniority' in the area. I know that's a stupid reason, but that's the way several of those guys thought, especially Big Frank."

She paused to enjoy a sip of the tea, and Martha added, "I just can't even comprehend that kind of thinking and why that would even be important to anyone."

Abigail commented, "I'm certainly interested in any information you learn about the Parsons adopting one of the Nelson's children, especially since I also adopted one of the three children. He would have been older than you by two or three years, so by now he would be about 27 years old. I wonder if he looks anything like you, Martha," and they both laughed.

After thinking about that for a minute or so, Martha wanted to find pictures of the Nelson family, and compare some of her own photographs of herself now, as well as when she was a child, just to see if there was any hint of resemblance to one of them. She decided that she would like to look through her mother's old photographs of when she was a baby and before Abigail was married, just to see if there were any clues or items of interest in a few of the photos.

"What do you know about the middle child?" Abigail asked.

"I haven't been able to find anything on him yet. The orphanage didn't want to give out any more information to me, so I'm at a dead end with him at this point in time. Hopefully I didn't get that young girl at the orphanage in trouble. I was lucky to be able to coax the information about the Parsons from the girl that worked there, but I don't think I'll be lucky enough to get any information on the other boy."

Martha paused for a second and thought about what she had just said.

"Wow. I said 'other boy', but he's actually my brother. It's strange to think after all of these years I have two brothers out there that I haven't seen in over twenty years."

Abigail stared at the window for a minute, and Martha could tell her thoughts went back to the days before the Nelsons were murdered.

"I just can't remember anything about the Nelson's children. I heard that they had kids, but since I wasn't involved with their family at all, I was never around the kids. I've tried to remember if I ever saw you with the Nelsons when you were a baby, but the first time I remember seeing you was at the orphanage in Marquette after their deaths. Even when I went through the adoption process back then, there was no information available about the two boys, since they had already been adopted and the information was private. I didn't even know that the Parsons had the same idea that I had about adopting. I wished I had known, since I would have preferred to stay in touch with them all of these years and let you children get to know each other as you were growing up."

Martha looked her in the eyes and said, "Mom, you're the only mother I have known, and you've always been there for me. I would have liked to meet my biological parents, but you and Dad are the parents who raised me, loved me, disciplined me, kept me on the right path, provided for me, spent time with me, and you have been my world all of my life. I would never trade what you have given me all of these years."

This brought tears to Abigail's eyes, and she got up and hugged her daughter.

Chapter Thirty-Five

AT THEIR CABIN THAT EVENING,
Paul and Lisa came out of their cozy shower
and were in their robes. They walked in to the
kitchen where Lisa made them both something warm to
drink.

She suggested to Paul, "Let's not talk about Michael's arrest tonight. Try to call Dave again in the morning to let him know, and see if he can straighten things out."

Paul replied, "The problem is that Jake doesn't trust Dave, so Dave may not be able to do anything."

Lisa looked pleadingly at him without responding, and Paul laughed and said, "OK, no more talk about what's-his-name or what happened at the souvenir shop today. Who could resist your puppy dog eyes?"

After pouring a cup of hot chocolate, they discussed his childhood as they both lay down on the floor. Lisa put her cold feet on Paul's arm, which obviously startled him.

"Wow! Your feet are like ice."

"Cold feet, warm heart," she replied, and they both laughed. "I could really use a relaxing foot massage while we're lying on this rug in front of the fire," so Paul obliged her, as she asked him more about his family.

Lisa remembered, "You told me a couple of years ago that you were adopted as a very young child, and that your biological parents had died young. That was over twenty something years ago. Now that we're learning several interesting coincidences about a couple with children dying around that same time, what else do you remember?" Lisa enjoyed her hot chocolate and didn't pay much attention to the wind outside this evening.

Paul said, "The only other information that my adoptive parents had on my past was that I lived in this small town around this very same lake, and that's why I've always wanted to come up here. I never dreamed I would find anything out about my biological parents, but just wanted to visit the town and see what it was like where I was born. I don't want to jump to conclusions, but my first instinct is that Martha is my little sister."

Lisa had sensed the same thing, and said, "It's incredible how this vacation has turned out. I don't think it's an accident that we happened to come up here exactly this week. You and Martha have so many similarities, and we've all gotten along so well, I know in my heart that this story we're unraveling is your story."

Paul nodded, as he looked her in the eyes.

"It's looking more and more like I'm one of the sons of a couple that was murdered and left in this freezing lake. I was then adopted from the orphanage in Marquette and my new family lived south near Lansing, where I grew up, went to school, met my future wife, and married the girl of my dreams."

Lisa smiled and said, "Hopefully they were good dreams and not bad dreams," and he laughed.

"My little sister, or so it seems, had been adopted soon after I was, but she stayed in the same town all of these years, never realizing that she lived right near the graves of her biological parents, near the cabin where they had all once lived, and was this close to the people who killed them."

Lisa said, "We need to talk to her and Abigail and let them in on what we know about your past, and see if they believe you may actually be one of the Nelson's children too."

Paul replied, "It does seem a little crazy, but from what we're learning about the Nelson family, I'm almost certain, deep in my heart, that they were the ones."

Lisa nodded, realizing that his eyes stared right into her soul as he talked about his feelings, and she relished this rare opportunity.

Paul added, "My adoptive parents have been awesome my whole life, and I wouldn't trade them for anything. It's sad that my biological parents weren't able to raise me, but I am thankful for the people who stepped in and accepted me into their family. I can't change the past, and I'll always consider my adoptive parents as my family."

Lisa thought about that and smiled at her husband. He was right though, since she had met his adoptive parents several times and they made her feel as though she felt part of his family already. No matter how good the Nelsons may have been, Paul was definitely raised by wonderful people and was indeed fortunate to have such loving parents.

As Lisa sipped on her hot chocolate again, she heard the wind howling louder outside, and asked, "Could that have been a wolf?"

Paul, who still concentrated on massaging Lisa's cold feet, said "There are wolves around here, but I believe that was just the wind. Then again, maybe it might have been one of the ghosts."

Lisa laughed, then kicked him a little bit, but was soon serious again as she brought up a concern she had thought about.

"If someone was indeed killing those locals who were involved with the Nelson's murder twenty-four years ago, rather than revengeful ghosts, the most likely suspects would be the Nelson's surviving family members, especially their grown children. So far, almost nobody even knows that they had any children, or if they do know, they haven't been talking. If Martha and Abigail put two and two together, connecting you to the Nelsons, there's a chance both of them might even suspect us as the murderers. I don't think that's a possibility, since they don't even know you were adopted. There's no way they could make any kind of connection."

She pondered that for a minute, and then Paul said, "For all we know, it may even be Martha who is taking revenge, but I have a difficult time believing that could be true. She seemed genuinely surprised when Abigail started revealing the story, but then again, she might be an actress and could be fooling all of us."

Lisa looked at him with a doubtful expression and drank her hot chocolate, but Paul continued, "What if Abigail had been instrumental in the plan, but had Martha, and even Dave, do the evil deeds, as Officer Haley seems to believe? Remember that Jake kept insisting Dave, who is an expert in cutting the ice and who has serious issues with several of the locals, was his number one suspect at first."

Lisa added, "I really can't picture Martha or Abigail having any involvement, but although I don't like having to admit it, Dave seems to be the most likely suspect."

Paul sat up, moving Lisa's feet to the soft rug. "This is a disturbing thought, but what if Dave is the older brother who was adopted first?"

Lisa made a face and exclaimed, "No way. That would make him Martha's big brother, and they're dating."

Paul replied, "What if they're not really dating, but are only using that as a cover for revenge and murder of the people who killed their parents?" Paul continued, "Think about it though. The Nelsons were a religious family, and may have named their children Biblical names, like Martha, Paul, and

David. If Martha is one of their kids, which she appears to be, then that's one Biblical name. If I'm one of their kids and it's still just speculation, then that would make it a second child with a Biblical name - Paul. Dave looks older than Martha, and may be older than me, plus he has a Biblical name."

Lisa commented, "Yes, but so does Jake, which is a nickname for Jacob, and he's the person who Dave suspects the most. Dave has lived here for years, but Jake just moved here six months ago. Two people have been found dead since then."

Paul agreed, "Yeah, I think you're right. Yet Dave doesn't get along with the older locals."

Lisa added, "But Jake doesn't get along so well with them either, even though he tries to fit in with them. What about his arrest of Michael earlier today? Maybe that was an attempt to steer attention away from himself and lead people astray."

Paul slowly nodded in agreement and said, "Yeah, that makes more sense. I think you're on to something."

Chapter Thirty-Six

THE SUN ACTUALLY TRIED TO PEEK through the 'permanent' cloud cover over Kisinaw Lake for a rare moment this winter, and people took advantage of this hint of spring by doing more outdoor activities than usual. The Johnsons took a walk along the road around the lake, waving at their neighbors who were out inspecting their yards or houses. The Erlandsons sat out in their front yard looking across the lake. They talked about what they needed to do to fix the shoreline this year after the ice melted, and considered doing something different when they setup their dock this year in late spring.

******

Paul planned to drive around to see a bit of the scenery before they finished their vacation and had to get back to work, so they took time this morning and afternoon to explore one of the frozen waterfalls and scenic viewing areas in the region that she had found and mapped out for them. Lisa had a knack for discovering great things to do when they went places on the weekends, and Paul was always fascinated by the sights she found to explore. Lisa wanted to remember that they were here on their 'honeymoon', since they didn't get a honeymoon when they were first married, but she couldn't keep the events from the past week out of her mind. They drove for a little while, and then parked when they arrived at the first site of the day. Paul had seen frozen waterfalls before, but this one was impressive, almost as wide as it was tall. Not quite as large as the American side of Niagara Falls, but just as beautiful.

His eyes followed the ice from the ground all the way up to the top of the falls, and he said, "I think we'll take the cable car to the top, then walk down the trail next to the waterfall," and there were no objections from Lisa. They hugged on the way up to the top, and were thrilled to see the frozen falls up close. The water sat there like a stone sculpture, not revealing what actually existed underneath the icy surface, and it felt as though the power of the water hibernated, just waiting for the right time to burst forth from the ice and announce to all with a thunderous roar that it had returned.

They did talk briefly about some of the grisly discoveries they had made while vacationing, even as they walked around the top of the big waterfall, but it didn't keep them from enjoying the beauty of this scene.

******

Three of the locals who meet at the pub regularly were ice fishing on this warmer-than-usual morning, and they tried to figure out whether or not they had enough beer to last them until lunchtime. They had already carved out a hole in the ice and started setting up to fish as the daylight welcomed this trio. Math wasn't their best subject when they were in school, but after each person had already gulped down a few cheap beers, none of them could figure out how many cans they would need until lunchtime based on the number of beers per hour each of them would drink. The conversation went on for much longer than it should have, when finally a fishing line was hit. After a good fight, one of the men pulled in a twenty-six inch Pike. Another of the men checked his line and felt that he had something on his too, so he pulled it in as quickly as possible.

The others watched as he struggled to bring it to the surface, and he said, "I can't believe how heavy this fish is. It must be your fish's grandpa." They all laughed, but he said, "I really need help here," so one of them reached the pole with a hook on it down into the hole to see if he could help pull the fish in.

He dug the hook into its side, and with another pull, they got it to come up through the ice. To their surprise, however, the head of a bearded man had popped up through the hole instead of a giant Pike, but his shoulders wouldn't fit, keeping the man from coming all the way through the ice. All three of them fell backwards in horror, as the frozen man stayed lodged in the hole, his shoulders tightly wedged in the ice when the fishermen pulled him up with such force by the hook and the line. The man's eyes and mouth were frozen wide open, but the three fishermen didn't recognize his bearded face. They quickly sobered up, and all three of them ran stumbling across the ice toward Old Deerfield, which was the closest building.

******

Paul had the camera, and asked, "Lisa, would you stand over there with the trees behind you?" He snapped pictures of Lisa posing at the top of the falls, and even snuck in a quick picture of Lisa losing her balance, scrambling not to fall down.

"Did you already take the picture?"

"I'm just about to take one, so smile big."

He chuckled to himself as he considered what her reaction would be when she looked through their photos of this trip and saw for the first time this picture of her slipping on the ice.

"Her expression is priceless. It's definitely an award winning photo," and he laughed again quietly.

He had enjoyed their ride to the top of the frozen waterfall, and looking down at the wall of ice from up there. It was certainly awe-inspiring, and was actually a nice break to get out into the cold air and do a little hiking. Paul had always liked rock climbing and hiking, and this fit right in with those activities. It gave him a chance to forget about the bodies found in the lake near their cabin rental, and focus on his wife as he had originally planned to do. As they were at the top, Paul took more pictures of Lisa with the distant snow-covered trees in the background. He remembered Dave had mentioned that off in that direction was a small chocolate factory that made its own sweets, so he knew Lisa would be eager to go there next. She told Paul that she wanted to sample a taste of their locally famous dark chocolates.

The trail around the top of the falls provided some of the best views, and Lisa said, "This must be unbelievable in autumn when all of the leaves are in full color."

They both stopped and looked around for a few minutes and he quietly relished the moment. He held Lisa's hand as they slowly made their way down the stairs, and was surprised at how quiet the falls were. Ordinarily, the water would be rushing beside them and the noise would be deafening, but in this state at this time of year, it was an eerie silence as Paul chose his steps wisely.

After following the trail back down beside the waterfall, Paul said, "OK, how about hot coffee and homemade chocolates?" while Lisa smiled, opened her eyes wide, and nodded her head.

Their cheeks reddened from the cold, and their eyes watered a little from the biting wind at the top of the falls. However, they were warmly dressed for this kind of weather and were as prepared as they could be. Even so, Paul was glad to get inside the SUV and start up the heater.

221

******

Officer Haley had come out onto the ice, and met with each of the three fishermen. He noticed a collection of empty beer cans around the ice hole, and asked them, "So you had a few beers already this morning?" He realized the three of them were not in the mood to be questioned about their liquid breakfast, and were still shook up about hooking a body on their fishing line.

They all gave him a look that said, "I don't want to be here right now," and Officer Haley turned back to look at the frozen man stuck in the ice fishing hole. He took off one of his gloves and rubbed his eyes. It was visible that he was frustrated and a little shaken up at having another dead body found in the frozen lake. He recognized the man as Robert Vallee, the hermit who had an argument with Dave Bramwell the previous week.

To make things worse, Paul and Lisa, had warned him only days before that they believed this man's life was in danger from the revenge of murder victims that had been buried for twenty years, a case that was originally believed to be accidental. This body was the third one found in this lake in only a week, and until now, there had only been three recorded deaths on this lake in the past fifty years or more. He knew that news would get around the town quickly, and he would soon face the gauntlet of concerned citizens who didn't think he had been doing everything that needed to be done to stop these murders. These kinds of things didn't happen in small towns like Kisinaw Lake, and he wondered if it would be better to be a police officer in Detroit or New York City.

Jake didn't find any clear connection between the three recent deaths and the previous deaths from years ago, despite the claims from Paul and Lisa, and he had even made a point of talking to the librarians to understand exactly what they knew about the old 'murders'. It was certainly a lead, but one with no evidence to go on. He had also questioned Michael Dufresne at the police station earlier, but Jake honestly didn't believe Dufresne had anything to do with the recent deaths. He accepted that Michael was a trustworthy man, well respected by everyone except some of the older locals, and Jake had appreciated talking to him. He only wished it had been under different circumstances.

Michael may have had a motive, but so did just about anyone who knew these men and had to deal with their arrogance and prejudice. Jake just didn't see any way that Michael could be involved with any of the three recent deaths. He tried to determine if Michael had an alibi for all three of them, but the problem was that each of the bodies could have been in the ice for several days. Anyone could have an alibi for the night before a body was found, but the body might have been put into the ice two days before discovering it, maybe more.

Robert Vallee had been the most likely suspect, since he knew the other two guys who were found dead, had a possibly scandalous involvement with them years ago in the Nelsons' deaths, and until today, that was a plausible theory. Vallee could have killed the other two men, then skipped town, never to be heard of again. Well, that was until these drunks pulled him up out of the lake.

Now he wondered about Abigail, who was the only living person who had come forward with knowledge about the Nelsons' deaths. Was she really the next victim, as she claimed, or was she somehow involved in these new deaths? He had heard that Abigail's daughter was dating Dave Bramwell, who could undoubtedly be the one doing the dirty work for Abigail. If the choice was between ghosts and Dave Bramwell, it was an easy one for Jake to make.

Chapter Thirty-Seven

PAUL HAD NO PROBLEMS FINDING the chocolate factory, and he thoroughly enjoyed the smells of fresh, hot, melted chocolate as it was being heated up inside the structure. It was a small place, but he felt welcome as the hostess led them inside to look around. Since Lisa was a chocoholic, Paul could hardly contain her excitement over the aromas that permeated the entire building, and she seemed to bounce from one window to the next, looking in at the assortment of items they made behind large viewing area windows. There were different types of chocolates created in each room, and Paul knew she would want to sample at least one of everything. He was thrilled to watch her have a great time tasting the sweets, and wasn't surprised when she decided on getting hot chocolate to sip on instead of coffee. Paul did the same, and was pleased to see that Lisa's mind was not on the deaths at the lake for the first time all week. He almost didn't want to leave, but he knew they had a long drive back to the cabin and needed to get started soon.

******

Suddenly, the voice of an angry man sounded over the commotion as Jake tried to stop more people from getting up close to the crime scene out on the ice.

"Jake Haley! I need to have a word with you about Michael Dufresne. You know he's innocent, yet you locked him up anyway."

Without turning to see who it was, Officer Haley sighed, as he recognized Dave Bramwell's voice.

He said to himself out loud, "I really don't need to deal with this right now," but he had no choice.

Jake tried to say calmly, "Dave, I called you out here to help me pull Robert Vallee up out through the ice and preserve a potential crime scene. I don't need an argument now."

"Paul told me about Michael Dufresne being taken into custody yesterday as a suspect. I've worked with Michael for years, ay, and I know he would never even hurt a fly, let alone another human being. I know that the men who were frozen in the lake weren't the nicest of people, but they were still human, and I can tell you that Michael couldn't be involved."

Jake thought he was prepared for an argument with Dave, and turned to face him, but saw a fury in Dave's eyes that he wasn't expecting as he quickly marched up and stood only inches from Jake's face.

"I'm warning you now, Haley. You'd better let Michael go, then apologize to him and his family for taking him in."

Jake wanted to step back to avoid the conflict, but he stood his ground and tried to reason with Dave.

"Listen Dave. Evidence was presented to me yesterday that placed Mr. Dufresne as a possible suspect, and it justified bringing him in immediately for questioning. He's not under arrest, but is still a potential suspect."

Dave responded, pointing his finger in Jake's face, "Yeah, lies from a couple of those losers who hate everyone except themselves. You should know better than to listen to them, when you have a person in town as trustworthy as Michael Dufresne. They treat him like dirt, and he still stays here and is one of the most honest and reliable people in town."

Jake brushed aside Dave's pointed finger with a warning, "Dave, you need to back down and talk rationally," but Dave only argued more.

"Back down. By taking him in, you gave in to those prejudiced, self-centered, owners of this town who have been pushing around anyone they don't like for years. It needs to stop, and you need to stand up to them."

"Now you listen here. I was given a tip, and it's my responsibility to follow up on it. If it was legitimate, we could have wrapped up this case. I now believe it wasn't legitimate, and I made the decision to let Mr. Dufresne go after my questioning. Now that he's no longer my primary suspect, and Robert Vallee is no longer a possibility, you should know that you've been moved back up to number one, and if you keep this up, I believe I may have enough cause to take you in right now."

Dave paused for a few seconds as they both breathed heavily and exhaled clouds of cold air, then said, "You have got to be kidding."

Jake continued, pointing down to the ice hole, "You recently had an argument with Mr. Vallee here, where he pulled a gun on you, and Paul is a witness. It's well-known around here that you don't get along with some of these older folks that you say own this town, so there is enough of a motive here to justify it. I would be well within my rights to take you in for questioning and I don't think anyone would complain one bit."

Dave continued to fume still, and turned around while running one hand through his hair, putting one hand on his hip. He gazed out at the shoreline where people had gathered to watch the action, then slowly looked at each person there.

Dave said, "I don't believe this," then marched toward the crowd of people, leaving Jake to stare at him as he stormed off across the ice.

Jake had wanted Dave to help him remove the body from

the lake, but he decided it would be best to let Dave go now.

Once Dave was out of sight, he then asked a few of the young men on the shore, "Bryce, Wayne, and Preston, would you help me pull Mr. Vallee up on to shore?"

The men walked toward Jake, and they all worked together in silence to finish the unpleasant job.

******

On their way back to the cabin, Lisa had fallen asleep in the passenger seat since it was getting late and already very dark outside. Paul drove on a road with no streetlights, with tall trees on both sides of the road, so the darkness overwhelmingly tried to cover them. It almost seemed as though it might extinguish their SUV's headlights like a black hole if they didn't hurry up and get back to the cabin. Paul had enjoyed great scenery and delicious food today, and had a very special time with his wife. He figured it was a trip they would both remember for the rest of their lives. Just then, something ran in front of the SUV, and Paul slammed his foot down hard on the brakes.

He was shocked to see a medium sized grey wolf trotting across the road, acting as though nothing had happened, as Lisa asked him, "What are you doing?"

Before he could respond, a second grey wolf ran in front of the SUV, with the headlights providing a stunning view of this casual jog in her predecessor's footsteps. Both Paul and Lisa just stared at the object in their headlights with their mouths open. Paul was speechless. Neither had ever seen a wolf in the wild, so this was indeed a chance of a lifetime.

Lisa was now fully awake, but Paul could tell she had difficulty putting her thoughts together into words as she stuttered, "D-D-Did-Did you see that? We just had a wolf run in front of the SUV. Did you see it Paul?"

Paul watched as the second wolf was quickly enveloped in the darkness past the headlights, and said, only slightly above a whisper, "That was the second wolf. I hit the brakes so I wouldn't hit the first one, and while we were stopped, the second one ran across the road. I can't believe we just saw that."

They both looked at each other and shared a silent kiss as his heart still pounded from the sudden excitement. Then Paul slowly pressed on the gas pedal to start moving again, both of them peering into the hole in the dark woods where the wolves disappeared until it was out of sight behind them.

They were still about forty-five minutes away from the cabin, but Lisa stayed awake talking the rest of the way.

"There's no way I could fall back asleep now."

Sometimes Lisa's conversations were challenging to follow, causing Paul to zone out for a while as he pretended to listen intently, but tonight's chatter was a welcome sound to help him stay awake for the drive back to the cabin through the blackness of Upper Michigan.

Eventually, Paul turned off of the highway and onto the lake access road, then came out of the ice tunnel of trees that circled over the road like a white covered bridge. Lisa stopped talking unexpectedly, which surprised Paul, as he glanced over to see what she was doing. She leaned down staring up and out the front window, with her mouth open and eyes wide, so he tried to figure out what she looked at. He quickly pulled over and stopped the SUV so he could get a better glimpse, and a big smile spread across his face.

It was the most spectacular display of the Northern Lights that he had ever seen, and he said, "Lisa, this is an amazing end to an amazing day."

She nodded, saying "Go ahead and park at the cabin so we can look at it over the frozen lake."

He did just that, since they were only a minute or two from the cabin, and they got out of the SUV to walk up to the edge of the lake. They stood there arm in arm under a blanket Lisa brought from the SUV, with the unearthly green illuminations slowly dancing over them, reflecting off of the lake's frozen surface. They looked alive as the lines in the sky appeared to wave and hypnotize him. While he witnessed this scene, he wondered if the Sasquatch, UFO's, ghosts, or evil spirits were really so far-fetched, since the beauty of the aurora borealis was just as difficult for him to fathom. It was undeniably another world out here.

Despite the almost unbearable cold air at their outdoor theater, this was better than watching any movie, and they stood in silence for a long time gazing up at this impressive display of lights.

Chapter Thirty-Eight

THE NEXT MORNING WHILE THEY were still in bed, Lisa looked at her husband and asked, "Paul, was everything we saw yesterday just a dream?" and Paul played dumb.

"Was what just a dream?"

Lisa frowned and hit him with a pillow, while Paul laughed and tried to get away. They were dressed in their 'long-underwear and socks' outfits that they seemed to like so much on the cold mornings, and she chased him around the cabin with the pillow. Sometimes the cold weather makes animals playful in the mornings, and it seemed to have the same effect on Paul and Lisa here.

She said, "We hiked around a beautiful frozen waterfall, saw a wolf run across the road...,"

"Two wolves," Paul interrupted.

"Aha, so you admit it wasn't a dream then?"

"OK, OK, you're twisting my arm. You convinced me it wasn't a dream. I admit it."

Lisa continued, "We had wonderful snacks at the chocolate factory, then when we made it back to the cabin, we saw an incredible display of the Northern Lights over the lake. I am so thankful we came here for a vacation."

"I certainly agree," Paul responded and gave her a hug and a kiss on the cheek.

Lisa mentioned, "Wow, we really slept in late today. It's almost time for lunch."

"We must have needed it. Plus, I didn't mind snuggling up to you all morning under the quilts with it being so cold outside."

"Would you start a fire in the fireplace while I get dressed, my handsome mountain man?"

"Of course, madam. Anything for you."

Paul worked his magic on the fireplace, and within minutes, warmth permeated the living room, where they both went to thaw out while putting on their outfits du jour.

"I think we should do whatever we can to fit in with the locals today, so let's wear these clothes I picked out."

Paul didn't argue, and just put on the same kind of clothes Dave would wear. They were comfortable, and Lisa looked gorgeous in her outfit, so Paul would be glad to show her off to the townspeople. They played around inside the cabin for a little while, taking photos of each other in the different rooms, until Lisa gasped with a surprised expression.

"Oh Paul, another dark chocolate," she exclaimed as she picked up a small candy bar Paul had hidden by a lamp in the living room, then tackled her husband onto the couch with a loving bear hug.

It took him by surprise, since he had forgotten about this piece, but he went along with it, as if he had much of a choice, laughing hysterically at his chocolate-crazy wife.

Paul drove around the lake to the pub again for an early lunch with Lisa, and as he stepped into Old Deerfield, he saw a few of the familiar faces that they were both getting to know. There was generally a different crowd that came here in the evening compared to the afternoon crowd, but Paul realized that many of the people were there at both lunchtime and dinner time.

By the second or third step inside the door, he felt light-headed again, and noticed that the sounds appeared to be muffled, while things moved slowly as if in some kind of dream. He tried to nudge Lisa to let her know it was happening now, but he couldn't reach her. One person they recognized sat with a group of men at the big table in the back, laughing loudly as usual. Tim sat in his typical spot at the bar, and he waved to them as they walked past him. Lisa hadn't seen Tim here in the lunchtime crowd before, but figured it made sense for him to have lunch here on the days that he had a job to do on Kisinaw Lake.

Paul tried to wave, but his arm didn't seem to be under his control. He continued walking behind Lisa, and Tim seemed to watch him with interest. Paul wondered if Tim could tell something was going on as his slow steps pounded the wooden floor like a Frankenstein monster. The hate-filled voices infiltrated his head, and he tried to look around to see who shouted, but his head turned so slowly he thought it would take forever to scan the room. Then just as quickly as it had started, Paul realized he was already at the table, and everything was back to normal again. He almost told Lisa, but was hesitant to mention it now. She looked over at the giant fireplace and said, "How about this table Paul?"

It seemed as though she should have been able to tell that his footsteps were unnaturally loud, but neither Lisa nor anyone else acted as though something out of the ordinary had happened. He nodded, knowing that the decision had already been made to sit at this table, and she just gave him the opportunity to make him think it was his decision.

He thought to himself, "Well, it's over, so there's no sense in discussing this weird feeling I've been getting. It must just be in my mind that I walked odd or heard the angry voices, since nobody else reacts to any of this."

******

"I'm hungry for one of their delicious fried lake perch lunch specials," said Paul.

Lisa responded, "I'm looking forward to their 'famous' marble cheesecake with a raspberry topping for dessert. A few days ago, the waitress told me that when the berries are in season, the cheesecake gets covered with ripe blueberries or raspberries, and that makes it even better. Since its winter, however, I'll have to settle for a raspberry flavored sauce."

Paul and Lisa both looked at the old photos on the walls as they turned in their seats near the window across from the bar, and Lisa noticed a photograph of four young men and a young woman sitting at a table laughing. It actually looked like it had been taken at the same table Lisa had selected to sit at this afternoon, since the same fireplace was in the background of the photo. This picture stood out as she remembered Abigail talking about her hanging around with four guys on that fateful evening twenty-four years ago.

"Paul, do you think this is Abigail in the picture, with those people who could have been involved with the Nelson's deaths?"

Paul looked at the old photo, and replied, "It may be Abigail over twenty years ago, but I wonder what the odds would be that these boys were the same ones from that night."

Tim stepped away from the bar toward them and said, "I couldn't help but overhear you asking about that old photo. The woman in the picture is definitely the older librarian, Abigail."

Surprised at the comment, Lisa turned to see Tim standing next to Paul, and stopped in her thoughts for a few seconds. Before she saw who spoke, she thought Tim's voice sounded a lot like Paul's for some reason, and when she looked at the two of them standing there next to each other, she noticed that they were just about the same height and had the same hair color. She even thought they had the same profile and combed their hair the same way. Lisa had never noticed it before, but there were definite similarities between Tim and Paul.

The waitress brought drinks to their table, and Paul said, "Thank you."

"I'll be right back for your order," she smiled and walked through the doors to the kitchen.

While the guys still stared at the picture, Tim said, "The two on the right are the two men who were found in the lake recently, Eddie and Little Frank, while the one on the far left is the missing hermit, Robert Vallee. The ugly man next to Abigail was a mean man called Big Frank, who died on the lake a long time ago."

Lisa was surprised at their luck, and Paul asked, "How do you know all of this? We thought you've only been here on the lake for about a year."

Tim smiled and said, "Most people here think I am from out of town, but my parents grew up here years ago and knew them all. I was actually born here, and my father even had that same picture at home as I grew up. He had been friends with a few of these men at one point in time, but they had a falling out somewhere around the time that the picture was taken. My father told me all kinds of stories about the people he knew on the lake up until his death about twelve months ago."

Tim took a drink, while Lisa looked at Paul in disbelief, not knowing what to say.

Tim continued, "When my mother passed away a few years ago, me and my father buried her up here at the big cemetery off of the highway near town, since she had always loved this area. Then when my father died in the past year, he was buried up here next to my mother, and I decided then to move here to see what it was that my parents liked so much about Kisinaw Lake. I've been staying at that cabin on the lake, just a short walk from this pub, which is where they all used to visit, and close to my parent's graves. After being here a few months, I see why they wanted to be buried here. I like the slower pace, the wildlife, the peacefulness of the lake, and many of the people in the area are great to work with, despite what you see with the older locals."

Paul said, "So then you really are more of a local than people realize," and Tim smiled, looked around with a mock caution, and nodded.

"Don't tell anyone yet. It is amazing to see how rude several of these people can be to people who they think are 'outsiders', and I don't want to spoil their fun. I now own that cabin, so I'm a legitimate 'local' again."

Tim sat down with them and took another drink.

"So what do you two think about this area?"

Without even thinking, Paul replied, "The scenery is beautiful, the restaurants are great, and most of the people here are awesome. If it wasn't for a murderer in town, this place would be my second home."

They all laughed, and Lisa added, "We've met some of the nicest people around the lake and in town, and have actually thought about buying a place here so we would be able to come down regularly."

Tim said, "Hey, that would be great. We would be permanent neighbors then."

Lisa looked over at Paul and commented, "Then maybe Paul could learn a few things about woodworking from you. He wants so much to be able to build, restore, and finish wood the way you have done around here."

Tim held up his glass and said, "Well, here's to my new apprentice," and they all touched their glasses together with good laughter and took a drink. Tim asked, "Paul, when you came in just now, you looked as though something was wrong. Are you OK?"

Paul stammered, "Oh, uh, I was feeling a little light headed at first, but I think I'm just hungry."

Lisa looked at him and asked, "Did it happen again?"

Paul replied, "Yeah, sometimes when I first walk in here, it feels like things slow down, faces are blurred with mean expressions, and I can't clearly understand the talking going on."

Tim said, "I've felt that same feeling when I'm around a few of these older guys who hate everyone. It took me by surprise at first, but now I kind of expect it. It's been almost a warning sign that I'm not around friends, but it happens less and less now."

Lisa said, "That's strange. I wonder why you two have had this happen and not me."

Paul shrugged and said, "I have no idea. Just be glad it doesn't happen to you. It's an unusual feeling, and a little scary."

"Could it be related to the evil spirits Michael talked about?" asked Lisa, but Paul didn't want to think about that. Being targeted by evil spirits could indeed be a frightening prospect.

Finally, Tim looked at Paul, and then added, "The ugly guy in the picture, Big Frank, was killed on the lake over twenty years ago. I heard from my father that there was more to Big Frank's death than just a boating accident," and nodded once while Lisa noticed his eyebrows went up knowingly. Nobody spoke for a couple of seconds as Tim shifted his eyes to Lisa's, then drank the rest of his drink. He mentioned, "I need to get back to my cabin to get ready for work. I'll see you all later."

Paul and Lisa both said, "Bye Tim," then looked back at the photo again as Tim got his coat and walked out the door.

Lisa excitedly exclaimed, "Paul, we need to get to the library fast to talk to Martha. I have a theory that's going to blow your mind."

Chapter Thirty-Nine

LISA STARTED REVEALING WHAT WAS on her mind, encouraging her husband to pay the bill without even ordering lunch, and leave right away to meet with Martha. Paul explained to the waitress that they weren't going to be able to eat yet, and just paid for their drinks. They both ran to the SUV and climbed in, and Paul quickly drove Lisa around the lake road, then out onto the highway. They had just began to make their way in to town to visit the library, when Paul saw Dave's rusty old truck speeding toward them, passing his SUV on the highway. Before Lisa finished telling Paul her theory, Dave must have realized he saw Paul drive by, and then both Paul and Dave slammed on the brakes, pulling off the highway on opposite sides of the road. Paul parked on one side of the road, while Dave parked on the other side, and all four of them met in the road near Paul's SUV with everyone talking at once.

Paul said over everyone else, "Listen, we just talked to that carpenter guy, Tim Parsons, who knows a lot about Martha's mother and the other four men who were involved with the Nelson's deaths."

"Who did you say?" Martha interrupted.

Paul repeated the name, "Tim Parsons. He's a guy we met in the pub last week that lives on the lake. Remember, we met him at that old farmhouse?"

Martha said, "I remember, but you didn't say his last name before. You're not going to believe this, but I'll bet that he's the oldest son of the Nelsons - my oldest brother."

Paul stared at Lisa, and then Lisa said, "You may not believe this but I think Paul is the other brother - your other brother."

Paul wasn't surprised when Martha looked in disbelief at Lisa, Paul, and then at Dave. There was silence for several seconds with no traffic noises in the background, and nobody said anything. Paul almost expected a dog to bark somewhere off in the distance.

Finally he blurted out, "We need to make sure Abigail is safe. If Tim, who hasn't really been a local here for twenty years, knows details about the Nelson's murderers, and everyone involved has died mysteriously or disappeared in the past two weeks, then other people might know too and Abigail could very well be the next target."

Martha replied, "I already thought of that when Dave told me that the old hermit was found dead, and I made sure my mother was safe for now at the church."

Paul said, "Wait a minute. Robert Vallee was found dead?"

Dave replied, "Yes, he's no longer missing. Officer Haley probably knew all along exactly where the old hermit would be found. Now he's on a slab in the morgue or having his insides examined in an autopsy."

Paul stared at Lisa for a couple of seconds, his mind swirling with this new revelation.

"That makes three people who have been found dead in the lake since we got here," said Lisa.

Dave added with a smirk, "Yah, you should hear how many people keep pointing that out too. You guys are the prime suspects for many of the townspeople."

Paul replied, "Wow. I thought Robert Vallee was probably the one who killed the other two men, and then he just left town. I didn't expect to hear that he had become one of the dead as well."

Dave commented, "If I was a betting man, which I'm not, my money would be on Jake Haley."

Paul tried to put his thoughts together, ignoring Dave's comment about Jake, and then asked, "What's going on with Michael Dufresne?"

"Jake took him in for questioning, and then let him go within an hour. Seems a little fishy, and I let Jake know that I wasn't very happy about it."

Martha added, "Yes, and you almost got yourself arrested."

Lisa exclaimed, "What?"

Paul asked, "What happened?"

Dave held up his hand and said to Paul, "Look, you called me and told me that Michael had been arrested by Jake for suspicion of murder. I was fuming. Then a few minutes later, I was called down to help Jake pull out the old guy from the lake, our buddy the hermit who pulled a gun on me. I wasn't in a good mood, and when I saw Jake out on the ice, I gave him a piece of my mind about what he did to Michael." Martha shook her head, while Dave looked at her, and then continued. "Jake then threatened me, saying that I was one of the suspects, and I stormed away from there. He must have had someone else help with the body."

Lisa then commented, "Martha, I believe you're right about Tim being the older son. It all makes sense. We know the Parsons were good friends of the Nelsons, and after the Nelson's deaths, the Parsons must have adopted Tim. Tim said that they moved away from here almost immediately, maybe driven away by Big Frank, and he even hinted that his adopted father, Mr. Parsons, might have been involved in Big Frank's death only a few months later."

Paul noticed that Martha and Dave both looked at her with interest at this news.

Paul said, "Let's head over to Tim's cabin to see if we can get more answers. I'll drive," and they all jumped in to Paul's SUV.

On the way over to the lake, Lisa told Martha, "We just met Tim at the pub for lunch, and when I heard his voice, I assumed it was Paul. Then when I looked up at him, Tim stood next to Paul and for a second or two, I thought I was seeing double. I never noticed it before, until they were both together. They looked and sounded so similar I got chills."

Paul commented, "I didn't notice any resemblance. He's nowhere near as handsome as I am."

Lisa replied, "I never did either until that moment, in that certain light, at that certain angle. It was incredible." Paul just stared at her for a moment, as Lisa continued, "Tim has been staying at the Nelson's old cabin for almost the past year."

Martha added, "I found that the Parsons are buried very near the Nelsons in the cemetery, and Mr. Parsons was buried there less than a year ago."

Lisa said, "Yes, Tim mentioned that he came up here to bury his father in the past year, and that's when he moved in to the cabin."

Martha questioned, "Do you think Tim knows the cabin he's at is the same cabin where the Nelsons had lived and were murdered in front of? Paul, that would be the same place where Tim, you, and I lived when we were little."

Paul told her, "Yes, he does know. Tim had joked with some of the people at the pub over the last few days about being in a haunted cabin."

He watched her expression as she just looked out the window in silence, obviously deep in thought, with tears streaming down her cheeks.

Dave asked, "Why would he have called it a haunted

cabin?"

"He told people that he's had nightmares there over the past few months that seem so real."

Lisa asked, "Could that be more results from the evil spirits that Michael Dufresne talked about?"

Nobody said anything, and Paul quickly maneuvered the SUV into Tim's driveway, parking behind Tim's truck. As soon as the engine stopped, Paul jumped out, followed by the rest of the crew, then ran to the back door and knocked on it. Nobody answered, so they all darted around the cabin to the lakeside.

When they got to the front door and knocked, Paul whispered to Martha, "This was our parents' cabin, where we were all born." The younger librarian just looked at him and nodded her head with no expression. Paul added, "I wish I could remember any of it."

Excited that Tim might really be his brother, he was also nervous about how to approach Tim about it. Could Tim already know about his family relationship with Paul and Martha? Was he aware of his biological parents and their deaths? There were so many unknowns, and the possibilities just churned in Paul's head.

After nobody answered, Lisa checked to see if the door was unlocked and found that it opened right up.

Dave said, "Hey, I just heard something in the woods next to the cabin," and they all stopped to listen. Sure enough a person was walking on a path that followed the lake, and Paul heard branches being stepped on and cracking. Lisa closed the door again, while Paul observed the other three with apprehension. Without saying a word, they all followed Paul down the path into the woods next to the cabin. He noticed fresh footprints in the snow, and quietly looked down as they all quickly added their prints next to them.

Chapter Forty

TIM BREATHED HEAVILY AS HE walked through the snow in the woods beside his cabin, and saw the frozen lake in front of him. It was still cold enough to cause pain in his lungs as he breathed it in, but he kept marching along. He progressed out onto the lake's surface, but slipped down the embankment, sliding onto the ice. He got up quickly, and began walking cautiously. Tim knew that it was not as thick now as it had been in a month ago, so he stepped carefully. He soon heard someone calling him, and turned, slowly looking up to his left. He followed the shoreline until he saw the cabin, but heard the ice crack below him. Tim noticed the four on the shore watching him as he tried not to fall through the ice, and he saw that they all stepped with care out onto the frozen surface toward him. Tim tried to balance when he heard it crack again. There was a terror on his face, just before he fell through. Paul motioned to the others to stay back and ran toward him, as Tim grabbed onto the ice, keeping his head and shoulders out of the freezing water.

******

Dave said, "Martha, call 911 on your cell phone," while he called Michael Dufresne at the souvenir shop.

"I'll call Michael too, since he may be able to get here before the police and he'll have supplies we may need when we get him out of the freezing water," and Lisa nodded.

Paul cautiously moved toward Tim as fast as possible, but he felt helpless as he saw Tim fall backward and go all the way under water. By the time Paul got to the hole in the ice, he had pulled his jacket off and there was no sign of Tim, so without hesitation he dove into the frigid water to get him.

Lisa was already in tears, as was Martha, but when Paul jumped into the lake, she screamed, "Paul!" Martha turned her head into Dave's chest, and he held her for a second or two.

Dave then said gently but forcefully, "I have to get to the edge of the hole to help Paul get out," and he moved forward with caution.

******

Paul knew he couldn't stay in this cold water for long, but he figured that Tim wouldn't have moved very far from the hole after he fell through. He tried to look around underwater, reached the bottom, and still didn't see anyone or anything. Unfortunately, it was dark, with very little sunlight showing through the ice to help him search, so that made things more difficult. Paul looked up at the ice, but only saw a little bit of light at the hole where Tim fell through. He reached around him in the dark water, but found nothing. Confused and disappointed, he returned to the surface, and was pulled up right away by Dave, shaking his head in frustration as the rest of his body shivered from the cold.

Paul said with chattering teeth and heavy breathing, "I can't understand it. He should be right around the hole in the ice, but I couldn't find him. I need to go back down."

Dave looked in Paul's eyes and asserted, "No way, Paul. You need to get inside and get warm right away. I'm not letting you go down again."

Paul insisted, "He's going to die if we don't get to him now," and he tried to go back into the water again.

Lisa and Martha both shouted, "Paul!" through their tears, and Dave held on to him firmly.

"Lisa, if you take Paul into the cabin and get a fire going, get some warm clothes for him, I'll go down and see if I can find Tim. I'll join you in the cabin in a few minutes."

Paul didn't argue, and Martha just wiped her eyes with both hands as she sobbed even harder. Lisa helped Paul get up, as Dave took off his jacket and boots, and then slid into the frigid water with a painful sounding groan. Paul saw agony in Dave's eyes, and knew exactly what he just felt as Dave disappeared under the ice. Lisa and Paul made their way across the ice to the cabin, and went right in through the unlocked front door.

"I'll look for towels to help you dry off, while you get out of those wet clothes now," she demanded as she walked out of the family room and he chose not to put up a fight.

She then started a fire while he still shivered by the hallway, struggling to get the freezing clothes off of himself.

******

While Dave searched under the water, Officer Haley came running up to the edge of the lake, and carefully made his way out onto the ice next to Martha.

She said through tears, "Dave's down there looking for Tim now. Paul and Lisa are in his cabin warming up since Paul had jumped in after him."

Jake whispered, "How long has Tim been under there?"

"It may be close to five minutes now," as Jake shook his head. He was visibly frustrated, since Tim was one of his best friends in this town.

"How long has Dave been down there?" he asked.

"A minute or two."

******

Indeed Dave had already spent a couple of minutes feeling under the ice for any sign of Tim, and tried to look for him as much as possible, knowing that he wouldn't have much light to work with down here. His eyes scanned the dark water below him, but he saw nothing. Dave then decided to get one more breath of air, and go down to the bottom for one last effort. He looked for the hole in the ice, but it wasn't where he expected it would be. His eyes showed a little bit a panic, as he quickly searched the underneath surface for the break in the ice. To his relief, he found it and climbed out for a much needed gulp of cold air. It burned his throat as he gulped it in, but it gave him relief after using up all that he had down there. He was glad to see that Martha and Jake both waited for him there and they pulled him out of the water. Dave tried to speak, but the cold made it difficult for him.

"I want to go down one more time, and then I'll get out."

Jake countered, "No, Dave. You need to come up now and get out of those wet clothes." Dave argued, but Jake said forcefully, "Dave, I'll go down now. Tim's my friend too, OK?"

Martha said, "I'll take you to Tim's cabin to get warmed up."

Without waiting for Dave to argue, Jake pulled him out of the water, and Martha wrapped his jacket around him. She picked up Dave's boots and put her other arm around him. Jake pointed to the smoke coming out of the chimney and told her, "Please get him into the cabin near the fire, and get him into some dry clothes. I'll go down and see if I can find Tim."

Martha nodded, and Dave replied, "I searched all under

the ice, but didn't go deep, down to the bottom. That's where I was going to look next."

Jake nodded, and said, "Thanks Dave. I really appreciate all of your help. I'll see you in the cabin as soon as I find him. Wish me luck."

Jake pulled off his jacket and boots, and then slipped into the cold water with an audible gasp as it took his breath away. Dave knew that it felt like a thousand needles had just poked him wherever the icy water touched him. He also noticed that the expression on Jake's face showed obvious discomfort at the cold temperature of the water, but he watched Jake take a deep breath anyway and vanish into the black hole.

Chapter Forty-One

MARTHA TOOK **D**AVE BACK TO Tim's cabin as fast as she could, walking right in to get him by the fire and put on some blankets. She saw Paul still shivering under a couple of old quilts, even after he had gotten out of his wet clothes and dried off.

He kept insisting, "I should have been able to save him."

Martha said, "You did all you could do. You should be thankful you're both alright."

Lisa came out with another towel and dry clothes for Dave, while he warmed up beside Paul at the fireplace.

"Jake went into the water when Dave came out so we need to go check on him to make sure he gets out and warms up too," Martha added.

Paul replied, "I'll go back out there," and put on thick socks and a pair of Tim's shoes to go help Jake. Martha noticed that the hiking boots fit Paul perfectly.

While in the cabin, Martha knew there wasn't much hope of Tim surviving after being under the cold water for this long, and she looked around the cabin with a sadness that she hardly comprehended. Nobody said anything, as Lisa and Martha looked at the pictures on the wall, the knickknacks on the mantle and on the shelves, and they walked from room to room. Martha found a copy of the same picture Lisa saw at the pub, this one having names next to each person in the photo. She also noticed that all of the faces were 'X'd' out with a red marker except the young girl in the picture, who she recognized as her mother, Abigail. Martha gasped when she saw this, and held her hand over her mouth.

******

Jake was down near the bottom of the lake, determined that he would find Tim in time. He knew there was still a lot of area to cover, since the lake was at least twenty feet deep here, so he moved quickly, yet methodically. He tried to calculate what direction Tim would have gone if he fell straight through the ice, but Tim wasn't there. He moved around with his arms outstretched, hoping to bump into Tim even just a little. Jake knew he needed to get back up and catch another breath of air soon. His body moved slower now, and the thought of hypothermia crossed through his mind. Discouraged, he looked up to the surface for the hole that he had come down through. It seemed so far away, and he still wanted to look just a little more before going back up. He wasn't sure if he would have enough air to search anymore.

It seems so peaceful down there, and he felt as though he was about to lose consciousness.

******

Dave had changed into dry clothes, and Martha knew he felt better now that he was by the fire. She watched as he sat near Paul and put on his boots, but neither said a word. Lisa went into Tim's bedroom and Martha followed.

Martha said, "This is really a cozy little cabin, isn't it?"

"Yes, it's just beautiful. I can't believe you and Paul both lived here when you were kids," and Martha wiped a tear from her eye.

Martha looked through a journal on the table by his bed,

and was astonished at what she read. Tim documented his nightmares in vivid detail, as well as describing the murders of Eddie, Little Frank, and Robert Vallee. This journal and the photograph with the faces crossed out were incriminating enough to prove that Tim was the killer.

"Lisa, I think you need to read this. It almost looks as though the journal was written by two different people, since the happy parts are very neat and legible, but the parts that mention the deaths of the men on the lake are done with a sloppy handwriting, as though they were written in a hurry or he was extremely stressed."

Lisa read a few pages and mentioned, "Look how hard the pen was pressed down when he wrote the murder sections, like he wrote with a tremendous amount of anger. Yet, the next page tells of work he did on Old Deerfield, and it's written neatly again with a happy tone. It's as though he was possessed at times, yet back to normal most of the time."

They walked out by the fireplace again, and Lisa said, "In these journals, Tim mentioned stories he remembered from his childhood, before the Parsons adopted him, and he expressed his anger over the murder of his biological parents. It's almost a 'Jekyll and Hyde' style of writing, as though he's two different people, neither aware of each other's activities or thoughts."

Martha added, "It also looks like he remembered our biological parents, or was told stories by the Parsons. I wonder if he remembered his brother and sister at all. I wished we could have talked with him about us when we were kids."

Lisa mentioned, "He writes about how good the Parsons were, and how thankful he was to have them as adoptive parents. One story describes how he believed his adoptive father secretly came back to Manitow and sabotaged Big Frank's boat, and explained that's what caused Frank's 'boating accident' on the lake the year after Tim's biological parents were killed. Tim would have been about six or seven years old at the time."

Martha continued, "Tim wrote that Mr. Parsons was extremely sorry for what he had done, and regretted it for the rest of his life. Revenge didn't bring about what he expected it would, and even though he had killed the person responsible for his friends' deaths, it didn't give him any satisfaction."

The room was hushed for a few seconds, and then Martha asked, "If Tim knew that revenge didn't help Mr. Parsons, then why did he come back here for revenge himself?" Nobody said anything, and after several minutes, the girls went back into Tim's bedroom.

******

Paul said to Dave, "Jake went in after me to look for Tim, but he hasn't come inside to warm up. I'm going to go out and see if he needs help."

"Yeah, he should have been here by now."

******

Jake was now close to blacking out, but he didn't try to fight it. He let his arms start to float up as he just stared into the blackness in front of him as though he welcomed it. Suddenly, there was a splash that snapped Jake out of his trance. Something pulled his arm up and he had the sensation of being dragged through the water. Within a few seconds, his head was out of the water, and he gasped for air. Even through his semi-conscious state, he realized that Michael Dufresne had arrived and jumped in just in time to bring him up to safety. Jake couldn't speak for several minutes, as Michael made sure he was breathing, and then helped him walk, sometimes drag, across the ice toward Tim's cabin. They came bursting through the front door, as Paul, who was on his way back outside at that moment to look for Jake, helped to get them both closer to the fire.

The racket immediately drew Lisa and Martha to the living room, and Michael asked, "Are there any dry clothes that we can change into?"

Lisa answered over her shoulder as she ran into another room, "I know where to get some now," and she returned with shirts, pants, and two more towels. "I don't think Tim's clothes will fit you Michael, unless you can fit into these large pajamas."

Michael was out of breath, but smiled and said, "Thank you, Lisa."

"Martha and I will go into the kitchen to look for hot chocolate, coffee, or soup, while you and Jake get out of those wet clothes," and Martha followed Lisa out of the room.

******

Jake looked at Michael and finally said, "Thanks Michael. I owe you my life."

"What happened?" Dave probed.

"I stayed underwater too long, underestimated the effects of the cold water, and was about to pass out. I thought I would die under the ice, when Michael jumped in and pulled me out. Another minute and I would have been a goner."

Dave looked at Michael and asked, "How did you know where to find him? You didn't even know he was down there, did you?"

"When I got out onto the ice, I saw nobody on the surface, but Officer Haley's jacket and a pair of shoes were by the hole. I suspected someone was down there, and waited for a minute to see if he would need any help getting out of the water. It was quiet, and then I saw something shimmer in the water. I think it was Officer Haley's watch or bracelet. He took too long to come up, so I jumped in to see if he needed my help."

Jake looked up into Michael's eyes and whispered, "I'm not wearing a watch or any jewelry," while he watched Michael just stare at him, obviously considering what Jake just said, without saying a thing. Jake offered Michael his wrists and neck to show he had no jewelry or anything that might have sparkled in the water and he saw the puzzled look in Michael's eyes as he examined Jake.

Martha and Lisa came back into the living room, and Jake observed Martha as she paused to look around the room.

"Look at all of these men freezing from being in the icy water. I've never heard of such a thing." In any other situation, this would have been funny, but Jake could tell it was difficult for anyone to laugh at this time.

The ladies held up several bowls of hot soup, and Lisa said, "Michael, now it is our turn to offer you a taste of delicious hot soup."

Dave and Paul smiled, because they knew how much Michael liked soups, but Jake knew they were forced smiles.

"Martha, I don't remember if you've met Michael, ay, but you've heard me mention him before. Anyway, he makes the best soups over at the souvenir shop, don'cha know, and always invites us to try some. I guarantee he won't turn down a chance to taste a bowl of hot soup, especially now."

"It's nice to finally meet you, Michael."

"The pleasure is all mine," responded Michael and his hand swallowed her petty little hand.

Jake saw that both Lisa and Martha had been crying for a while, but he had nothing to offer that would cheer them up.

With dusk transitioning to darkness outside, Jake finally accepted the fact that there was no hope of reaching Tim in time. He knew that Tim was most likely now dead, and had difficulty letting go of his best friend, his only ally in this town. He watched out the window as the mist slowly took over the lake and all within it, and he experienced anger as it glided up onto the shore outside, moving through the trees, past the cabin. Jake thought it was declaring the finality of Tim's death, taking him away once and for all, and he didn't like it.

The men were all in dry clothes now, and they gathered around the fireplace as their bodies craved the warmth offered by their soups.

Jake figured they had all been thinking it, but Paul finally said, "I don't believe there's any chance that Tim survived," and Jake shook his head in agreement.

"I'll arrange to have people search the lake for his body."

Paul continued, "We've been researching more, and we all believe that Tim was the oldest son of the Nelson family."

Jake turned his head in surprise and looked at Paul.

"Even more interesting is that we believe I'm the middle son, and Martha is the youngest daughter."

Jake's mouth dropped open and he looked over at Martha, not knowing what to say.

Michael smiled and said, "Now the family has all come together after all these years."

Lisa added, "Based on what we've found, it looks like Tim had come back here after being away with the Parsons for almost twenty years, and planned the murder of the people who killed his biological parents. Once the Parsons had both died and were buried here in town, Tim moved into the cabin he grew up in as a small child, right where the Nelsons were killed."

Jake asked, "How did he know who killed the Nelsons?"

Martha handed Jake the photograph with the faces 'X'd' out and said, "It looks like Mr. Parsons confided in Tim exactly who was involved in the murder of his friends, and may have even confided to Tim that he killed Big Frank in revenge for forcing his family out of town."

Jake's mind reeled from all of this new information, and

wondered if he would be able to absorb it this evening. He felt like shutting down, since he was on overload, but he forced himself to take it all in. He had a responsibility to gather the facts, verify with further investigation, and present them to the rest of the town.

Martha held out a piece of paper for Lisa, and said, "My mother mentioned I was baptized as a baby at the Lutheran church when I was still with the Nelsons, and it gave me an idea. I was so excited when I stopped by the church today and found the records from twenty-four year ago for the Nelsons, my parents, but with all the chaos of the afternoon, I forgot about it. Unfortunately, all of the excitement has left me."

Martha could tell Lisa was very interested, and watched her as she saw that it listed Stephen and Laura Nelson, both age twenty-six, their son Timothy Stephen Nelson age four, Paul Andrew Nelson age two, and Martha Rebecca Nelson age nine months. Paul came closer and read it with her and Martha looked into his eyes in silence. She could tell that he noticed the middle son's birthday was the same as his as he pointed to the date.

Barely above a whisper, Paul asked Martha, "Is your middle name 'Rebecca'?"

"Yes, and is your middle name 'Andrew'?"

Paul nodded. "This is all the proof I need to show that we're linked to this family."

Martha added, "Tim probably never knew that his biological brother and sister were in the same town at the same time, although it's likely that he remembered some things about us from his childhood, and was told about us by the Parsons."

Jake said, "Tim was such a great guy. I just don't see how he could have been involved with killing these people, even if they allegedly murdered his biological parents and threatened his adoptive parents."

Lisa replied, "Just wait until you read Tim's journals in his own handwriting. You won't believe what was going on in his mind behind the nice guy we all thought we knew. No wonder he had such horrible nightmares. Something tormented him, pushing him to the point of murder, and it looks like it made him schizophrenic. A talented carpenter that loved life, loved this area, and a revengeful man who had an intense anger toward the men who killed his biological parents."

By now, the fire in the fireplace had burned down and was only embers.

Dave added, "Not much of a ghost story, ay?" then the lights went out and the cabin went dark.

Chapter Forty-Two

THE NEXT DAY, OFFICER HALEY met with Paul, Lisa, Dave, Martha, and Abigail at Tim's cabin and talked with each of them for a while in the yard as they stepped into the hints of sunshine. When they all approached the front door, Paul was reminded of the previous night's horror by the search team out on the ice, just a stone's throw from where he now stood. They took their turn filing into the cabin with the solemnity of a funeral service, with Jake bringing up the rear. Looking out the window, Paul saw Michael Dufresne arrive a few minutes later, and noticed that he brought his wolf, Miikawa. He observed curiously while Michael waited outside for a couple of minutes, walking around the cabin with the wolf. Paul was drawn to him, and his eyes wouldn't release Michael from their stare. He continued watching as Michael knelt occasionally in the snow-covered grass, and when he eventually came inside, Paul noticed everyone enjoyed petting Miikawa. She obviously helped to take away much of the tension of the morning, but Jake had to bring it all back.

"For whatever reason, we've not been able to find Tim's body, even though we've had a team searching the lake for almost two hours, on and off."

Dave responded, "That doesn't make any sense. He

should just be sitting there in this small area in front of the cabin waiting for us to find him." Dave looked over at Paul, Lisa, and Martha and added, "I'm sorry if that sounds callous, but it's a fact."

Jake replied, "I know Dave, but he's simply not there. I don't know what else to say about it. They're still going to keep looking, and expand the search area. Based on the evidence, it's assumed that Tim Parsons is dead, and that he was responsible for the deaths of the three people found in the lake over the past week or so. I've looked through his journal and his pictures, and as difficult as it is for me to believe it myself, I'm convinced that he murdered those men."

Paul asked, "Is there any chance he was setup, the way Michael was accused with an anonymous tip that was false? Maybe someone else wrote those angry entries in his journal and planted the photograph."

Jake paused for a few seconds, and then looked at Paul. "I want to believe that, and trust me, I really do, but I don't think there's a chance anyone else could have orchestrated this or helped Tim in any way. It looks like he worked alone, with revenge constantly on his mind, and hunted down the men responsible for the murder of his biological parents, the same people who made life miserable for his adopted parents. According to Tim's journals, Big Frank fought with Mr. Parsons more than once, and two of the gang apparently even hurt Mrs. Parsons. Mr. Parsons told Tim several of these stories before he died, so Tim had probably been planning it over the spring and summer, maybe even before he moved here.

Then while he lived here, I think he was anguished about the murders he committed, and filled with guilt, since he said he kept having terrible nightmares. The nightmares may have been his conscience reminding him that what he had done was wrong."

Abigail said, "Well, it wasn't the ghosts of the Nelsons who came back for revenge, but the ghost of that family's past coming back to haunt those who were responsible, and I mean Tim." She looked at Martha and Paul, and then added, "Your older brother."

Martha added, "The sad thing is that revenge wasn't the answer, and Tim should have known that. It's not what the Nelsons would have wanted and it's not what the Parsons would have wanted. I just can't understand how Tim would have made those choices. The Nelsons were my parents too, as well as Paul's, but I would have never considered murder or any kind of revenge."

Michael said, "I am certain that you are correct, and that this was not done by ghosts at all. I believe that Tim was tormented by evil spirits when he came back to town, and may not have even come back to his birthplace with revenge on his mind."

Paul looked at Michael with interest, and he continued. "It sounds as though Tim was bothered, or haunted, by something while he was here. Evil spirits could have influenced him to do things that he would normally not have done, resulting in bad choices that were out of character for Tim."

Lisa asked, "So if Tim was influenced by evil spirits, what would keep any one of us from being influenced in the same way?"

Michael scratched Miikawa's neck and smiled as he said, "Many people believe that the wolf is a symbol of protection against evil. When I first came into this cabin last night, I felt an evil that gave me great fear. Yet, since I have been here today with Miikawa, I feel that the evil is gone."

Paul asked, "That could just be coincidence though, right?"

"Perhaps. I had always thought that I was Miikawa's protector since she was a pup, but there have been times when

I believe I have been protected from evil over the past few years. Many of the Ojibwa say that the wolf spirit protects me, and other people say I am protected by a guardian angel. I am not going to argue about it, but will always be thankful for the protection. Plus Miikawa is a good companion. Anyway, I believe something has taken the evil spirits away from this area, but whether it was Tim who took them with him, the wolf spirit or angels who chased them away, or something else, I do not know."

"I would have never suspected Tim, but I certainly never considered ghosts or evil spirits," replied Paul, as he saw Abigail smile sheepishly when Martha gave her a hug. "I still think Robert Vallee was the most legitimate suspect though."

"Until he showed up frozen in the lake too," commented Dave.

"Just a minor glitch in that theory," said Paul with a grin.

"You know, I think everyone in this room was a suspect at one time or another," Jake pointed out.

"Even you, Jacob Haley," commented Dave. At this, the room remained for a couple of seconds.

Jake said, "Since Tim legally owned this cabin, by law it may now go to his nearest relatives, which appear to be Paul and Martha, if you can indeed prove the relationship. I don't know if Tim had a will, but we'll check on that."

Paul looked at Martha and said, "It's so strange. I just told Tim that Lisa and I are considering buying a cabin here for vacations, and he commented that we'd be neighbors. It was as though he planned to be here for years to come. It just doesn't make sense that he would have been involved with something so sinister."

Jake commented, "Paul, I would certainly welcome you and Lisa here as neighbors and friends, and I'd like to reach out to Dave and Michael as new friends too." Jake looked at Dave, then at Michael and added, "I've had reservations about both of you in the past, for one reason or another, but I believe you're both people that I want to get to know better. I hope you'll accept my apologies for getting off to a bad start. I don't care what anyone says about you, you two are OK in my book," and he reached out to shake hands with each of them.

******

While people talked, Lisa and Martha sat on the couch near the fireplace, looking through a photo album of old pictures. Martha found several that had the Nelson family in them over twenty years ago, showing Tim, Paul, and Martha as little children with their biological parents inside this cabin, some outside the cabin, and some by the lake just before the Nelsons were killed. Martha was overwhelmed when she saw these, and started crying. She smiled and looked over at Lisa, who also had tears rolling down her cheeks. They didn't speak, but hugged each other in silence.

Lisa showed Abigail the photos of Martha as a baby, and the older librarian had tears of joy, since she had never seen these old pictures of her little girl that young.

******

Before heading back home toward Lansing, Paul and Lisa met with Dave and Martha at the cemetery just off the highway. They all strolled along the path to the Nelson's grave and Martha said, "Look at this. The Parsons are buried right next to the Nelsons, but we didn't know enough to make the connection before."

Paul added, "Now it makes perfect sense, with them being close friends."

Lisa said, "When we first came here, I noticed fresh flowers on both of these sets of graves, and I'll bet it was Tim who put them there. One batch of flowers on his biological parents' grave and another batch on his adopted parents' grave."

The cool breeze carried the silence over the nearby graves like a whisper announcing a secret to the dead.

"This may be why I thought the Parsons' name sounded familiar," commented Martha. "I probably saw their name on the gravestone, and when I heard it later from the orphanage, the name rang a bell but I didn't put two and two together." She looked at Lisa, then over to Paul. "It's interesting that you two came to town this year, especially since we got to know each other, and we both were able to meet Tim briefly. I really don't think it was a coincidence."

Paul returned her gaze and gave her a brotherly hug.

He replied, "If we had waited until next year to visit this area, we may not have ever met, so in a way, Tim brought us all together."

Dave looked at Lisa, shrugged, and gave her a hug, while she laughed at his comical expressions.

Lisa said, "I'm going to miss your accent, Dave."

She saw his perplexed expression as he replied, "Accent, ay? I don't even think I have an accent. You two are the ones with an accent."

That brought a smile to everyone's face, and Martha shook her head as she stared up at her silly boyfriend.

Dave added, "So Paul, I guess it's in your blood. You're a Yooper after all."

"It looks like I am, ay?

More laughter as Paul shook hands with Dave, and Martha hugged Lisa one last time at the grave site before they departed. Each of them slowly made their way off the path through the ankle-deep snow, back to the cemetery parking lot.

******

So despite the sorrow of losing a friend and learning the unexpected truth about Tim Parsons' anguished secrets, the town and the lake were able to release a foothold of the prejudice and hatred that had gripped it for generations and Jake noticed everyone in the area had a more positive outlook. These murders could have been a major obstacle for the town, even strengthening existing divisions, but he saw that the townspeople somehow made it a catalyst for change in the right direction. Several people who were previously unknown to each other, but apparently destined to come together, had formed a bond of friendship that would not be easily broken.

Jake was determined he would no longer take sides with a few older prejudiced men who were now almost extinct in the town, but would stand against them to show that he couldn't be swayed so easily by them anymore. He would work together with Dave and the local Ojibwa population to earn their respect, and planned to spend more time with Michael, Dave, Martha, and Abigail. Paul and Lisa told him they expected to visit Kisinaw Lake regularly, in every season, and would get together with their friends from this area each time they stopped by. Dave and Michael even began visiting Old Deerfield and were welcomed by Jake and the other locals who stopped in regularly.

Paul said to Michael before they left, "This place was called Gitchi Manito because of the healing aspects of the area, and I can see why they felt that way then. Something about the lake is so relaxing, the woods are peaceful, and most of the people we've met are great to be around. There is healing in this place, not only physical, but deep inside. I feel it and I want it to be part of my life."

Michael just smiled with a twinkle in his eye and shook

his hand.

The ice was certainly melting in this area, and the winter was already promising to turn into a beautiful new spring season. Of course, spring in this area often still had ice in the lake and frost on the gardens even into June, but it was still a welcomed change for a town that had undergone a new awakening from a long, cold winter.

Epilogue

MICHAEL DUFRESNE AND HIS wolf, Miikawa, explored the shoreline around Kisinaw Lake near the creek that ran along the property line of Tim's cabin, and he looked up at several of the taller trees.

"If only you could tell of the things you have seen in your lifetime. You stand over the lake and witness many things over many years, but never reveal the secrets that you keep."

He remained silent for a few seconds, as though waiting for a response from the trees, and he caught a glimpse of several white birch trees leaning out over the surface of the lake.

"It looks as though you want to help, to reach out to those who have perished in the lake unjustly, maybe to show us or teach us something with your long fingers outstretched."

To Michael's surprise, Miikawa then discovered a hole in the ice, about twenty-four inches in diameter, only recently frozen over in the surface ice where the creek flowed into the lake. It was unusual, since most people wouldn't be fishing right at the lake's edge, until he realized how close this hole was to the break in the ice where Tim had fallen through the previous day. He knelt down in thought and considered that it was only a short underwater swim from that hole to this one by the creek, wondering if Tim would have faked his own death in an attempt to stop any further investigations.

Michael stood up and noticed that this area was partially blocked by trees between the new hole and the one where Tim fell through, and figured it would be possible for a person to come up out of the water at this hole without people from shore or someone at the other hole seeing him.

Michael glanced over his shoulder to look at the trees that seemed to point him in this direction, and wondered if he should thank them for the information. His eyes traced upward at the taller trees near this new hole in the ice, and he just nodded his head as he walked back toward the cabin. In the past, Michael had felt some kind of evil presence watching him whenever he was around this lake, but today it seemed comforting, with no reason to fear and no feeling of danger lurking behind the trees.

Miikawa soon found large footprints in the woods on the other side of the creek that could have come from this hole near the shore, while Michael pondered the situation a little more.

"Tim, are you truly finished with your revenge for the murders of your biological parents and are you at peace, or are you still a real threat to this community?"

Michael felt in his heart that Tim was finally free from whatever had been haunting him, but he needed to talk this over with Jake and Martha right away.

Rick Gangraw lives with his wife and children on the East coast of Florida, and wishes he could spend more time at his family's cabin on a lake in the Upper Peninsula of Michigan. He has traveled to over twenty-six different countries and has visited almost all fifty states in the US. When he's not dabbling in fiction, he enjoys sports, hiking, kayaking, camping, and researching family history.